I showed her a picture of Michelle Obama and left looking like the Dalai Lama. After an hour with the flat-iron, my ear-length hair was straight, but didn't have an ounce of the body or softness that my weave had. I was instantly transported to my childhood when all my class-mates had long pigtails, while my hair jetted out of my rubber bands like cocktail wieners. Tears pricked my eyes as Tameka removed the cape and I paid the receptionist. When I stepped outside, the wind blew and nothing moved. It was as if my hair had been glued to my head, not a strand moved out of place. My friend was gone.

UNBEWEAVEABLE

KATRINA SPENCER

Genesis Press, Inc.

INDIGO VIBE

An imprint of Genesis Press, Inc.
Publishing Company

Genesis Press, Inc.
P.O. Box 101
Columbus, MS 39703

Copyright © 2010 Katrina Spencer

ISBN: 13 DIGIT : 978-1-58571-426-1
ISBN: 10 DIGIT : 1-58571-426-7
Manufactured in the United States of America

First Edition

Visit us at www.genesis-press.com
or call at 1-888-Indigo-1-4-0

DEDICATION

This book is for my best buddy, my best friend, and Miss Weavy Wonder herself, Kasandra Lightfoot. You deserve all the happiness in the world.

ACKNOWLEDGMENTS

I believe it takes a village to raise a writer. A few people in my village I'd like to thank are, first and foremost, my family. To my parents, Kenneth and Norma Lightfoot, thank you for continually pushing me to keep going and to never give up. Mama, you're my point person, the person I write for. When I hear your laughter at a scene I've written or see your tears, I know I've done my job. I couldn't do this without you. To my mother-in-law, Sonia Spencer, thank you for always asking, "How's the writing thing going?" Just the fact that you ask endears you to me forever. To my sisters, Kasandra and Kimberly Lightfoot, thanks for putting up with me and listening to me whine about how hard writing is. To William Moore and little Trey-Trey, thanks so much for your support and for staying close. To Niki Lightfoot and Jordan, I'll never forget your words when I gave you a copy of *Six O'clock*: "It's like a *real* book!" I love you, girl. To Kim Cruz and Kenneth "Little Man" Lightfoot, thanks for always being in my corner. Words can't express how much I care about you. Thanks to Leonard Lightfoot for taking the time to read *Six O'clock* and sincerely loving it. Thanks to all my aunts and uncles, cousins and everyone. Shame on me for not telling you about my journey sooner.

Thanks to all my friends, but especially Joyce Jenkins for your tireless editing, for letting me drag you to writing events and for giving me strength when I had none. Thanks to Denice Walton, for always asking about my writing and actually *buying* a copy of *Six O'clock*.

Thanks to all the readers of *Six O'clock*! I've gotten so much support for my first novel. All I can say is, Wow. Thanks go to Diana Jagan, keep writing! It's hard, but you will find your way. Thanks to all the clients of Behave Hair Salon that gave your hard-earned money to support my first novel. Love and miss you all. Thanks to Jay and his wife Sahie, and everyone at the Beauty Spot. The discounts on the weave have kept me looking stellar and won't be forgotten. It's been real.

Last, but certainly not least, thanks go to my husband Ronald and my daughter Isabelle. Ronald, what can I say? You are my *"good gift and perfect present."* You bring out the best in me. My darling Isabelle, you are my rainbow in this dark world. Who knew that you would be so smart, so fiercely independent, and so funny? Words cannot express the joy I have in being your mother. Without either of you, I would not be the woman I am today, and it is because of you that each day I strive to give my best. I love you.

The lovely hair
that Galla wears
is hers—who would have thought it?
she swears 'tis hers;
and true she swears,
for I know where she bought it!
—Marital

PROLOGUE

July 15, 2009
Snip, Snip.

"Why you taking your weave out so early? This is some good hair," Tameka said, her scissors gliding through my weave as another track fell to the floor.

"You know, just trying something different," I said, looking at the weave that cost a month's rent surrounding me.

"You should at least save some of this hair," Tameka said, smacking her Juicy Fruit in my ear.

"No, that's okay," I said, feeling the stainless steel blades of the scissors remove my weave, my heart, my life.

"Don't worry, you got a cute face. You can still rock a short 'do. So what you in for today, a relaxer, a shampoo, what?"

"Um, today I just want to remove the weave. I can wash it at home."

"What? Girl, in the three years I've been doing your hair you've never washed it yourself. Now stop playing and tell me what you really want."

What I really wanted was to keep rocking my weave. It was my best friend, my baby, my soul. I couldn't live without her. It wasn't fair that this was happening. First my job, now my weave? What else could go wrong?

"You have a lot of confidence to do this, you know. My man would have a fit if he saw me without my weave. You don't have to worry about that, though. You don't have a man."

Another track hit the floor and I cried.

SWEATING LIKE A BABY NIGERIAN

January 7, 2009

"No, not acceptable. This is a Pulitzer-prize winning author," I said, flipping my weave over my shoulder. "This doesn't do him justice. Do it over," I said, handing the review back to Cassidy Sommers, my assistant.

"Yes, Mrs. Stevens," Cassidy said. At barely five feet, she stood the height of a pubescent teenager.

I picked up the phone on my desk and noticed Cassidy near me, hovering. "Yes?"

"Did you want me to write the whole thing over? Or just—"

"Are you brain-dead, Cassidy? I swear, you are a complete waste of space sometimes. Yes, write the whole thing over. I want it e-mailed to me in an hour."

"But Mrs. Stevens, its 6:00—"

"And?"

"It's almost time to go home."

I gave her a withering glance. Her lip twitched and she finally hung her head. "I'll stay."

"Oh, I *know* you'll stay. And you won't leave until you have that book review, right, Cassidy?"

She nodded.

I flicked my hand and she left my office. I called Bill Greenly, one of the executive editors at *Spirit Magazine*. As I waited for him to pick up, I twirled strands of my jet-black locks around my pinky finger.

"Bill here," he said in his usual rushed tone.

"Bill, it's Mariah. Everything set for tonight?"

"Everything's still a go. She doesn't suspect a thing."

"Great. I'm leaving now. Want to get ahead of the traffic."

"Good idea, wish I could but I'm swamped. I'll be there, though. Wouldn't miss it."

"All right, see you there." I hung up and grabbed my Michael Kors jacket from the back of my chair. I pulled off my flats and slipped on my black, patent-leather, five-inch Christian Louboutin heels and left my office.

"Good night, Mrs. Stevens," Cassidy said as I passed her desk.

"One hour," I said as I stomped passed her desk, not bothering to look at her.

"Yes, Mrs. Stevens."

I nodded at the few editors that were still in their glass-enclosed offices, while their wrinkle-browed assistants scrambled to finish last-minute details for the magazine's August issue.

I pushed the down button on the elevator and crowded in with everyone else leaving for Jasmine Cole's retirement party. I couldn't remember the last time I'd left this early; several months? I squinted, and rifled through Valentino bag to find my Gucci sunglasses to block out the sun glinting across the Manhattan skyline.

"Leaving early?" Paul Shepard, one of the entertain-ment editors, asked me as we both exited the building.

"Yes," I said, pushing open the heavy glass door.

"Here, let me," he said, trying to open the door for me. I shrugged his hand away and stepped through.

"Just trying to help."

"Didn't ask for it," I said, waving for a cab.

"You going straight to the party?"

"Yep."

"Need some help getting a cab?"

I looked down at him, which was easy to do. In my heels I was well over six feet. "Do I look like I need help?"

He backed up. "No, I was just—"

"Just what? Look, you're new here, Paul, so I'll give you a hint." I blew out a long, hard whistle and a cab screeched up. "I never need help."

I got in the cab and slammed the door. I laughed as his face filled with surprise.

He would get used to me, just like everyone else at work did.

I rattled off the address to the restaurant and dug my Blackberry out my purse. I checked e-mails and fired back replies as I dug into my purse to grab a silk scarf to change my black Chloe dress to something more appropriate for the evening. After finishing the last of my e-mails I leaned my head back onto the leather seat and closed my eyes.

Jasmine Cole was retiring. Jasmine was editor-at-large of *Spirit Magazine*, a monthly glossy targeted to upscale African-Americans. I've worked for *Spirit* for seven years (nine if you counted the two years I interned), and stomped my way up from measly intern to book review editor. But now with Jasmine retiring—well, that opened up a whole new level for me. *Editor-at-Large*. I liked the sound of that.

"Here we go, Butter restaurant," the cabbie said, pronouncing "butter" like "budder." "That'll be $11.35."

I handed him a ten, a dollar bill, and two quarters, and waited on my change.

He threw 15 cents at me, and I reached down on the filthy floor to grab my dime and nickel. I slammed the door of the cab, smoothed down my dress, and proceeded to walk to the entrance of the restaurant. I'd practiced my walk for years and knew how to walk hard and fast enough that I caught the wind in my hair. It fluttered behind me like a black silk cape as I pulled open the doors to the restaurant.

"Reservation, ma'am?" the maitre d' asked.

"Spirit Magazine."

"Yes, of course. Right this way." I followed him upstairs where about fifty or so people were mingling and drinking cocktails. I noticed Jasmine right away and walked over to the table where she was sitting.

Like a vampire, Jasmine was one of those women who never aged. She was at least sixty-five, but she could compete with any forty-five year old in the wrinkle department. Her light brown hair was pulled back into a low ponytail that showcased her dark, intelligent eyes, high forehead and long, graceful neck. Her only jewelry were large hoop earrings and a wedding band on her left hand.

She spotted me, excused herself from the men around her, and stood. "Mariah, I'm glad you made it. Gentlemen, I'll talk to you later," she said, grabbing my hand. We air kissed and she asked me to walk with her to the bar.

"Of course," I said, trying to pull my hand from her grasp, but she held on tight and was still holding it when we got to the bar. She ordered herself a gin and tonic, while I ordered a glass of champagne. She finally let go of my hand to grab her drink and, as I watched her twirl her straw around and take a sip, I thought her eyes looked glassy. She sighed and faced the crowd that was gathered in her honor. "Phonies. All of them. A bunch of brown-nosing wannabes," she said.

"Excuse me?" I almost choked on my champagne. I never heard Jasmine talk so freely before.

"Oh, don't be so naïve, Mariah. Half of these people here are smelling around after my job."

I nodded and looked around the room.

She laughed.

"You, too, huh?"

I looked down and she laughed again.

"You're not fooling anyone, Mariah, especially not me." She took another sip of her drink. "You're not getting it."

"What?"

She put her drink on the counter. "My job. You're not getting it. Listen, Mariah, I like you—"

"But not enough to give me a recommendation?"

She touched my shoulder and I shrugged her off.

"You're a good editor, Mariah. Ambitious, too. Be careful with that."

"What's wrong with being ambitious?"

"I created this magazine. Stayed up all night designing layouts while my kids called their nanny 'Mama.' I thought I was giving them the best—the best schools, the best clothes . . . the best of everything. Turned out all they wanted was me." She sighed. "I just wanted *Spirit* to be the best. And it was. But now I'm leaving, and my kids don't know me and my husband . . ." She turned and looked at me. "Ambition can be good, Mariah. But make sure this life is what you want."

"I want it." I wanted it so bad I could taste it, already imagined myself in her office. "I don't have anything stopping me. No kids, no husband—"

"You're not even dating?"

I fingered my weave and said no.

"So this job—"

"My career is all I have."

"*Job*. In the end, none of us have careers. As snazzy as the word sounds, this is still just a job." She blew out a ragged breath. "Mariah, the magazine isn't—"

"There you are!" Matthew Ryland, the executive editor, said, striding over to us. "I've been looking for you. There's someone I want to introduce you to."

"Hello, Matthew," I said. He shook my hand and led Jasmine away. "We'll talk," she said, over her shoulder.

I scanned the crowd for a few more minutes, finished my champagne and left. I'd done my duty.

~

I decided to walk home. After a quick change back into my flats I walked the five blocks to my apartment, across Houston Street and another two blocks to my brownstone. A quick nod to Henry my doorman, a check of my mail and then I pressed the up button to the elevator, hoping I wouldn't have to make idle chitchat on the climb to my eleventh floor apartment. I wouldn't be so fortunate today as I looked at one of my neighbors smiling at me.

"You have beautiful hair. Can I touch it?" she asked, her white wrinkled hand already out. I let her, confident that she wouldn't feel a braid or track. At $2,000 a pop, Tameka kept my braids thin as floss. She could run her hands through my hair all day and not feel a thing.

"Soft, too," she replied. The elevator's door opened and we both walked in.

"Thirteen please," she said, and I punched in her floor and mine. I kept my head down looking through my mail while she went on and on about her son.

"You sure are pretty. What did you say your name was?"

"I didn't."

"Oh. Well, I guess you didn't. My name's Shirley. But you can call Mrs. Jenkins."

"Okay."

"You remind me of one of the girls that my son dated. She didn't have your pretty hair, her hair was nappy."

I stiffened.

"She was so pretty, that little colored girl."

The elevator doors opened. "What color was she?"

"Um, what?"

"The girl. What color was she?"

She just stared back at me.

I laughed. "Good night, Mrs. Jenkins."

"Good night, um, what did you say your name was?"

"I didn't," I said as I watched the elevator doors close. I unlocked my front door and walked in, immediately taking off my shoes so as not to scratch my Brazilian cherry wood floors.

Home is where the heart is.

You wouldn't be able to see my heart if you looked around my tiny, yet expensively furnished apartment. Not one crumb lay on my black granite counters, the stainless steel appliances shone, and every pillow on my couches was fluffed with the perfect bend in the center, just the way I liked them. I examined the floors and found a single hair staring back at me. I picked it up. It was blonde.

I went to the phone and dialed Kathy's cell phone.

"Yes, Mrs. Stevens?"

"Kathy, did you come clean this morning?"

"Yes, Mrs. Stevens. I come every morning—"

"Well, could you explain to me why there's a hair on my living room floor?"

"Um, I don't know, I dust-mopped—"

"How many times?"

"Three. Just like always, Mrs. Stevens. Not everything can be perfect, though—"

"For the amount of money I'm paying you, my apartment *better* be perfect. Let this be the last time, Kathy."

I clicked off before she could answer. My belly began to burn, as it often did after I drank alcohol, and I poured myself a glass of milk. Everyone thought my weight-loss was from plain old diet and exercise. Only Cassidy knew about my stomach ulcer, which either had me in pain, or left me vomiting my food after I ate. Milk seemed to help, that and my never-leave-home-without-it bottle of Maalox. I walked to my bedroom and slipped out of my work clothes and jumped into the shower. After scrubbing myself clean, I got out and pulled on a pair of red velour drawstring pants and matching tank.

The ringing phone startled me and I checked the caller ID to see it was my best friend, Norma Rodriguez.

"Happy anniversary," I said into the phone.

"Thanks."

"So how's dinner going?"

"Roast? Check. Rosemary red potatoes? Check. Salad drizzled with raspberry vinaigrette? Check. Husband? Not in sight."

"He's late and you're over there sweating like a baby Nigerian."

"First of all, how do you know about baby Nigerians' perspiration levels?"

"I watch the Discovery Channel. You learn all sorts of things."

"You're a nutcase, as usual."

"That's why you love me. Calm down, I'm sure Chris will be home soon. At least your dinner's finished."

"Yes, but it's not like him to be late. Especially not today. You know three years is a long time, maybe he got in a car accident—"

"Pretty difficult considering he doesn't have a car. He's fine."

"What if he cut his finger at work and he's at the hospital right now?"

"Then someone from the restaurant would have called you. He's fine. Calm down."

I heard her exhale over the phone line and I laughed.

"What did you get Chris this year?"

"Nothing. He said this year we wouldn't give gifts, just spend time together."

"That's sweet. Now seriously, what did you get him?"

"Nothing!"

"You know that I'm just teasing. And honestly I do think that's sweet."

"What are you doing home so early anyway? I thought you were going to some party?"

"I did, I left early. Jasmine isn't going to give me a recommendation."

"You mean the lady who's retiring? Why not?"

"I don't know. She says I'm too ambitious. I would think that would be a good quality."

"In your field, yes. Maybe she already has somebody in mind."

"Probably. She started mentioning something about the magazine, but we got interrupted. It was probably nothing."

"Don't worry, it's not over 'til it's over. You might still have a chance."

"Yeah, maybe. Let me let you get back to it." We said our good-byes and I hung up.

Spirit Magazine is the only thing I'm good at.

I looked up from my journal and reached for the remote on my nightstand so I could turn the volume down on an old episode of *Seinfeld* blaring loudly in the background.

Jasmine didn't seem to think that being ambitious was a good thing. And why not? Nobody ever said anything to Donald Trump as he marched his way to the top, why shouldn't I? I've worked too hard all my life to not have the big payoff. I deserve this promotion.

I chewed on my pen.

I've given up a lot for Spirit. *I can't remember the last time I had a man; college, maybe? I have a stomach ulcer the size of Texas that burns like fire even now.*

I reached over to my nightstand, grabbed my bottle of Maalox and took a swig. I belched and then finished writing.

If I don't get it, I don't know what I'll do. Who am I without Spirit? *What else do I have going on in my life besides this magazine? Norma is out there celebrating her third wedding anniversary and my biggest companion is—*

I looked around my bedroom. A stack of books was on my nightstand, all needing to be reviewed for the magazine. My alarm clock, a lamp, and my trusty bottle of Maalox stared back at me.

My biggest companion is my bottle of Maalox. How sad is that?

I slammed my journal shut, and went into the bathroom to begin my nightly ritual of pin curling my weave.

"Baby, how are you doing tonight?"

My weave looked back at me. I shook my head and the strands flung in my face. "Yeah, you're doing fine, just need to get you ready for bed, okay?"

My hands grazed over my skin, and the childhood taunts of Tar Baby rang in my ears. I pushed the thoughts back and brushed my weave out, picked up a small section, and then rolled it between my fingers until it lay flat against my scalp. I secured it with a bobby pin and picked up another section. As my fingers kept rolling my long tendrils, my stomach eased and all was right with the world.

SPIRIT

It takes me about two hours to get ready for work. Getting up at five a.m. would be hard for most people, but not me. I needed all that time to transform myself—and a transformation it was.

It starts and ends with my weave. My hair—still pin curled from the night before—is protected from getting wet with a plastic shower cap. Before I leave the shower I douse myself in vanilla-scented body oil and then let my skin air dry. The oil turns my skin to the color of wet tar, and as it dries I brush my teeth and floss.

The oil gives my skin a radiant glow and I don't have to worry about turning ashy all day. My skin used to get so ashy it looked like I rolled around in chalk. I walk to my closet and get goose bumps as I look at my clothes, all organized by color, designer and season. The closet was one of the reasons that I'd rented the apartment in the first place, and even though it was bigger than my living room, it was well worth it. My hands caressed Christian Dior, fondled Balenciaga, and petted Chanel daily, and it was something I never took for granted. I pulled out a turquoise Michael Kors turtleneck, a black Gucci pencil skirt, and a black Narciso Rodriguez wool coat. It was January, and blistering cold outside, even for New York. I contemplated wearing my brand new suede

Christian Louboutin boots, but with the weatherman forecasting thunderstorms I decided against it, and pulled out a pair of black leather high-heeled Manolo Blahnik Mary Janes from last season. After getting dressed and admiring myself in the mirror for several minutes, I expertly applied my makeup, then snatched the plastic cap off my weave, removed the bobby pins and finger-combed my long tendrils into place.

"Are you going to behave for me today?" I asked as I kept fingering my weave. It looked liked it was going to be a good hair day. I smiled.

Man, I look good.

I checked for lipstick stains on my teeth and then turned off the lights in the bathroom.

I grabbed my digital camera from inside one of my kitchen drawers and took a quick profile snapshot of my hair. I didn't have time to catalog it like I did most mornings, but I would get to that this evening.

Looking fabulous for another day of work, and in record time.

I live in Manhattan. Yes, my apartment is expensive (I pay a little over five hundred bucks per square foot, but who's counting?) but everything is in New York. Beverly—aka Mommie Dearest—had given me a nice chunk of change when I graduated NYU to help me get started, and I used a lot of it to keep up the lifestyle I worked hard to create.

I couldn't remember the last time I'd driven a car—probably ten years? Maybe longer. I walked to work most days, except when it rained or when it was so cold your snot froze on your upper lip, but that just gave me an excuse to wear my fabulous coats.

The wind blew my weave hard across my face and I tossed it back and shivered inside my coat.

My mind kept going back to Jasmine and what she'd said at her retirement party.

As snazzy as that sounds in the end, it's just a job.

Being a waitress—that was having a job. I had a *career*. I was going somewhere. No one at the magazine had made editor at my age. That was an accomplishment. Yet, she made it seem like in the end it hadn't been worth it. Jasmine might be regretting her decision, but I wouldn't. I didn't have any kids. No man. I shivered more in my coat as I crossed the busy street.

I looked up at the sky and couldn't believe how deceiving the bright sun made everything. I wouldn't regret putting my career first. This is what I was born to do, what I was trained to do. I had to succeed. I ignored the nagging in the back of my head that said, *But what if you don't?*

I took a deep breath, the cold air constricting my lungs but clearing my head. I was fine.

Spirit Magazine was on the eighth floor of the Trump Tower. I started interning there while in college, and always thought that I would end up somewhere else until I saw her. Toni Morrison. I was invited to help at a photo shoot where she was to be on the cover and I couldn't believe how humble she was. She made me feel smart, like I could do anything. Books had always been my first real love; when Beverly punished me for doing something bad, she didn't realize that she was rewarding me by giving me more time for my precious books. So seeing her, and knowing that I could see other legends like her made me stay. Getting your book reviewed by *Spirit Magazine* catapulted several black authors to best-sellerdom, and it was nice to know that I had something to do with that. The work was grueling, but on some days it didn't feel like work at all—no one got upset if they saw me sitting in my office reading.

I ignored Sam, the security guard, as he waved— every morning to get my attention—and waited for the elevator. I squeezed in with a bunch of other people and made the trek to the eighth floor. I got off, pulled open the heavy glass door with *Spirit* engraved in white italics and proceeded down a long hall, nodding at the usual suspects as they hustled around to get their layouts ready. Our office was designed in a square with editors having offices around the perimeter and everyone else in the center in low, no-privacy-having cubicles—affectionately nicknamed "The Pit."

"Good morning, Mrs. Stevens."

"Good morning, Mrs. Stevens, your hair looks pretty."

I was gracious enough to nod my head to everyone and pushed open the door to my office. I slung my Prada bag over my chair and sat down, ignoring the huge pile of books that awaited review.

Cassidy came in with my coffee—black—in her hand. She said a quick hello and didn't say anything else. It took me weeks to train her that I didn't like a lot of conversation in the morning.

I slid my MAC compact out of my purse and powdered my face. My dark skin glowed like a firefly. I constantly had to powder to keep the oil at bay. I fluffed my weave, making sure my real hair was smooth and blended, then closed the compact and placed it back in my purse.

"Did you finish that review?"

"Yes, Mrs. Stevens. I sent it to you last night. Was it okay?"

"I had to do several edits on it, Cassidy. Tell me something, do you want to be okay in this business? Or do you want to be excellent?"

"Excellent."

"Excuse me?"

"Excellent," she said, her voice louder.

"Good. Let's try to do that next time."

"Yes, Mrs. Stevens. Your schedule is up, you have a meeting in ten minutes with Mr. Ryland."

"That's new. Why wasn't I told about this sooner?"

"I don't know. He asked for an emergency meeting."

I flicked my hand and she left the room.

An emergency meeting? What was that all about? I called Bill to see if he had any scoop.

"Bill here."

"Bill? What's going on with this emergency meeting? Matthew's never done that before."

"I think the magazine's in trouble," he said, his voice a little higher than a whisper.

"What? How? I thought our circulation was up last month—"

"Not enough, I heard. I think Matthew's been getting a lot of pressure from the publisher. Said we're losing advertisers."

My mind went back to last night. *So that's what Jasmine was trying to tell me.* Her baby, her magazine, was losing money.

"The market's bad right now. It'll turn around."

"Let's hope so. See you in a minute."

I hung up, grabbed a yellow legal pad and walked down the hall to Matthew's office. I nodded at a few of my colleagues that sat in The Pit and I could see eyes green with envy glare my way as I continued down the hall to the meeting.

Matthew's office was arranged in dark shades of cherry wood, and was as sparse and lean as he was. There were a few chairs around his desk, and I wondered why we weren't meeting in the conference room. He was on the phone when I came in, and I nodded at some of the editors that were littered around his massive desk.

While he talked he kept pulling on his tie, loosening it further from his neck. I felt a chill creep up my spine and I fingered a piece of my weave and twirled it around my pinky. He hung up, loosened his silk tie even further and sat back in his chair.

"Hey, Mike, please close the door behind you," he said as one of the lifestyle editors filed in.

"Everybody here? All right, guys, I'll cut to the chase. The magazine has seen better days. We're losing a lot of our advertisers, and we need to cut some space. Everyone has to cut their space by half."

"Half?" I screeched. "Matthew, I only get one page as it is, you want me to cut it down to a measly half a page?"

Other editors started grumbling and he held up his hand. "Guys, things are looking bad. I'm going to level with you; this next issue could be it. For all of us."

My heart seized.

"You mean—"

"You know what I mean," he said, his dark brown eyes meeting mine. "I need everyone to put in their best effort."

"And if that doesn't work?"

He scratched the back of his neck. "Let's just say you won't have to set your alarm in the morning."

SINKING SHIP

"Mrs. Stevens?"

"Yes, Cassidy?"

"Just letting you know that I'm going home."

"All right."

"You need anything else?"

"Did I ask you if I needed anything?"

She shook her head. "Good night, then."

I flicked my hand and she left.

I looked around the office and saw other editors sitting at their desks, all rearranging their pages and trying to figure how to work their ideas into half the space. Half a page wouldn't do Abraham Williams justice. He'd just won the Pulitzer Prize for his latest book, *Fatima's Story*. It was the journal of Fatima Nzhinge, a black slave who kept a journal full of her sketches of what went on around her. You could see her progression as she learned to read and write a few words, syllables really. The words were so haunting and pictures so dramatic and chilling I cried when I read it. I couldn't cut his interview into half a page! He didn't deserve it, and neither did the magazine. My stomach burned and I crunched on a Tums.

I wouldn't do it. Matthew said to send out my best, and this is it. I was not cutting one word of Abraham's interview, and I was adding the review, too. I looked at the other books slated for review this month—a cookbook with recipes specially tailored for diabetics, and two novels, one of which was our book club pick of the month. How was I supposed to fit all of this on half a page?

"Knock, knock."

I jumped.

"Sorry, didn't mean to scare you," Bill said, coming in my office and taking a seat.

"No, no. I was just thinking."

"Heavy news today, huh?"

"Yes. How did you know?"

"People have been talking. How did you *not* know the magazine was in trouble?"

"I knew we'd lost some subscribers and advertisers, but I just figured we were in a slump."

"Yeah, a slump that we can't dig our way out of." He sighed. "I've already found another job."

"What?"

"Yeah, put in my resignation today. Matthew didn't even blink. Just told me to hand in my boards."

"What are you going to do?"

"My wife's business is really picking up. I told you about her bakery, right?"

I nodded. "Sweet Tooth Bakery. I think I've gotten a cupcake there once."

"Right. Anyway, one of her managers quit on her—just as she was planning to open another location in Brooklyn. I never believed that her little business would grow so fast . . . Anyway, she needs my help."

I sat back in my chair. "Wow. You go from *Spirit* to a bakery. I know the economy's bad—"

"The economy's shot, Mariah. And I told you, her business is growing. I can't take this kind of stress anymore. You work and work and work, and for what? The magazine will always be called *Spirit*, not *Bill*. Besides, you know I've always wanted to own my own business. Even if it means that my wife is the boss."

"Yeah, but you didn't even give this a chance, Bill. You're leaving?"

"This is a sinking ship, Mariah. You need to get out, too."

I shook my head. "I've worked here too long. I believe in *Spirit*. I'm staying."

"Don't be a fool, Mariah. You're a talented editor, one of the best. And you can write. The market is crowded enough as it is; why don't you find somewhere else before it's too late?"

"No. *Spirit* is where I belong. We can pull through. It's happened before."

"I think you're making a mistake."

"It's mine to make."

"You're right. And maybe this place will turn around." He got up and left, throwing "Good night" over his shoulder.

"Wait," I said, getting up from my desk. I walked toward him as he waited by the door. "If you're leaving, do you think you could ask Matthew to give me more pages?"

"What?"

"Abraham Williams deserves better than this. Half a page? Come on."

He looked at me for the longest time and then nodded. "I'll see what I can do."

I caught a cab home. It was a little past two in the morning when I left. I didn't care whether Bill got the extra pages for me or not, I was still turning in a full page. I'd explain to Bill in the morning why I needed the space.

I was home in minutes and was sliding out of my heels. I poured myself a glass of milk and threw a handful of saltines onto a saucer and opened my window in the living room. I sat down, feeling the frigid air blow into my face. I munched on a cracker and thought about what Bill had said.

Was I making a mistake? Should I pack up and leave, too? I had to believe that everything would turn out okay. But with Jasmine gone, and now Bill, what if *Spirit* was going under? Where would I be?

You're a smart girl, Mariah. You have six months of savings, you'll be just fine. Don't panic.

I took a deep breath and took a sip of my milk. *I was fine. Better than fine. I was great. Everything would be okay.*

LET ME BE ME

My sanctuary when I'm feeling stressed? The salon. I walked in and rattled off my appointment to Ty, the receptionist.

"You're here early, Mariah. Tameka's running behind. Is there something I can get for you while you wait?"

I looked at my watch.

"How long?"

"Maybe fifteen minutes?"

"Let her know if it's a minute longer I'm leaving."

"Of course."

I sat in a leopard-print chair in the waiting area and played on my Blackberry while I waited.

Fourteen minutes to the dot Tameka walked up.

"Ready?"

I looked at my watch. "One more minute and I would have left."

"And go where? You can pull that attitude at work, but you better drop it here. Come on," she said, waving me back to her station.

I smiled and followed her.

Tameka didn't put up with any of my mess, and as much as I pretended that it bothered me I loved how she let me be *me*. The salon was the only place that I could be myself—had to be since Tameka was the only person I trusted to see my real hair.

"You're just getting a shampoo and your weave tightened, right?"

"Yep."

She draped me and I followed her to the shampoo bowl. I sat back and closed my eyes as she vigorously shampooed my hair, the tea tree shampoo tingling my scalp and invigorating my senses.

"Hard week at work?"

"Hard life," I said.

"What's wrong?" Tameka asked, slathering my hair with shampoo again.

"You read the magazine, right?"

"*Spirit*? Sometimes."

"What? I thought you said the salon had a subscription?"

"Had. No offense, *Spirit* can be a little over my head. Some of the topics aren't relatable to everybody. Why can't you guys have someone regular on the cover?"

"Abraham Williams is regular."

"Who?"

I sighed. "Abraham Williams just won the Pulitzer Prize for Fiction this year. He's amazing."

"Why can't you guys cover Beyoncé or Vivica A. Fox or something? Why does it always have to be somebody so . . ."

"Inspirational?"

"I was going to say boring, but okay." She tapped my shoulder and I lifted my head, heavy now with water, as she towel-dried my weave. She sprayed an antiseptic on my scalp to prevent it from itching and then I followed her to her station.

"Did I hurt your feelings?" she asked.

"No, but . . ." I trailed off. Is that how people saw *Spirit*? As boring? Was it? *I* loved it, but was that enough? *Spirit* was my life. What would I do without it?

"All right, ready for the dryer?"

I nodded and I followed her to the dryer and let her pull the hood down over my head, where I let the sound of the air drown out my worries.

"Are you sure you should be doing this?" Norma asked as she sat on an ivory silk-lined ottoman in the dressing room.

"Why not?" I asked, as I slipped the purple Diane Von Furstenberg dress over my head. I turned and looked at myself in the mirror. I looked great. The wrap dress accented my thin waist and long legs, and my dark chocolate skin glowed.

Norma grabbed the tag near my wrist. "This dress is over $3,000! Have you lost your mind?"

"Lower your voice," I said. After getting my hair done, I met up with Norma and now we were in a dressing room at Saks.

"You told me the magazine was having trouble. Are you sure you should be out buying a whole new wardrobe?"

"First of all, it's just a dress."

"A $3,000 dress," she muttered.

"Anyway, it's been a week already and I still haven't heard anything. Matthew gave me the extra pages I needed and when people read the interview, they'll be uplifted and look forward to buying our next issue. Don't worry."

"I'm not, but I'm wondering how *you're* not. How can you be so calm?"

I wasn't. I'd thrown up three times today, and my stomach and chest burned so much that I was drinking Maalox like it was water. But I pushed my fears down and kept working. That mentality had saved me before, it would save me again.

I saw her disapproving glance in the mirror and turned to face my friend. Her dark brown eyes glinted with worry and she kept twisting her wedding ring around her finger, a nervous habit she'd acquired since getting married.

"I don't like you doing this, Mariah."

"Just relax, okay? I've got it covered."

I knew she had a point to some degree. But Norma couldn't possibly understand how I was feeling. Norma was a wedding photographer. She had her *own* business. Her time was scheduled by her own hands and she could never comprehend the meaning of the word *boss*.

"Well, it is a nice color on you," she said, her eyes scanning my dress.

"Thank you," I said, turning back to the mirror and spinning around so the dress twirled around me. "Now stop worrying about me and help me find shoes that match."

IT'S MY LIFE

"What?"

"You heard me, Mariah. It's over. Last month was our last issue."

I was standing in Matthew's office Monday morning. I hadn't even sat down yet before he told me the news.

I sat down, my throat burning. "With no warning? Matthew, you can't—"

"No warning? Mariah, where have you been for the last year? We've been in trouble for a long time—"

"In trouble, yes, but not enough to shut down this magazine! This simply isn't done—"

"It's done every day, Mariah. *Vanguard* did it, *Prestige* did it—"

"Those were urban magazines. It was bound to happen for them. They're readers are average—"

"And ours aren't?"

"No. *Spirit* is for the upscale reader—"

"Upscale or not, people aren't reading. Look, Jasmine knew *Spirit* was going down, but she refused to modernize and change the magazine. In the end she was forced to retire because of that. She got off easy."

"Easy? Are you crazy? She loved this magazine!"

"But not enough to save it. I'm sorry, Mariah. It's over."

"It can't be."

"It is."

"It's my life. This magazine is my life. What am I supposed to do now?" I slumped in my chair and I could hear Beverly telling me to sit up straight. Matthew droned on and on about how some of the staff would stay over the next month, but I couldn't hear, I couldn't think. I closed my eyes to block out the brightness of the room.

"Mariah? Mariah?"

"What am I supposed to do?"

"I don't know, but I would start by cleaning out your office. And remember your laptop is property of *Spirit Magazine*—that stays."

He stood, signaling that our meeting was at an abrupt finish. Matthew offered me his hand and I shook it—barely squeezing his fingers—and walked out of his office. It seemed that everyone at the magazine knew what was going on. Except me. I passed my colleagues in the pit and saw their eyes turn from envy to pity. I kept my head up until I got to my office, and then sank into my chair.

The hair is the richest ornament of women.
—Martin Luther

THERE'S HOPE

Later that evening, I sat on the floor of my apartment with a bottle of white wine and India.Arie playing from the stereo nearby. I couldn't bear calling Norma and hearing her voice singsong 'I told you so.' The severance check I got wouldn't even cover one month's rent, and even though I had enough savings to cover me for a couple of months, I was worried.

What am I going to do? I wrote over and over in my journal, filling up two pages with the question.

Spirit was the first job I'd had, the *only* job I ever had. Jasmine's words danced in my head—*in the end, it's just a job.*

Let's see, I have no man, no kids, but it was all for something. It wasn't just for a job, it was for a career. Careers are *not* jobs. Yes, I got paid for it, which was the definition of a job, but careers left you feeling fulfilled. Isn't that what *Spirit* had done for me? Left me feeling fulfilled? I didn't know. The hardwood floors made my butt ache, but I wouldn't get up. Couldn't get up. I sat on the floor, still wearing my dress from work, and tried to trust in India.Arie's words.

India is right. There is hope. I'm talented, right? I wrote, taking a sip of wine straight from the bottle, not caring what it would do to my stomach later.

Yes, I'm a talented, smart woman. I will find a new job. I won't let this economy beat me down. No way. I'll write a great résumé, hit the ground running and find a new job. No, a new career. But right now, I better hit that unemployment line.

―

Name, the form asked as I scribbled my name down on the form. *I don't belong here,* I thought as I looked around the room. Vacant, stunned eyes glanced back at me. I kept my head down, trying not to look at anyone else in the room, trying to pretend that I didn't need any help, that I really didn't belong here.

"Mariah? Mariah, is that you?" a voice said behind me. *This is the last place I wanted to get recognized . . .*

I turned around and looked at Catherine Phillips. We both had interned at *Spirit* years ago. While I stayed, she went off to write brilliant editorials for the *New York Times.* Even in my five-inch boots, Catherine held my gaze—she was as tall as she was wide, with dingy blonde hair and grey, sallow skin.

"I knew that was you! Looks like the economy got us both," she said, reaching in for a hug.

"Um, economy?"

"You lost your job, too, right?"

"My job? No, of course not! I'm in here for a friend."

Catherine raised her eyebrow. "A friend, huh? Your *friend* must have hit on hard times. So where are *you* working now?"

"Um, *Spirit.*"

"*Spirit?* Where we interned together? Working there was worse than watching paint dry. How could you stick in there for so long?"

"Actually, it was—is a wonderful place to work. I love it."

Catherine caught my slip and stood closer to me. "Still in here for a friend?" She laughed, a thin raspy whine, and starting digging in her purse. She pulled out a stick of gum and folded it into her mouth.

"Yeah, times are getting hard," she smacked. "I thought there was no way that they could get rid of me. Felt like I was that Beyonce song, um . . ." She snapped her fingers to jog her memory.

" 'Irreplaceable'?"

"Yeah! 'Irreplaceable'." She shrugged. "People just aren't reading anymore. Not on paper, anyway. Everything is on a computer screen."

"How long have you been out of work?"

"This here is my second round of unemployment. I got a job a couple of months after getting laid off, and then turned right around and got laid off again."

"But you're college educated. You'll write somewhere else."

She laughed again. "Nobody's hiring now. And especially not newspapers. Magazines either, for that matter."

"But your husband is managing everything, right? You're still making out okay?"

"Oh, I'm making it. I was going to leave him before all this happened. Now I can't afford to get divorced."

"I'm sorry."

She shrugged again. "Such is life." She looked at me then, as if finally seeing me, and said, "I remember dressing like that. Amazing when bills start to stack up what'll you'll sacrifice." Her hands ran through her thin, lifeless strands.

I looked down at my Coach boots and True Religion jeans. *I thought I'd dressed down . . .*

I crumpled the form in my hand and said my goodbye to Catherine. I walked outside into the sharp, cold air and threw my form away into a trash can on the sidewalk. My hands were shaking, not from the cold, but from the fear of what Catherine said, the fear of having to sacrifice too much.

I grew up in Texas—Houston, to be more exact—a thousand miles from the island of Manhattan. I was raised near Rice University, in a neighborhood where the houses sat back on small hills that faced the tree-lined street. I can't remember a day when my mother, Beverly King, worked. Coming home from school she was always there, sitting in the sunroom with her embroidery hoop, the sun glinting down on her hair and skin, making her glow.

"How was school?" she would ask, without even lifting her head from her hoop.

"Good."

"Well, start your homework. Henrietta will give you a snack before dinner."

I nodded and would run off to my room, eager to get my homework done so I could watch TV.

My sister Renee would always arrive before me. She would be sitting in the living room watching TV, eating her snack of grapes with sliced cheese.

"You always beat me."

"I come straight home," she would say, smacking on a grape.

"Did you do your homework?"

"Nope."

"Then you shouldn't be watching TV," I said, flicking it off with the remote.

"Hey! I was watching that!"

"You know the rule, homework first," I said.

"Mama said it was okay."

"Yeah, right," I said heading into my room to start my homework.

A few minutes later Beverly was in my room, hands on her hip.

"What is this I hear about you turning the TV off?"

"She didn't do her homework, she ain't—"

"Ain't?"

"Sorry. We're not supposed to watch TV first."

"*You're* not supposed to watch TV first. Renee will do her homework later."

"That's not fair!"

"Life isn't fair. The sooner you realize that the better. Homework now. Don't you want to go to college one day?"

"Yeah, but—"

"No buts. Start on your homework."

"Isn't Renee going to college, too?"

Her eyes turned to slits. "Don't worry about Renee. Just worry about yourself. Independent woman, remember?"

I nodded.

Independent, self-sufficient woman. That's how she raised me. In some ways I'm glad. All the years of putting homework first made high school easier, and taking tests and writing essays were a breeze for me. Renee struggled in school and the things I found easy were hard-earned for her. While I came home with A's in English and got pats on the head from my stepfather, Anthony, Renee would get a party for landing C's in home economics. My belly would burn when I would see the new cashmere sweaters she would get just for baking a cake, while basic math equations left her floundering. *College*, I would chant as I kept my nose in the books.

The one thing my sister Renee was good at, the thing I envied most, was how she attracted men. It was the thing Beverly groomed her for, always reminding her of her appearance, making sure she cooked well and knew how to run a house full of servants. Because of course every woman had servants to manage, right? It seemed my mother's efforts paid off when Renee married Peter Chamberlain three years ago. Her happiness was short-lived when he died last summer.

"I want to be a wife, too," I used to say to Beverly.

She always laughed when I said that, as if me wanting to be a wife was as ludicrous as going to the moon.

She would pat my head, her hand fluffing my cotton ball-like hair.

"College is best for you. Your hair and skin tone . . ."

"What?"

"Well, let's just say that you are very, very smart. Stick to the books, not to the men."

So that's what I did. A week after high school graduation I hightailed it out of Houston and went to New York with my best friend Norma.

"You what?" Norma shrieked into the phone five minutes later.

"Laid off. I know."

"What are you going to do for money? Please don't tell me you don't have any savings left."

I bit my lip and fought back tears. *Suck it down, suck it down. You will not cry . . .*

She sighed. "I take that as a no."

"No, no. I have a little money. But it's not going to last forever. What am I going to do?"

"I told you not to buy that dress—"

"Right now is not the time to tell me that. Just be my friend, Norma."

"You're right. I'm sorry. Well, you still have options."

"Okay, name them."

"Well, since you got laid off you're eligible for unemployment. Have you filed already?"

"Yes." After taking a walk, and getting a cup of hot cocoa, I willed myself back to that unemployment office and did all the necessary paperwork. Thankfully, Catherine was gone.

"Okay, well, that's a start—"

"That's the end, Norma. Unemployment doesn't even pay half of what I used to make. I can't live on that."

"You could call your mother—"

"No."

"Your sister?"

"No! No family phone calls."

"All right. Well, if it was me I would cut back on my expenses and just live on the bare necessities. No shopping, no restaurants, no hair appointments—"

"Gotta stop you right there. No hair appointments? I can't do that." I felt traumatized by just the thought of removing my weave. I picked up one of my jet-black strands and twirled it around my pinky.

"Look, you don't have a job, remember? You're going to have to do a lot of things you don't like."

"I'm *not* giving up my hair," I said, twirling furiously.

"Fine," she said. "Just start looking for another job and cut back on your expenses. You'll be okay. You could come work for me—"

"And do what? Stand around and hold the light for you? No thanks."

"You'd have a job."

"I don't want a job. I want a career!"

"Fine. But you know beggars can't be choosy. Sooner or later you're going to have to do something that pays the bills."

"Yeah, maybe. But that's a last resort. I want to find something that fulfills me—"

"You could work at the restaurant with Chris."

"No! Don't you get it? I don't want to be some waitress or your assistant. Making food and taking pictures are not especially life-changing, you know."

"Oh, and telling people what book to read is?"

"Yes! I help change the way people think and how they look at the world—"

"By reading some trashy novel?"

"*Spirit* doesn't cover trashy books! We cover literary novels, and—"

"In case you haven't noticed, no one reads literary novels but stuck-up literatis!"

"That's not true! I read literary novels."

"Exactly."

"You know what, thanks for offering me the job, but I'm college educated—"

"So am I! We went to the same school, brainiac. Taking pictures and making food is an *art*. Not something that everyone can do. And Chris and I happen to own our own businesses, another thing that takes talent, hard work and discipline. Remember that before you start turning up your nose at everything. I was just trying to give you options, remember?"

"I know you both work hard—"

"We do."

"Sorry. I'm just frustrated, all right? Didn't mean to offend you."

"Fine." She blew out a breath. "So I guess you're going to try working at other magazines?"

"Yeah. I'm going to touch up my résumé and get ready to get back out there."

"That's positive thinking."

"And at least I have a great dress for interviews."

"See? You're thinking better already."

BILL COSBY'S CHEST HAIR

"I'm sorry, Mrs. Stevens, but you don't seem qualified for this position."

I stared blankly at his soft white face and shook my head. For the past several weeks I had been on over ten interviews, magazines and newspapers mostly, with all of them repeating the same answer—*you're not qualified*. It seemed reviewing the latest literary novel was not something that was desired at other magazines. And the fact that *Spirit Magazine* was the only place I'd ever worked didn't bode well for my résumé.

"Look, don't you have *anything* open for me?"

He took off his wire-rimmed glasses and sat back in his black leather chair.

"I'm going to be honest with you, Mrs. Stevens—"

"Please call me Mariah."

"Okay. Um, Mrs. Stevens, you don't have the experience we need right now for our newspaper. *New York World* gives hard-hitting political and editorial pieces. From what I read off your résumé, your job consisted of reading books and giving reviews. That really isn't our thing here. We need a copy editor—do you think that is something you're skilled at?"

"No. But I'm a fast learner, and I can be trained—"

He put his glasses back on and wrote something down. Without looking up he remarked that he would call me if something came up for me, and I left his office with a $3,000 dress on and $727 in the bank. I walked outside to a gust of wind that blew my long weave across my cheek, caressing it like how I longed a man would do. I did everything I could think of to save money, but my weave was the only thing that I held on to, it was stitched to my hair, interlocking us together. I was as much a part of it as it was a part of me. It was who I was, my weave, and I refused to let it go. I said as much to Norma over lunch—which she paid for.

"It shouldn't be that big of a deal," she said, tossing her long brown hair over her shoulder. "It's just hair."

"Of course you would say that—*your* hair is long."

"Well, you've been wearing a weave for years. Maybe your hair is long, too."

"Not this long. Besides, my hair is so tight and kinky that it looks like Bill Cosby transplanted his chest hair onto my head."

"Gross. I don't want to imagine Bill Cosby without a shirt on, thank you very much," she said, sipping her iced tea.

"Something has to give. I don't have enough money to pay my rent next month. If things got really bad, do you think . . . you know—that I could move in with you and Chris? Just for a little while?"

Right after we graduated from NYU, Norma's grand-mother bought her a tiny, two-bedroom condo near Central Park. Tall, wide windows encompassed the entire apartment with light, and the hardwood floors shined like new pennies. She immediately asked me to move in, and I was both excited and relieved that I didn't have to find a place of my own. Life had been fun and carefree then, I was an intern at *Spirit*, and Norma was just getting her photography business off the ground. I'd still be there if it she hadn't ruined everything and fell in love with Christopher Rodriguez, a handsome chef that she met at one of the weddings that she photographed. It was love at first sight for them, and he slowly came over to the house more and more. They would sit together on the sofa, snuggled in each other's arms, while I would be in my tiny bedroom reading, or wondering why the latest man I'd been dating had dumped me. After Chris proposed, I knew I needed to find a place to stay—both for their privacy and for my sanity—but I didn't think I could afford the neighborhood that grew so dear to me. My first week as book review editor at *Spirit Magazine*, I mentioned my position to Bill and he helped me find an apartment, albeit totally out of my price range.

"Bill! I can't afford this place."

"Sure you can. Things might be tight—"

"You've seen my paycheck, Bill. Food would be a *luxury* if I stayed here."

"Well, you have friends. Eat at their house."

Problem solved. Most evenings I would eat at Norma's house, and not once did Chris make me feel like the third wheel that I often was.

"It may be a little crowded—" Norma started.

"I know Chris has turned my old bedroom into his office, but that's okay, I'll sleep—"

"I'm pregnant."

I sunk back in my seat.

Pregnant.

I should have been congratulating her, telling her how happy I was, but I couldn't shake off the realization that she was leaving me again—first by getting married, and now this. Norma was my plan B; I didn't have any other options.

"That's great," I finally said, taking a bite out of my Caesar salad, crunching on a huge Parmesan crouton.

"You don't sound too pleased," Norma said.

I knew I hurt her feelings, but I couldn't wrap my mind around it. Everything was happening so fast. I had been so careless with my money, always thinking there was time to earn more. But now I was unemployed. And with thirty creeping up like a thief, my stomach trembled with the eggs in my ovaries that would never be fertilized. Where was my husband? Why didn't I own my apartment that I could fill with children? I had no one to lean on, a lesson I've known all my life, but the full realization had hit home today. Who told Norma it was time to grow up?

"No, no, I'm really happy for you—"

"You don't act like it." She sighed. "I'm sorry about what happened to you, and you know if things were different we would love for you to stay with us, but the apartment will be crowded enough as it is."

"I know, I know. Don't worry about me; I'll be fine. Let's talk about you. Have you picked out baby names?"

I plastered a smile on my face and listened to my good friend talk about her future bundle of joy as my heart squeezed with the knowledge that I would have to figure this out on my own.

ASSISTANT

I had another interview scheduled for that afternoon with *YOUTH*, a hip young magazine for the eighteen-to-thirty set. It was a much different take than I was used to, but it was one of the last magazines that was hiring.

"Mrs. Sommers will see you now."

"Sommers? You mean—"

I took a sharp inhale of breath as I saw my former assistant, Cassidy, in the large office. She was seated behind a modern opaque glass desk, and was on the phone when I entered. We both waited by the door until she waved us in.

She hung up, and her assistant spoke: "Mrs. Sommers, this is our last interview for today, Mariah Stevens. Will you need anything else?"

"No, Sheila, thank you. Please Mariah have a seat."

I couldn't hide my shock as I lowered myself into the white leather chair.

"Cassidy, how did you—"

"I'd prefer if you called me Mrs. Sommers."

"Cassidy—"

"Mrs. Sommers," Cassidy said, in a tone that let me know she wasn't playing. "Now let's see your résumé."

"Cass—I mean, Mrs. Sommers, do you really think that's necessary? You know I'm qualified for this position."

"I'll be the judge of that. Your résumé, please."

I dug in my bag and handed it to her.

"You've only worked at one magazine?"

"*Spirit Magazine* has been the only magazine I've worked for, yes. But you can see that I've held many—"

Cassidy held up her hand.

"I can read, Mariah."

"Mrs. Stevens," I corrected.

Cassidy stopped reading and held my gaze. "Excuse me?"

"My name is Mrs. Stevens. You've called me that for three years."

"Mariah, I've called you Mrs. Stevens when I was your assistant. Do I look like your assistant now?"

"No."

"What?"

"No."

"So I will address you as Mariah, and you will address me as Mrs. Sommers. Is that clear?"

"Crystal."

"Good. Now, I'm well aware of your qualifications, but I think you're a little over-qualified for this position."

"As an entertainment editor? How so?"

"I'm sorry, is that what you thought the position was? No, *I'm* the entertainment editor for *YOUTH* magazine. If you got the job you would be *my* assistant."

"Assistant?"

"Yes. But that's *if* you get the job."

"But I thought you have an assistant already?"

"Sheila's getting married and is relocating with her husband. You wouldn't have that problem, now would you?"

I stiffened. "I hardly think my marital status is any of your business."

"You mean your *lack* of a marital status, don't you?" She chuckled to herself and then finished reading.

"You're enjoying yourself, aren't you?"

"Excuse me?"

"You enjoy seeing me in here groveling for a job."

Cassidy sat back in here chair. "You know what, Mariah? I do. I enjoy the fact that someone like you would be in here needing a job."

"Someone like me?"

"Yes. Someone who loves to make other people miserable. Someone who thinks that having a high-paying job and a college degree automatically make them better than everyone else. Someone who does this," she said, flicking her wrist, "to signal to someone that it's time for them to leave her presence."

"I don't do that."

"You don't anymore. Because you don't have the power to do that to someone, the power to remove their dignity when you're supposed to train them to become better workers, better people, even. No, you didn't do that. But you know what? I learned anyway. I worked my butt off for you, and not once did you compliment me, not once did you say one nice thing to me. I was nothing but a waste of space to you."

"I never said that—"

"Please, Mariah. Spare me. You might not remember, but I do. And I won't forget it. But you know what? You did teach me one thing. You taught me how *not* to treat people. None of my staff will *ever* endure the humiliation you put me through. Never. So if you come in here thinking you could ever work for me, you have another think coming. We don't need your stuck-up attitude ruining our positive work environment."

She slid my résumé across her desk back to me.

I snatched it off the table and put it back in my bag. "I'm sorry. I had no idea—"

"You knew exactly what you were doing." She picked up the phone and flicked her wrist at me.

I flinched at the coldness of her dismissal and got up to leave.

"Mariah?"

"Yes?" I said, turning.

"Close the door on your way out."

SPAGHETTI AND MEATBALLS

The only thing that could save me after that disaster of an interview was a heaping plate of Chris's savory spaghetti and meatballs. I was on my second helping, my mouth full of garlic bread as I told them my story.

"Can you believe what Cassidy said to me?" I said, crumbs flying across the table.

Norma gave Chris a look and drank a sip of water.

"What?" I asked.

"What?"

"I saw that look. You think I deserved that treatment today?"

No one said a word.

"Hello!"

"Okay, you want the truth?" Norma asked.

"Uh-oh, maybe I should go in the other room for this," Chris said, standing.

"Sit down!" we both said.

"Now finish," I said, slurping a huge bite of spaghetti in my mouth.

"Remember that day a couple of months ago when I came to your job and ate lunch with you?"

"Yeah . . ."

"You were so rude and mean to your assistant. I felt bad for her."

I flipped my hair over my shoulder. "How was I mean to her?"

"You snapped your fingers at her, you name called—you were pure evil!"

"I was?"

"Correction. You are."

"I'll admit that I can be a little tough—"

She knocked on the table. "This table is tough. You're like—"

"Stainless steel," Chris offered.

"Yeah. Thanks, babe," she said, giving him a kiss across the table.

"Excuse me while I throw up," I said, making gagging noises.

"Anyway, you're like stainless steel. You mean well, you don't stain and you look perfect, but you wouldn't want to do a whole kitchen in it, you know? It'd be too—"

"Cold," Chris said.

"Exactly!"

"Maybe you should have left," I said to Chris.

He put his arms up in defense. "Sorry, just trying to help. Don't kill the messenger. How you treat people at work is the same way you treat men."

"And how do I treat men?"

"Like you don't have the time of day for them, like you don't need them, like they're beneath you—"

"We've never dated, Chris. How would you know how I treat men?"

"I did try to fix you up with my cousin Enrique, remember?"

"Oh. Oh, that. Well, that wouldn't have worked out."

"And why not?"

"He was a waiter in your restaurant, Chris. I don't do waiters."

"See! That's exactly the attitude I'm talking about," Norma said. "You act like you're better than everyone."

"I do not! It's just that some people out there aren't goal-oriented. I am, and that puts me on a different level than most people."

"Yeah, a *better* level. Admit it, Mariah. You had it coming today with your assistant."

"I don't think so. All my life people have been making fun of me. Norma, you remember how bad it was in school—"

"Everybody gets teased in school," Chris said. "Even the popular kids."

"Which you probably were," I added.

"True. But I still got made fun of."

"Not like me. Tar Baby, Cotton Ball, African Booty Scratcher—"

Chris spit up some of his wine. "What? African Booty—"

"Scratcher. I got called Blacky, Baldy, Chickenhead—"

"You had a very imaginative school," he said.

"You weren't the only one who got made fun of. Remember me? Wetback was one of their favorites even though both my parents *and* grandparents are American citizens. Remember how some of them wrote a fake yearbook and said that I was most likely to have eight kids and run a fruit stand? That was mean," Norma said.

Chris shook his head. "Oh, the trials of being rich."

Norma hit his arm. "It's not funny. Mariah and I were the only minorities at that school. They really tore into us."

"But your sister went to that school, too. She didn't get made fun of?"

I waved my hand. "Half-sister. And she doesn't count."

"Why not?"

"Because her father is white. She fit in with most of the kids at Druid."

He sighed. "Everyone gets made fun of. Including your sister. If you two hadn't been teased so much maybe you wouldn't have bonded and been such close friends. The point of this whole thing is that you can't make other people pay for your hard childhood."

"Wanna bet?" I said, taking another sip of my wine.

"Well, what are you going to do now?"

I shrugged and pushed my plate away. "Truth is, I don't know. That was one of the last magazines in the city. I can't concede to working at some neighborhood paper." I shivered. "No, I couldn't do that."

"You have your degree. Why don't you try teaching?" Norma asked. Chris stood and started clearing the dishes away. I mumbled a thanks when he grabbed mine.

"No. I don't want to do that."

Norma sighed and scooted her chair closer to mine. "Look, I know you have a lot of grand ideas about where you want to work and where you see yourself in five years, but right now, you just need to find a job."

I opened my mouth in protest and she put her hand over it. "You need some money coming in to handle your expenses. You barely could afford that apartment with the job you had. You're too smart to keep passing up jobs like this." She removed her hand and I nodded.

"You're right. I do need some money coming in." I twirled my weave around my pinky. "What kind of help would Chris need at the restaurant?"

She smiled. "Now we're talking.

I'M FINE

Chris owned a small tapas restaurant called Muave on Fifty-first Street. I wanted to hail a cab, but since I was pinching my pennies, I took the subway. The restaurant was doing well, especially after a well-known actor started making his rounds there. With several paparazzi outside whenever he came to dinner, it put Muave on the map, and a flattering review in the *Post* followed. Now reservations had to be made at least two months in advance.

I pulled the heavy wood door open and saw Chris sitting in one of the brown leather booths, talking to one of his waiters. He saw me come in and approached me.

"You ready for tonight?"

"Sure," I said. My stomach had already began burning even after swigging my bottle of Maalox like a wino on the subway.

"Look, I really appreciate you helping out. Becky's out sick, so you're really doing me a favor. Come on."

I followed him to the hostess stand where I would be standing.

"This is the layout of the restaurant," he said, pointing to the laminated seating chart on the stand. "It's pretty simple, really," he said as he gave me a quick overview of how to seat people. "You think you can handle it?"

"Um, I guess so."

He patted me on the shoulder. "You'll be fine. You're college-educated, remember? This should be a piece of cake for you. By the way, you sure you want to be doing this in those?" he asked, pointing to my five-inch Manolos.

"Sure. Why not?"

"Normally Becky wears flats. It's a lot of walking back and forth from tables, and you have to stand long hours at a time."

"Trust me, I'll be fine."

An hour later I was anything but fine. My calves shook as I towered over the stand, gripping it for dear life as I wrote down a reservation. I grimaced at the sight of a young couple walking in and tried to smile through the pain.

"Welcome to Muave. Do you two have a reservation?"

"Yes. Kendrick, party of two at eight?"

My finger trailed the book until I saw their name. "Ah, I see it right here. Let's find you two a table."

"Is he here tonight?" the young woman asked, her voice high with excitement.

"Who?"

"Jonathan Frankel? The actor from *Vows*? I heard he was going to be filming a new movie with Jennifer Aniston this summer. Anyway, is he here?"

"Sorry, I'm afraid not."

"Oh." Her date rubbed her back, trying to ease her disappointment.

"But you never know, the night is still young."

She smiled at the thought, her hope revived. "Yeah, he could always come in later."

I nodded and had them follow me to their table.

"Your waiter will be right with you," I said as I turned to walk back to the hostess stand. Attempt to go back to the hostess stand was more like it. The heel of my shoe caught on the hem of my pants and I skidded, stumbled, then finally fell hard on my hands, my wrists and knees taking the brunt of the fall. I could hear gasps of, "Oh, no, she fell!" "She looks hurt." "Somebody help her."

Please God, make the earth open up and swallow me whole.

I felt a pair of hands on my back, asking if I needed help.

"No, I got it."

"You sure?"

I nodded and stood, slipped again, then held my arms out for balance. After a few shaky seconds I limped back to the hostess stand, with the entire restaurant watching my every move. I gave them a wobbly smile to show that I was fine, but they didn't buy it. As people left, they kept asking if I was all right. "I'm fine! Thank you for asking but I'm fine," I said, for about the tenth time. But this time, even I wasn't buying it.

"Heard about your tumble. You okay?" Chris asked later that evening.

"I'm okay," I said through clenched teeth.

"You did a good job, all things considered. How'd you like it?"

"I don't think this is for me, Chris."

"Of course it isn't. It's just something to tide you over until you find something else."

"I know, but I don't think I'll last that long. This would have been cool if I was still in school, but I didn't go to college to be a hostess. I mean really, can you imagine anyone my age working at a restaurant?" I laughed.

Chris stiffened.

"No, but I didn't mean you—"

"Of course you didn't. Here," he said, handing me an envelope. "Hope you don't mind being paid in cash."

I peeked in and saw two $100 bills.

"Chris, this is too much—"

"It's fine. I appreciate you helping out, but I can see this was a bad idea."

"I'm sorry. I didn't mean you—"

He walked away. "Of course you didn't."

THE DEPARTMENT STORE

A month later and it had come to this. I was forced to sell everything. My apartment looked like a department store with all my designer duds spread over my sofa. I left myself a few pieces for interviews and casual wear and added up what all my clothes were worth.

"What do you think I can get for all this?" I asked Norma.

"I don't know, how much did you spend?"

I shrugged.

"Let me guess, about six figures?" Norma asked, fingering a Burberry coat and holding a pair of patent leather Jimmy Choo pumps.

"No way," I said, laughing. "No, just a little over $30,000. You think I could get at least $20,000 for 'em?"

"Maybe," Norma said. "Most of this stuff is still in really good condition. How much do you need to keep afloat for a few months?"

"My rent is $3,500 a month—"

"What? Thirty-five hundred dollars? Are you crazy?"

"Hey, you can't talk. You don't have rent to pay."

"Still, that's high. Maybe you need to move—"

I put my hand up. "There are a lot of things I'm giving up, but my apartment is not one of them."

"I thought your weave was something you weren't giving up?"

I ran my hand through my adopted long locks. "That, too," I added.

"I can't believe you're willing to get rid of all this stuff. Aren't you sad?"

"I'd be sadder if I had to give up this apartment." I shrugged. "You have to do what it takes to keep what's important."

"All this for your weave?"

"My weave is a part of me; I can't give it up. I wouldn't ask you to give up your baby, would I?"

She clutched her stomach. "That's different."

"Not to me."

She looked around the room again. "How are you going to pack all this stuff to Margaret's?"

Margaret was a resale luxury boutique. I've never bought or sold anything there, but the store was known for their fair prices.

"They're sending someone over here to look at everything. I told them this was too much stuff to bring."

"When are they coming?"

The doorbell was her answer. I went to answer it and was greeted by an older woman and a young gentleman.

"I'm Sylvia Donners, and this is Steven Plath. We're from Margaret's."

"Come in," I said, opening my door to let them in. Sylvia's jet-black hair was pulled back in a tight bun, which made her eyes slant, giving an Asian flair to her appearance. Her body was short and compact, and as I shook her hand I got the feeling that cleaning floors was her previous job. Steven had a Lurch-like quality to him. You felt he would only talk if you spoke to him first.

"This is my friend Norma," I said, as Norma stood up to shake their hands. After the brief introduction, Sylvia came deeper into the apartment and looked at all the clothes that I had placed around my small living room.

"You have a lot of beautiful things," she said, eyeing a pale pink Chanel jacket. "But you have a lot of inventory. It will take us a few hours to catalog everything. Is that all right?"

"Sure, make yourself at home."

Norma and I waited in the bedroom, looking through several magazines, until Steven peeped in and said they were ready.

"Well?" I asked, walking back in the living room.

"You have a beautiful collection here. Especially for someone as young as you; how old did you say you were?"

"Oh, I'm not that young, I'm only twenty-nine."

"Twenty-nine is young in my book. Well, you have excellent taste, my dear. I've called over to Margaret's to speak to my boss, and I've been approved to offer you $9,500."

"For everything? That's nothing! All my clothes are worth at least triple that," I said.

"I know. But the market has seen a downturn with designer clothes. Women just aren't spending the money they used to." She thought for a moment. "What about an even $10,000?"

"I need at least double that," I whined.

She shook her head. "You're not going to get that price from anyone. Tell you what, I can give you $12,500. But that's my final offer."

I looked at Norma and she gave me a thumbs up.

"Deal," I said, shaking her hand.

"So what are you hoping for?" I asked Norma as she hopped up on the exam table.

"Chris and I just want a healthy baby."

"Girl, please, it's me you're talking to. You don't have to act so politically correct."

"Well, I really want a little girl."

"Really?"

She shook her head and started to cry. "I'm sorry; I've just been too emotional lately."

I got up and hugged her. "It's okay. That's normal."

"And to top it off, Chris is running late. This is his baby, too!"

"He's coming, he's just stuck in traffic. Don't worry, everything is going to be fine."

"What if the baby isn't healthy? What if they find something wrong?"

"Girl, calm down! Your baby is fine."

She took a deep breath. "You're right. I know you're right." She patted my hand. "I'm fine."

I sat back down. "So I figured out my expenses. I fired Kathy, cut my cable and Internet, I'm doing my own manicures and pedicures, I eat at your house every evening—"

"And we love having you."

"Thank you. I bought an iron, so I'm ironing my own clothes—"

"Oh, no, the horror!"

"Hush. And I called my credit cards and got them to lower their interest rates. So with all that, I would need to find a job in two months. Or things are going to get really tough."

"You can do it. The offer still stands for working with me."

"Thanks. You know I really appreciate it. But after things went with your husband, I don't think mixing friends and money can go well. Besides you can't afford to pay me what I need to keep afloat."

"True. But if you got another apartment—"

"No."

"I've seen some really great places in Brooklyn."

"Absolutely not. Brooklyn? Gross."

"Hey, don't turn up your nose. Brooklyn is coming up." She paused for a minute. "You know your money would last longer if you would start doing your own hair."

"What? No, ma'am."

"How much does it cost for Tameka to do your weave?"

I ran my fingers through it. "I pay about $3,000 to get it sewn in—"

"What!"

"Including the cost of the hair," I added.

"That's ridiculous."

"I said that *includes* the cost of the hair. Look at my hair," I said, standing up so she could touch it. "Every penny is well worth it!"

"Not when you're *counting* your pennies. Mariah—"

I put my hand up. "My weave is not up for discussion. I'll find a job. Everything will turn out all right."

Chris came in, ending our conversation, and I watched him shower her face with kisses, and she tried to pretend to be mad, but then broke into laughter. My stomach squeezed and I looked away. When had a man ever kissed me like that?

"Thanks for covering for me," Chris said, giving me a hug.

"No problem."

There was a knock on the door as Norma's doctor entered. Dr. Mitchell was a stocky man with the neck of a bull and the smile of a child. He said his hellos and got right to business.

"And how have you been feeling, young lady?" he asked Norma.

"Fine. Great, actually. I can barely tell I'm pregnant."

"You just started your second trimester, that's normal."

After a quick pelvic exam and a few more questions, a technician rolled in the ultrasound machine.

"This is it, baby," she said, looking into Chris's eyes.

"No, this is just the beginning."

The lights were dimmed and Norma's belly was slathered with a clear gel. The doctor skimmed his scope across her stomach and the room filled with the sound of her baby's fast heartbeat.

"Oh my God, Chris!"

"I hear it, too. It's wonderful."

"You guys want to know the sex of the baby, right?"

They looked at each other and nodded.

"Well, the baby's positioned perfectly. Her legs are right open."

"Her? Did you just say her? Chris we're having a baby girl! A baby girl!"

"A beautiful baby girl!" Chris said, his eyes full of tears. He kissed her full on the lips as his tears fell onto Norma's face.

"That's so wonderful," I said. "I'm happy for the both of you. I think I've had too much coffee today." I twitched my foot. "Need to go to the ladies' room."

I needn't bother excusing myself; they were too busy looking at the monitor of their baby girl.

I left the room, and walked—nearly ran—to the restroom. I went for the handicapped stall, closed the door and burst into tears.

I had worked so hard all my life for this? To be almost thirty and unemployed? To be without love, even the *hope* of love? Beverly's word's chimed in my head—*"Not every woman is made to be a wife. Career first."*

I built my life around those words, trusting them—no, *needing* them to be true. But I was alone. So utterly alone.

NO OPTIONS

July 15, 2009

Three months later, I was jobless and penniless. The money seemed like it would last longer, but it slid out my hands quicker than sand through an hourglass.

I'd already said my goodbyes—I talked to my weave a full hour this morning in the bathroom mirror—but the reality of what I was doing was starting to hit full force.

So here I was doing the one thing I swore I would never do.

"I really wish you would have let me apply a relaxer to your hair. It's really thick," Tameka said, running the shampoo hose over my head like a vacuum on carpet.

"Maybe next time," I said. Of course there wouldn't be a next time. This would be the last time she would see me.

"You okay?" she asked, seeing a tear run down the side of my face. "Did I get shampoo in your eyes?"

"Just a little bit," I said. She didn't know that my eyes were stinging from the loss of my best friend, not from the burn of shampoo.

The warm water felt good against my scalp. My head felt lighter, but my heart felt heavier, as if the weight of the weave had moved to my heart. Tameka refused to let me leave the salon without getting a shampoo and blow-dry, even though she said I needed a relaxer. I couldn't afford the $225 she charged me for the take down and shampoo, let alone another $150 for a relaxer. I told her to do her best with her ceramic flat-iron. She gave me a long look and said she would try. After struggling fifteen minutes to wrap it, she finally sat me under the dryer and told me to look through some pictures to find hairstyles I liked.

I showed her a picture of Michelle Obama and left looking like the Dalai Lama. After an hour with the flat-iron my ear-length hair was straight, but didn't have an ounce of the body or softness that my weave had. I was instantly transported to my childhood when all my classmates had long pigtails while my hair jetted out of my rubber bands like cocktail wieners. Tears pricked my eyes as Tameka removed the cape and I paid the recep-tionist. When I stepped outside, the wind blew and nothing moved. It was as if my hair had been glued to my head. Not a strand moved out of place. My friend was gone.

The first time I got a weave in my head was my high school graduation. My hair was about ear-length and I couldn't imagine going across the stage with my cap on and nothing coming out underneath. I'd already missed my prom. I couldn't keep on going missing events because of my hair.

"Why don't you get your hair professionally done?" Norma asked. We were sitting in my room flipping through fashion magazines.

"I told you what happened last time I got my hair professionally done. No thanks."

"Her hair is pretty," Norma said, handing me a copy of *Vogue*. It was Naomi Campbell, standing facing the camera, her long hair in a sleek middle part down to her waist, her lips carrying her trademark pout.

"It's fake, though," I said, handing the picture back to Norma.

"So? It's still pretty."

"There is no way that Beverly will let me get a weave in my hair."

"Tell her it's for your graduation present."

I shook my head. "But I don't have any money. Unless . . ." I opened one of my dresser drawers and pulled out a credit card.

"I could use this!"

"But that's for emergencies only."

I pointed to my head. "Don't this count as an emergency?"

"I don't know . . ."

"Stop being a party pooper. All I need to do is find a hair salon that does extensions."

We rifled through the phone book and found a one-page ad for Extensions Hair Salon. *'If You Can't Grow It, I Can Sew It. Money Back Guarantee.'*

"Let's try this one!"

The salon had a cancellation for Friday, and with graduation on Saturday morning, it was perfect.

I was greeted at the salon by a woman named Stephanie and told to have a seat. A lady named Josie introduced herself and led me to her station. Her hands went through my hair, inspecting my scalp as she asked what kind of weave I wanted.

"Your texture is dry so I would recommend a full sew-in."

"A sew in?"

"We braid your hair down in small cornrows. Then we sew in tracks to the braids. It'll give your hair a break and allow it to grow underneath the weave while you still get to rock a cute 'do."

"That sounds great. I want that."

"You have a picture?"

I pulled out the magazine with Naomi Campbell.

She laughed.

"You sure you want your hair that long?"

I nodded. "I'm graduating from high school and I want it long."

"This is over twenty inches. The longest hair we have here is eighteen inches. Is that okay?"

"That's fine."

She told me she would be right back and left for a few minutes. When she returned she held a board with pieces of hair stapled to it.

"This texture is called Kinky Straight. This is the closest texture to your real hair." I felt it. It felt hard, just like my hair.

"What about this one?" I asked my hands caressing the straightest hair I'd ever seen.

She laughed. "This is Silky Straight. It won't be a good match for your hair. Trust me, get the Kinky."

"But the whole point of this thing is to get something that *doesn't* look like my hair."

"But you still want to look natural. Tell you what, why don't you try this one?" she said, pointing to a relaxed section of hair. "This is called Yaky Straight. It's close to your hair, but straighter. You'll have to flat-iron your real hair more often to blend—"

"That's fine. I don't want anything called Kinky sewn in my hair."

She laughed. "Do you want to match your color, too? Or did you want a different color?"

"I hadn't thought about color. What do you think?"

"Your hair is a 1B, a dark brown. I think you should keep it."

"Okay."

"All right, you ready?"

"Yes."

"Let's get started."

After a shampoo and quick blow-dry, Josie sectioned my hair and started braiding it down in tiny braids around my head. I was surprised by the tightness of her grip and kept feeling my hairline to make sure it wasn't bleeding.

"This your first weave, right?"

"Yeah."

"Don't worry, it'll loosen up in a few days. You want it tight to last a couple of weeks."

"So I can shampoo this?"

"Of course. Think of it as your own hair. You can do whatever you want with it."

As she finished my weave, she told me how to wrap it at night to keep it from getting tangled, to never go to bed with my hair wet, and to always make sure my real hair was down so none of my tracks showed.

"And here you are," Josie said handing me a mirror.

Tears sprung to my eyes as I saw the girl looking back at me. I was beautiful. No, better than that, I was gorgeous, a supermodel.

"Wow."

"Nice, huh?"

I got up and gave her a hug, and she walked up front to the receptionist and gave me my bill.

"A full head of weave is $500?"

"Yes."

"Okay . . ." I handed over the credit card and was sweating bullets until it was approved.

"How do people pay this every month?" I asked as I signed the receipt.

"Honey, you'd be surprised what people do to look good."

STEEL WOOL

"Are you serious?"

"Yes."

"Why can't you keep looking for other jobs—"

"I have $227 in the bank. I can't afford to keep doing this. I've already called and she agreed. Believe me, I wouldn't if I had a choice."

"Don't you have some jewelry you can pawn—"

"I've already done that. I didn't get half of what I paid for 'em."

"I can't believe that you're moving back. What will I do without you?"

I was sitting on her couch the next day. She was a little more forgiving when she saw my new look, although she did say now she understood why my hair was such a big deal. With no job, no money, no hair, no man, and, looking at Norma's growing stomach, no friend, I did the only thing I could think of—I called Beverly and begged her to come back home. After several pauses on her part and explanations on mine, she offered to send some money for a plane ticket. I would leave in two days.

"You're going to have a beautiful baby girl. You won't need me," I said, hoping she replied that she would always need me.

She did, of course; she was my best friend, after all. I nodded as she said the words I desperately needed to hear at the time.

"What are you going to do with all your things?"

"My sister offered to ship them to Houston."

"That was nice of her," Norma said.

"I guess," I said, my eyes welling up with tears. She pulled me in for a hug and I cried long and hard. Ugly, animal-like groans and hiccups escaped my throat.

"It's okay, it's okay," she said, rubbing my back. "It's just hair."

"Look at my hair!" I wailed, sitting up, wiping my eyes. "It's hideous! It's so short—"

"It's not all that bad."

"Not that bad! I look like Florida Evans!"

Norma burst out laughing. "From *Good Times*? I thought you weren't allowed to watch that show?"

Beverly refused to let Renee and I watch *ethnic television*, as she called it.

"What's wrong with *Good Times*?" I asked her once, after she caught me trying to watch an episode.

"There are no *'good times'* in the ghetto!" she shouted.

"Girl, give it some time," Norma said. She reached out and touched my hair, then shrank back.

"It feels like a Brillo pad."

"Looks like one, too."

"Maybe your sister can hook you up, you know, help you re-train your hair to its former glory?"

"What former glory? This is how my hair looks. It straightens a little bit with a relaxer, but it mostly looks like steel wool on my head."

She patted my hand.

"Maybe you can buy a wig."

Hair brings one's self-image into focus;
it is vanity's proving ground.
Hair is terribly personal,
a tangle of mysterious prejudices.
—Shana Alexander

COTTON BALL

I was five years old when I realized that I was ugly. Well, not exactly ugly, but not as pretty as my sister Renee. We were at a party, I can't remember what kind, and my mother introduced us to her friends using our nicknames—Cotton Ball for me, and Princess for my sister. And she did look like a princess with her long wavy brown hair that fell below her waist, her brown eyes with flecks of emerald, her light skin the color of whipped cream.

Being ugly wasn't even the worst part; it was the dim in my mother's eyes when I entered the room, like a lamp that's been cut off; her smile toward me just wouldn't be as bright as it was for my sister.

"Am I ugly?" I asked her one day after school when the teasing was really bad.

She dropped her embroidery hoop and looked at me. "Do you think you're ugly?"

I shrugged.

"Well, do you or don't you?"

"I don't know."

"You have a brain, Mariah, and you better start using it. Being ugly is one thing, but being average?" She clucked her tongue. "That's something else altogether. You're smart. And that's what makes you beautiful."

It wasn't until I got much older that I realized that she never answered the question.

Beverly is beautiful. The kind of beauty that even women have to stop and stare at. Her hair grayed prematurely, and when most women would look to Clairol to solve that problem, she didn't see a problem and never colored her hair. For some reason it never aged her, just enhanced her beauty even more. And Beverly knew she was beautiful. Her beauty was as insignificant as her pinky finger—she always had it and, therefore, didn't realize its importance.

"How do I look?" she would ask, twirling into the living room before she went out for a night on the town with Anthony. Her hair would be down, shiny grey strands running through it like a river of silver, her lips painted a dark red that matched her dress.

"Mama, you look—"

"I was asking Renee," she would say, not even turning to look at me. "So, Renee, what do you think?"

"You look gorgeous, Mama!"

"See how it twirls and spins?" She would spin around the room, her dress fanning around her like a red umbrella.

"Mama, you are so pretty!" Renee would get up and dance around the room while I put my nose further in my Judy Blume book.

She'd kiss both of our cheeks, remark on how fast a reader I was, and leave us for a night of dinner and dancing.

That's what it felt like growing up with Renee—I could be in the center of the room and she could stand in the corner, and somehow I was invisible. Renee came in the room and cast a ray of sun around her, and everyone wanted to be near her so they could bask in her warmth. I was the cloud that passed over the sun, a brief annoyance that was permitted only because soon the sun would shine again.

Our favorite game growing up was beauty pageant. Renee would gather her long hair in a ponytail. I would wrap a bath towel around my head and pretend for once in my life that I had long hair. I would swing it around, pretending that the blue, pima-cotton towel was my magnificent, beautiful long hair. We would dress ourselves in sheets, wrapped up like Grecian women. We had three rounds as all beauty pageants did— talent, swimsuit, and evening. Beverly was the judge and always gave me the swimsuit round as I pranced around the living room in my pink, polka-dot swimsuit. But Renee always won. Always. Yeah, Beverly would make it a close call, saying if my voice hadn't gone flat while singing "I Believe Our Children Have a Future," then I would have won. Or if my evening gown had been tied more elegantly around my waist then I would have won for sure. The more I lost, the more I wanted to play until we were in junior high and Renee said she didn't want to play anymore.

"It's just a game, Mariah. It's not real life."

For her, maybe. But to me it was as real as anything could be.

FRENCH TOAST

Life has a way of throwing a monkey wrench in your plans. I swore three things that would never happen to me: I would never take out my weave, never lose my job, and never, never move back home. Yet here I was, on a plane back to Houston.

I can't remember the last time I didn't have a plan. But I feel my stomach churning, and for once, I don't think it's my ulcer. What am I doing here? But more importantly, how long was I going to be here? Beverly booked a one-way ticket to Houston, which gave me the impression it would be a long time before New York was my home again.

So many changes. And everything happening so fast.

I put my pen down and reached up to twirl a lock of weave around my finger, and was brought back to a cold reality.

Oh, that. No weave. That was the hardest thing of all. What was I going to do without her? Who was I without her? One thing's for sure. Never say never.

I got off the plane in a dreamlike state, praying that at any moment that I would wake up and find myself back in my small, but lovely, apartment in New York. I walked past everyone and waited patiently for my luggage, a nondescript black bag that wasn't anything like the Louis Vuitton luggage that I sold a week prior. I was surprised to see my half-sister waving and carrying on at the entrance.

I groaned. I hoped to postpone our reunion, but now here she was—her hand waving, her long, wavy brown hair dancing around her head, her light skin sparkling in the sunlight.

"Welcome home!" She hugged me, engulfing me in Chanel No. 5. "I'm so glad to see you! It's been over a year, oh my goodness, you look great!"

Great? I looked a lot of things, but *great* wasn't one of them. She gathered my luggage and stowed it in her black Escalade while I hoisted myself in the passenger seat, but not without admiring the dark leather interior, high-gloss wood grain details, and chrome accents.

"It's good to see you, too, Renee," I said as I buckled my seat belt. She heaved herself in the driver's seat and looked at me.

"I mean it, Mariah, I really am glad to see you." She smiled at me and put her hair behind her ear, revealing four-carat diamond stud earrings that sparkled and glinted so much, I literally needed sunglasses.

"Are you hungry? We could stop and get some breakfast before heading to the house?"

"No thanks, I ate a little on the plane."

"That's not real food. Let's go by Sal's and treat ourselves to a real breakfast."

Sal's was the diner in a part of town we rarely frequented, yet it somehow became the after-school hangout. Their prices were small, portions were big, and ambiance was low but the food was good and the closest thing to homemade. We drove there with her talking about all the things she had been up to, me politely nodding at the appropriate pauses. She noticed that I was quiet for most of the ride and would only answer questions when asked. I wasn't in the mood for conversation and tried to emit enough negative energy so she would get the point and stop talking. It worked. The rest of the trip she was silent.

We pulled up in front of Sal's, and I wasn't surprised that it hadn't changed much in the twelve years I'd been gone. The white paint on the wood frame building was peeling and chipped and the steps up to the front door groaned with our weight. A black sign with stick-on black letters told us to seat ourselves and we sat in our usual booth near the rear of the restaurant. We grabbed our menus from the table; mine was splattered with ketchup or hot sauce, and I grabbed a napkin from the stainless steel dispenser and cleaned the plastic menu.

"I'm having French toast. What are you having?"

"Probably just an egg white omelet."

"That's it?"

"Not all of us are blessed with the skinny gene, Renee. Some of us have to work to stay thin."

"You look great; you don't need to lose any weight. In fact, you look a little thin."

"Good. Bony is the look I'm going for."

Our waitress approached with two glasses of water, and we placed our order.

"So, Mama said you lost your job. I'm sorry about that."

I shrugged. "Technically I didn't lose my job. The magazine folded. So me being unemployed has nothing to do with my job performance."

"Okay, that's good, I guess? Well, you don't have to rush to find anything. I mean, you can take your time to find a job. Maybe you could find something you really enjoy."

"I enjoyed my old job, Renee."

"Oh yes, of course. I know that, I was just saying that you didn't need to rush. I'll support you in any way I can."

"I'm getting unemployment—"

"But that doesn't pay much, I'm sure. Don't worry, while you're here, let little sis take care of you," she said, patting my hand.

"Thanks," I said. I slipped my hand away and started twirling my straw around in my water. Getting support from Renee was the last thing I wanted right now, but I was so low, I had to take what I could get.

"So I haven't heard from you since Peter's funeral last year. What else has been going on in your life?"

"Why are you so interested in what's going on in my life?"

"I just wanted to know—I mean . . . I haven't seen you in forever. Every time I call you or ask to visit you, you're always so busy. What has you so busy that you can't see your baby sister?"

"Work mostly. Just going out and doing things—"

"You and Norma are still friends, right?"

"Yes."

She nodded. "She wrote to me a couple of times after Peter died. I'll never forget that."

"She wrote to you?"

"Yes. What's wrong with that?"

"Nothing," I said. Our waitress reappeared with plates of food, and I stared at the huge omelet before me that was stuffed with bacon and sausage and covered in cheddar cheese.

"Excuse me. This doesn't look like an egg white omelet."

"It ain't one. That's just a plain 'ole omelet. If you wanted to eat healthy you came to the wrong place." She walked off while I stared at the massive omelet on my plate.

"I can't eat all this."

Renee was dousing her French toast with maple syrup. "Why not?"

"This isn't what I ordered."

"Just relax, Mariah. Eat what you can and then just bag the rest for later."

I sighed and dug into my omelet, grease turning my lips shiny as wet gloss.

"Good, huh?"

I nodded as I took another huge bite, forgetting about calories and what it would do to my hips and my ulcer. I just kept eating until, several minutes later, it was gone.

I sat back in the booth, feeling stuffed and satisfied.

"I forgot how good the food is here."

"You forgot about a lot of things. Let's hope you start remembering."

GREASY

I remember being eight years old and Beverly combing our hair in the morning, getting us ready for school. It took all of five minutes to do Renee's hair, just a quick brush and her waves fell into a long ponytail that swished behind her like a horse's mane. She gave my hair the same attention, even though my hair needed much more time. With Beverly's hair being so straight, she wasn't accustomed to dealing with hair like mine; she and Renee shared the same texture. So dealing with my short ethnic hair was a challenge that Beverly was not up to taking.

I would watch in horror as short, curly hairs landed without a sound on my white t-shirt as she brushed my inch-long hair in a ponytail. Keeping my hair in a ponytail required the skill of a magician—in minutes my hair would sprout free from the rubber band, my edges sticking out like porcupine quills, the rubber band only holding the hair in the center of my head.

You can imagine the friends I made with my hair looking like Cealy from *The Color Purple*. I was the only black girl in the entire private school of Westmont Elementary. Well, take that back, there were two other black girls there, but their hair would shine, and be almost as straight as their white counterparts. Curious, I asked one of the girls what they used on their hair.

"Your hair is nappy. You need a perm."

"And some grease," the other one chimed in. "That's why your hair is sticking up all over the place."

"Yeah, nappy head, some hair grease. Ain't yo' mama told you about hair grease?"

I nodded and walked away while they chimed "nappy head" and "tar baby" behind me.

The next day I told my mother about what the girls said and she shook her head.

"Grease is so ghetto, and the bane of black folks. My mama thought I needed grease, too, and she used to slather the stuff all over my head. It made my pillowcases so dirty and grimy. I refuse to use that stuff. Look at Renee's hair," she said. "See how long and pretty her hair is? She doesn't use grease at all and her hair is long."

"But Mama, Renee's hair is different than mine. She don't need hair grease."

"Don't?"

I sighed. "Doesn't."

"And neither do you," she said.

I wouldn't let the matter drop. The teasing at school worsened. It was bad enough to be dark, but did I have to have nappy hair, too? Beverly gave in after weeks of me crying and took me to a hair salon.

She huffed and puffed on the drive over, upset because upon seeing me her stylist said he didn't do ethnic hair.

"I can't believe I have to drive all the way to the ghetto to get your hair done. You better appreciate what I'm doing for you. You hear?"

"Yes, ma'am. And I do. Thank you."

"I made your appointment already. Just tell the woman what you need," she said, leaving me at the front entrance. "I'll be back to pick you up later." She peeled off, leaving me coughing at the dust that kicked up in her wake.

I walked in the salon, with its peeling black and white linoleum tile floor, black leather couches, and the smell of burnt hair and hair spray tickling my nostrils. I sat down on one of the couches hoping someone would notice me, but after thirty minutes of being ignored, I walked up to the receptionist and told her that I had an appointment.

"With who?" she asked, making a loud pop with her gum.

"Don't know."

She sighed, letting me know her full irritation with me.

"Name?" she asked.

"*My* name?"

"Well, whose name do you think I want?"

"Mariah Stevens."

"You're late. You're for LaQuisha. 'Quisha, your one o'clock is here!" She told me to sit down, that she'd come and get me when she was ready for me.

I waited several minutes and then a tall, thin woman approached. Or rather her scent approached. Her flowery perfume was overpowering and I blinked back tears as she told me to come on. I followed her, mesmerized by her long hair that was curled in perfect spirals, each of them shiny as patent leather. Different colors were intertwined throughout, some blue, green, pink—her hair was like a rainbow. It was beautiful.

She placed three telephone books on her purple styling chair, picked me up fast and plopped me down in the chair. She threw a black plastic cape around my neck and started touching my hair. She whistled.

"Your hair is dry." Several strands of my hair stayed in her fingers and she shook her head.

"How you getting your hair done today?"

"A perm."

"A perm? You sure? Your hair is a little dry for chemicals."

"That's what I want," I said, my voice firm. After getting bossed around so much today I needed to be strong about what I wanted.

"Where's your mama? I need to talk to her—"

"She not here. But she told me that I needed a perm. So that's what I want."

"You sure she didn't say a relaxer? She said a perm?"

I thought back to what the girls at school had said. "Yep, a perm is what she said."

"Okay. Let's get started."

She went to a back room and came back with a jar of cream. She put Vaseline around my hairline and then applied the slippery goop all over my head. It smelled like the water that sat under my house after a hard rain. I held my nose as she worked, and then she led me to a dryer where I sat on top of telephone books again, as she lowered the hood on my head.

"Sit here for ten minutes—I'll be back."

Just when I thought the smell would smother me to death, she appeared, and led me to the shampoo bowls. I sat with my knees in the chair, my head bent down over the sink like Beverly had me do every evening.

"TaWanna, take a look at this girl!" LaQuisha said, bent over from laughter. A woman came over and laughed long and loud. "That's a shame. This is probably her first time at a beauty salon."

"What did I do wrong?" I asked.

She didn't answer, just kept laughing. She pulled me up from the chair and I stood waiting for her to return with the dreaded telephone books. She sat them in the purple vinyl shampoo chair and patted them. I climbed up and she pushed the back of the chair down until I was at the level of the shampoo bowl. I realized my mistake and felt my ears burning. She rinsed the goop out and shampooed my hair, her plastic bangles clanking together. She finished and towel-dried my hair and we made the trip back to her chair, telephone books and all.

She grabbed a clear plastic bin off her station. It was filled with rollers of all different shapes and sizes. These rollers were different than the ones that Beverly used; these had what looked like rubber bands attached to the ends.

"What are those for?"

"I need to rod your hair to finish the process."

I was too short to see myself in her big mirror hanging above her station but I could feel my hair, and for the first time it felt soft as warm butter and just as slippery. It was straight. I felt like singing.

"Will my hair look like yours?"

She laughed.

"This is a weave. Synthetic hair."

"A weave?"

"It's not my real hair. I stitch this hair into my hair to make it look longer."

"Can I get that?"

She laughed again, and patted my shoulder. "You're too young for this. Maybe when you grow up."

A hair weave, I whispered, imprinting the words upon my brain. *That's what I want.* She put the plastic bin in my lap and told me to hand her rollers as she needed them. We fell into an easy rhythm. She pulled a long cotton strand from a box on her station, and wrapped it around my hairline, and then told me to close my eyes as she squirted liquid all over the rollers. The smell was intense and reminded me of the few times Beverly let me go to the nail salon with her.

"What is this stuff?" I wailed.

"Just keep your eyes closed. It'll be over in a minute."

I obeyed until she was finished. "Now sit with this and then I'll rinse it out."

Thirty minutes later she was finished with the whole perming process and she pumped up her hydraulic chair so I could see myself in the mirror.

I was a boy. I was Little Richard incarnate.

My hair was curly, short and so greasy I was afraid to stand next to a stove for fear it would catch on fire.

"It's ugly!" I cried, while LaQuisha patted me on the shoulder.

"Your hair is short. When it grows you'll love it."

I dried my tears and nodded, praying that what she said was true. I waited another hour for my mother to appear and when she did she stifled a scream.

"What did they do to your hair? It looks like it's been covered in lard!"

"It's a perm. The lady said when it grows it'll be pretty."

She reached out to touch it, and then backed her hand away. "This won't *ever* be pretty. Which one of these ladies did your hair?"

I pointed and watched as Beverly walked over to LaQuisha's station. I couldn't hear everything that was said, but could tell by her wild arm movements that Beverly was upset.

"How am I supposed to take care of this mess?" she screamed, pointing to me. "I can't go walking around with this grease monkey, she looks horrible!"

The salon was quiet as she snatched my hand and dragged me out.

"I told you not to get a hairstyle where you needed grease. Don't lean back in the seat," she snapped, as she put the car in reverse. I sat rigid in my seat, keeping my head still.

"They told me I need to buy some stuff to keep it shiny."

She glared down at me.

"It's shiny enough. Looks like I could fry a whole chicken from the grease on your head."

"Sorry."

"You're not going to school tomorrow. I need to take you somewhere else where they can fix that disaster on your head."

"I need to go get the stuff for my hair—"

"You're not going anywhere, Mariah."

"Fine. Beverly."

"What did you call me?"

"I called you Beverly. What's wrong—that's your name, isn't it?"

The slap came across my face so fast, I was left wondering if I'd imagined it. My eyes filled with tears as I held my cheek.

"You call me Mama."

"No."

The light turned red and we stared at each other until a horn blew and she was forced to turn her attention back to the road.

And I sat there, still as stone as she drove home, her mumbling about my hair all the way.

BEVERLY

My sister's home used to be in River Oaks, a part of Houston that was legendary for the size of their mansions. She said the house was too much for her so she bought a four-bedroom condominium in a part of town just as ritzy.

"You wouldn't believe it, but when the condo was getting built, I thought about you and asked for a fourth bedroom. I knew one day you would come to visit us."

"Beverly still lives with you?" I asked.

"Of course! Why wouldn't she?"

"How silly of me. Of course."

My heart slowed to a crawl as she pulled into her parking garage and we walked to the elevator that led to her condo.

She stayed next door to the Houstonian Hotel and was walking distance to the amenities of the hotel, fine restaurants and their top-notch spa.

"It's nice over here," I said, looking at the landscaped grounds, the tennis courts and the swimming pool.

"Isn't it? They have everything, a gym, pools, tennis courts, walking trails. They really spoil you here."

We exited the elevator and she gave the doorman her car keys and instructed him to bring the luggage to the eighteenth floor.

"Do you think Beverly is home?" I asked, as we stepped on the elevator that would lead to her apartment.

"Yes, she's home. She's waiting for you."

"Why?" I asked, as the elevator climbed to the eighteenth floor. We exited and I followed her down a long expansive hall to her condo.

"Why wouldn't she be home? It isn't everyday that you come to stay with us."

She unlocked the door to her condo and I sucked in my breath at its beauty. Dark, shiny hardwood floors were below my feet and the ceilings had to be at least twenty feet high. Floor-to-ceiling windows made up an entire wall and let in an abundance of natural light. My mother stood next to the window, the light turning her grey hair to a brilliant sterling silver. Her entire head was coiffed into a beautiful grey bob, full and thick as a woman half her age. She turned to look at me, her light brown eyes giving me a quick once-over, and the same look that I had seen for twenty-nine years resounded in her eyes. Sadness and another emotion I couldn't put my finger on crossed over her eyes. In a moment it was gone, quickly replaced with a smile. She walked toward me, her arms outstretched for a hug.

I opened my arms to her, and was taken aback with the ridiculous urge to cry as I fell into her arms. *Mariah, stop being so melodramatic! It's just a hug.*

She stood back and held me at arm's length.

"What happened to your hair?" she asked. She tried to touch it, but I pulled away from her.

"Hello, Beverly. How are you?" I said, refusing to answer her question.

She blanched at the mention of her name, then straightened her spine and said she was fine.

"How was your trip?"

"Okay."

"You look tired. Renee, show her to her room so she can freshen up." She squeezed my hand. "It's good to see you, Mariah. It's been too long."

I nodded, not accustomed to the attention, and followed Renee down the hall to my bedroom.

Even though Renee had downsized, her condo was still over four thousand square feet, and I found myself feeling small and lost as I listened to her describe her home.

"It's a split floor plan, me and Mama are on the other side of the condo and you're on the side with my office," she said, opening the door to a room with a mirrored desk and a laptop, thin as glass, perched on top.

"Feel free to use whatever you want in there; we rarely use it. Your room is over here," she said as I followed her further down the hall to the guest bedroom. "Here we go," she said flinging the door open.

The room was bigger than my entire apartment, with a king-size cherry sleigh bed in the center of the room flanked by two ceiling-high windows. The room was painted a pale grey and had shiny accents of crystal and chrome in the accessories.

"Your bathroom is here," she said, as I followed her deeper in the bedroom. "Everyone has their own washer and dryer, although most of the time we just send our stuff out to be cleaned. Kelsey comes every Monday and Thursday to clean, so just try to pick any clothes off the floor because she automatically assumes that they're dirty if you leave them there. Your luggage should be here in a minute." She paused suddenly as if she realized that she was rambling and turned to me. "What do you think?"

"I think it's great, actually. You have a beautiful home."

Renee beamed. "Thanks. I'm glad you like it. Mama said you had to stop your cell phone service, so I can take you to get another one. Oh, and I'll show you the storage unit where your old furniture is. Just in case you need anything."

"Thanks."

"Is there anything else you need, anything I can help you with?"

"No, not that I can think of right now."

She looked around the room and then nodded. "Well, I guess I'll let you relax a little bit. Unless you want me to show you around the condo? The kitchen and the other bedrooms?"

"Maybe later. Right now I just want to rest."

"Sure, okay. Well, let me know if you need anything."

She left the room and I sank down on my bed and blew out a ragged breath. After a few minutes I grabbed my purse and walked into the bathroom and was startled by my appearance.

I touched my dry, lifeless strands and shivered. I shook my head, and not one hair moved. I threw my head down and brought it up, the way I did to brush volume into my weave. Nothing. My hair just sat there like a helmet, frozen in place. I pulled it back away from my face. *Maybe if I just did this* . . . Nope. *What if I tried it like this?* Na-da.

I slammed my fist on the white marble vanity. "Do something! Don't just sit there! Move!"

This is the best I've got, babe. This is me. Better learn to accept it.

MEMORIES

Can you miss something if you never had it? Can you miss the sound of your father's voice if you've never heard it? I did. Looking up at my stepfather, Anthony, a man who neither looked like me nor acted like me, made me long for the father I would never know.

I only have one picture of him—the edges were so thin from my constant touching, that I had to have it framed.

"What was he like?" I would ask Beverly, stopping her from whatever task she was performing to answer my question.

"Oh, Mariah, why do you have all these questions? Your father is dead. Nothing will bring him back."

"I already know I look like him. I just wanted to know if I act like him, too."

Sometimes she would smile, other times she would just look off into the distance into a memory that I longed to know. "Sometimes, the way you sleep, he used to sleep just like you, curled up into a ball on his side. Just like a child."

"Did he love me?"

"Yes, he did."

"Would he—"

"That's enough for today, Mariah. I can't take anymore of it right now."

"But I want to know—"

"Enough! No more, not right now." Her eyes would fill with tears, and she would escape to her bedroom. On days when I really pushed her for answers, tears would run down her face and she wouldn't come downstairs for several hours.

"She's too upset," Anthony would often say, as we ate our dinner in silence.

"I just want to know more about him. Is that so wrong?"

"No, not at all. And you should want to learn more about your father. But his death was really hard on your mother. Try to understand that it's hard for her to talk about it."

I nodded, but I didn't understand. *I* was the child, it was hard on *me*, not her. *I* was the one who didn't have a father.

I would keep asking, keep trying to prod information out of her, but it was difficult, she just wouldn't open up to me. Every encounter would end in tears, hers, and frustration, mine.

It wasn't unusual for me to leave my room in the middle of the night and creep downstairs to get a cold glass of water. One night, I saw her. She was sitting in the corner of the family room, talking softly to herself, quiet tears going down her face. She was rocking back and forth, and her arms were around her like she felt a chill in the room. In one of her hands was a piece of paper— no, on closer inspection it was an old picture. I tried to walk away unseen, but she saw me and our eyes locked.

Her eyes were glassy and strange, and I felt that even though she was looking at me, she didn't see me.

"Forgive me," she mouthed.

A chill ran through me and I raced back to my room. I slid under the covers and put them over my head, trying to block out the sight of seeing my mother in such a state.

Forgive her?

For what?

If mentions of my father brought this much pain, then I wouldn't bring him up again. And soon I stopped pestering her. Questions of him were like a faucet that was turned off. First everything went at full blast, but then slowly slacked off until, after a couple of drips—nothing.

My mother was married to Anthony King, Renee's father. He was a constant fixture in our lives, and although he wasn't my father he still treated me as if I was part of the family—not his daughter, but like a niece he tolerated. Which was fine by me, since my mother insisted I call him Uncle Anthony. He traveled a lot for work, but we saw him on most weekends. I felt like an outsider when he came back home, the way they all cuddled together on the sofa to watch a movie—looking just like a postcard. Their skin was all various shades of vanilla and the few occasions I sat with them, I came in as dark as a raven, ruining their precious family time. I knew I was welcome to join them, but I didn't feel welcome—their conversation swirled around me like dust in the air and hard as I tried I couldn't hold on and get a word in.

Mentions of Anthony brought smiles and happy memories to my mother's beautiful face, while mentions of my father brought tears and regret.

The framed picture I have of him was of Beverly and him on their wedding day at the courthouse. He's tall and thin, with black, shiny skin and a short, neat Afro. Beverly could almost pass for a white woman; her skin was the color of milk and she was smiling brightly at the camera.

I wish I could say I was happy that I looked like him, that at least I had that to hold on to since he passed away. But life would have been so much easier if I looked like Renee. My dark skin and nappy short hair felt like a curse growing up in the constant blare of whiteness. My school was white, my neighborhood was white and so was my home—white. I saw with my own eyes how looking like Mama and Renee afforded them privileges that I would never gain. It opened doors for them, while I had to climb through back fences.

In school people often wondered why we had different last names; after all, we were sisters, weren't we?

"Were you adopted?" was the question my classmates often asked me. I remember going home to my mother and asking her the same thing.

"Of course not. Why would you ask such a thing?"

"The kids at school always say that I look different than y'all. And our names are different. Why does she have a different last name?"

"Don't say y'all. That's ghetto. Say you all."

"The kids say I look different than you all."

"You were not adopted, Mariah. You both have different fathers. You have your father's name, Stevens. Renee has King. That's the same reason you look different, you have different fathers."

"Why didn't you change my last name to King so we all could match? I stick out with Stevens."

"Baby, having the same name as us won't change anything. You still won't look like us, so what's the point? It doesn't matter."

"It *does* matter."

"Why?"

"Because I stand out! Because I'm a black, nappy-head dog. You should have changed my last name!"

I ran from her and to the safety of my bedroom, to my books and the homework that was a constant, which made me feel sane.

It took her two hours to come talk to me.

She sat on my bed while I sat at my desk reading a *Valley High* book.

"I thought you would have been proud to have Paul's last name. I know I was. I've made so many mistakes— too many to count, but your last name is not one of them."

She put her arms around me and I stiffened, turned my muscles to metal, and wouldn't give in.

"You don't love me," I whispered. "You kept my name different because you don't want people to know I'm yours."

She knelt down next to me. "Don't ever say that again. I love you, I do. And I'm sorry that you don't like your last name, but I'm not sorry it's yours."

She tried to kiss my head but I turned away from her. She sighed. "I'm sorry you're upset."

"Why did you have to marry somebody white? You should have married a black man so Renee would be as dark as me. Then I wouldn't stick out so much."

"You know what, Mariah? I don't think Anthony's skin color makes a difference in your sticking out. Now I'm sorry you had a bad day at school, but don't lash out."

She stood. "When you're feeling better I'd like you to come downstairs. We're about to watch a movie."

I never did go downstairs. There was no comfort at school in all its blinding whiteness, and my home life was just as bad. Was there any place that I belonged?

FREDDY KRUEGER

Three hours later I left my room and walked down the hall to the living room to face Beverly. My stomach felt queasy, and even though I knew the air conditioner was on, I could feel a faint trail of sweat sliding down my back. She was sitting on the sofa, holding a wooden hoop with her delicate embroidery inside. The room was still and quiet except for my footsteps. I knew she heard me approach, but she didn't do anything to acknowledge my presence.

I coughed.

Nothing.

I waited a few seconds for her to say something, but she just sat there, her needle going through the fabric—in and out, in and out. No response. Nothing had changed. Why after all this time had I expected anything different? Anger moved my feet and I turned on my heel to leave the room.

"Wait," she said, her cool voice laced with authority. "Sit."

I walked over to her and sat down on the chair across from her. She continued her embroidery, her needle going in and out of the fabric systematically, revealing beautiful pink and red roses. She stopped, placed the embroidery in a basket near the sofa, and looked up at me.

"I'm glad you're here."

I didn't say anything.

"Renee's happy, too. She can't stop talking about it."

"It seems like it. Did she leave?"

"She went to pick up a few things from the store. Things to make your stay here more comfortable."

"That's nice of her."

"We both want you to feel comfortable. I know things have been hard—"

I waved my hand. "I can handle things being difficult, Beverly. It's how you raised me, remember?"

The mention of her name made her wince. I stared at her and dared her to object to it. She simply sighed and picked up her embroidery hoop again.

"Some things never change, do they?"

"I guess not."

"So, how long do you think you'll be in Houston?"

"I don't know."

"Well, how long do you think you'll be here? Staying with us?"

"Not long. I want to find a job as quickly as I can."

"That's good. You want to keep busy. Now about your hair—"

I ran my hand over it.

"I've made you an appointment tomorrow afternoon with my hairstylist, Henry. He's very good and he'll get your hair under control and ready for Houston's humidity again. You'll need a relaxer, of course, and maybe with a few deep conditioners we can get that hair of yours to grow." She started to laugh. "Do you remember when you got your first relaxer?"

"How could I forget, Beverly?"

She took me to get a relaxer a day after I got the perm, not telling the stylist what previous chemicals I had on my hair. I left the salon bald as a newborn baby, with red chemical burns all over my scalp that crusted over into unsightly scars over the next week. It took several months for my hair to grow back, and another year before I would even try another relaxer. Walking around with my head looking like Freddy Krueger made the teasing unbearable, and it was then that I met Norma Gomez, the new girl at our school.

"You got burned or something?" she asked, sitting down next to me at lunch.

"Something like that."

She stared at my head for a few minutes and then started talking about her old school.

"My parents thought private school would be better."

"Look at them, the Wetback and Freddy Krueger! Hey, Mexican, why don't you swim back to the border and get me some tacos! I'm hungry!" Norma's face turned red, while I continued eating.

"Leave her alone, Michael," I said.

"It's okay," Norma said, grabbing my arm.

"It's not okay." I turned back to Michael. "You better leave us alone."

"What you going to do about it, Tar Baby?"

I don't remember hitting him. I don't remember the crunch of broken bone that his nose made when I hit it with my fist. I just remember being pulled off him and getting suspended for a week. The teasing continued, but it was different after that day. From then on, I said something back just as cruel.

Beverly's laughter jolted me from the memory. She kept laughing to the point that tears pricked her eyes. "Whew," she said, wiping her eyes with her hand. "You were always such a character. Your hair finally did grow back, though."

"That wasn't funny. I had a hard time with that."

She shrugged. "Honestly, Mariah, don't get so sensitive. You barely had enough hair to cover your head anyway. What did it matter if it all fell out?"

"I was ten years old! Do you know how traumatic it is for a ten-year-old to walk around bald?"

"I *knew* you would be like this."

"Like what?"

"Difficult. Mariah, I hope the time that you're here can be enjoyable. We really want to try to get along."

"That certainly sounds like what you're trying to do." I stood. "We finished?"

She looked at me. "I'm sorry I laughed. That was cruel—"

"Are we done?" I asked, my voice shaky. *Don't you cry, Mariah. Don't you dare cry in front of your mother.*

She nodded and I left the room and retreated to the patio.

The air was warm, but I couldn't feel it. I was cold inside, a chill spread through my bones, and I rubbed my hands together to fight against the cold that swept through me. It's been years since I came to Houston, and now I remember why I don't visit. Houston made me feel small, with its wide expanse of highways and unbearable heat. Houston made me feel like a child again. Or rather, Beverly made me feel like a child again.

Bringing up that memory of when I lost all my hair brought tears to my eyes. The teasing that I endured from that touched my kidneys and was made worse by the feelings that remained when I arrived home.

Renee used all her allowance money and got me a wig. At nine years old she managed to get a mail-order catalogue and bought a wig for my bald, scarred head. I wish her taste in wigs was as good as her intentions, because the wig made me look like Weezy from *The Jeffersons*. It was a tight-curled jet black synthetic thing that sat on my head like a hat. The teasing worsened, and so did my mouth. Even the teachers would get in on it, commenting that I should stay out of my grandmother's closet. I was appalled by their lack of compassion and retreated further into myself. Who could you run to when your own teachers were making your life as bad as the students?

"Stop that crying," Beverly said to me after school one day. I was holed up in my room and wouldn't come down to eat. Henrietta had fixed chicken enchiladas—my favorite.

"They keep making fun of me. Look at me! Why did you have to take me to another hair salon? I'm a monster."

She sat on my bed and, in a firm voice, she told me to sit up. I obeyed.

"I'm only going to tell you this once, Mariah. All this crying you're doing, has it helped you?"

I shook my head.

"Is your hair back?"

I shook my head again.

"Tears don't do anything. They are a waste of emotion. They'll never get you anywhere, won't do nothing for you but make you sick."

She touched the prickly wig that sat on my head.

"I'm sorry about your hair. I didn't know you weren't supposed to mix those two chemicals together. If I had—"

She looked down. "If I had I wouldn't have done it. But you can't be mad at me forever. And tears won't help you, baby. If they did, I'd be a different person. Okay?"

"Okay," I mumbled.

"Come with me," she said, taking my hand and leading me into the bathroom. She slid the wig off my head.

"Don't!"

"Now, look at yourself in the mirror."

I closed my eyes. "I can't."

"Open your eyes!"

I obeyed. I saw my bald head, with hair interspersed like a child playing peek-a-boo. I saw the angry black scabs and the white skin underneath from where I'd picked a few off.

"Your looks will never get you anything in life." She pointed to my head. "But this will. You're a smart girl, Mariah. And smart girls do not cry."

"Even when they get their feelings hurt?"

"Especially then. You lock those feelings away and push them out. Don't think about it. It'll make you stronger, tougher, *wiser*. It'll make you the best."

"No tears?" I asked, wiping away the ashy patches on my dark skin from the old trails of tears.

"No tears."

No tears was my motto in life, the thing I said to myself when boyfriends dumped me, when friends moved away, when pets died. *No tears.*

I said it over and over again, my tongue thick and heavy from the tears that were jumping at the chance to fall. But I didn't let them. I willed them back into that dark place where dreams die and where hope is lost. I kept chanting to myself until Renee touched my back and I jumped.

"I was calling your name. You didn't hear me. I just got back from the store. Are you okay?"

"No. I'm not. This was a mistake. What was I thinking of coming here?"

She sighed. "I know this can't be easy for you. But let me try to help. I promise to take care of you."

"That's not your job."

"I know. I just want to be there for you. I know she can be hard, but she loves you—"

I laughed. "I don't think Beverly is capable of loving me."

"That's not true. She does. She just had a hard time with everything. With Paul's death and all."

"I'm well aware of how I was brought into this world, Renee." I gripped the iron rails until my hands ached.

"I picked up some food. You must be hungry." She reached out and touched my hands, rubbing them until I loosened my grip on the railing. "It's okay, Mariah," Renee repeated over and over until I let go. She kept rubbing my hands as if they were cold.

"Let's go eat, okay?" Her voice was shaking.

I nodded and followed her into the kitchen. Paper bags of takeout from Pappasito's, my favorite Mexican restaurant, were on the black granite counters. I stood next to her in the shiny modern kitchen feeling dull and out of place.

"The plates are here," she was saying, pointing to a dark cherry cabinet. "And that's where we keep the glasses. Why don't you grab a couple?"

I grabbed three margarita glasses and set them on the counter. She placed one back in the cabinet, stating that she didn't drink anymore.

"Look, after the day I've had I need something besides Diet Coke. Got anything stronger?"

"No."

I sighed, and put the glasses back and pulled out regular glass tumblers. She poured Diet Coke in our glasses and added a squirt of lime.

"Come on, let's set all this up and sit outside. It's nice out today."

"I know. I was just out there, remember?"

Without looking at me she asked if Mama had talked to me.

"I guess. Why?"

"She was worried about you. I think she's as happy as me about having you back. She needs to tell you some things—"

"I think she shared all she wanted to share with me. She didn't exactly make me feel at home, you know."

She shrugged. "She's been having a hard time. She'll come around."

"A hard time? *I've* been the one having a hard time."

"I've wanted to talk to you about that. You sort of brought those problems on yourself. But don't worry," she said quickly, when she saw my glare, "you're here now and you can start over. Have a clean, fresh slate. Right?"

"I can't believe I'm back here," I said again. "I can't do this right now—"

"What? I'm sorry, I said something wrong . . ."

"No. I just want to be alone."

"But I wanted to celebrate—"

"Why would this be a celebration for me, Renee? Losing everything so I have to move back home with you? You think I'm excited about being here? I *hate* Houston. I *hate* everything about being here."

"But your family is here—"

"Correction. *Your* family is here. I don't have a family."

Her face crumpled in like a piece of tin foil.

"I'm sorry, I meant—"

"I know what you meant. Here," she said, handing me my soda. "I'll leave you alone."

"Sorry," I said to her retreating back. I couldn't tell if she didn't hear me or she just *chose* not to hear me.

DANCE, BALLERINA, DANCE

Watching my mother dance had been one of my favorite pastimes. She only did it when she thought no one was watching, so it was hard to catch her. But when she did—oh, how she took my breath away! She would dust off her dancing shoes and dance around the house, high up on tiptoes. She moved so easy, so graceful, I thought she could float on air.

I've seen pictures of her in her costumes, doing a performance of Swan Lake at her school, her tutu white as snow as she danced the lead.

"Why'd you stop?" I would ask her as she stretched.

She shrugged. "Just didn't want to do it anymore."

"Why, Beverly? You're so good at it."

She winced at the sound of me using her first name, but by then she'd gotten used to it and she didn't try to discipline me.

"I made some decisions that took me away from it. Sometimes being good at something doesn't mean you have to do it."

"Am I the reason you stopped dancing? You couldn't dance with a baby, could you? You regret having me, don't you?"

She caressed my cheek. "It's not you I regret."

"Then what *do* you regret?"

"Mariah, will you stop with the questions! I love you, okay? What more do you want from me?"

It was a question without answers. What did I want or expect from her?

On Beverly and Anthony's eleventh anniversary they flew to Paris for a week. We stayed with Grandpa, a place I would rather be anyway. When they came back and picked us up, they sat us down and gave us our gifts—*for being good*, they said.

Renee unwrapped a beautiful porcelain ballerina jewelry box. When she opened the lid, a soft melody played that brought tears to my eyes.

"It's beautiful, Mama! I love it!" I watched them hug and waited eagerly for my present.

It was wrapped in newspaper. I tore it away and stared at a snow globe. Of the Eiffel Tower.

"This is it?" I shrieked. "A stupid snow globe?"

"What's wrong with it?" Beverly asked.

"I don't want it! I want that!" I screamed, pointing at Renee's gift.

"Oh, Mariah, you can't have everything she gets. Your gift is just as special, let me show you."

I threw the globe on the floor, shattering it into hundreds of little pieces.

"Mariah!" Anthony said sharply. "What has gotten into you?"

My feet were wet from the water that leaked every-where from the globe. "Why do you try so hard to show that Renee is your favorite?" I asked. "Why can't you treat both of us the same? I want what she has, too!"

Beverly shook her head and pulled out another bag wrapped in tissue paper.

"Open it," she said, her voice shaking from anger.

It was a ballerina. A beautiful, black ballerina.

"Oh, Mama—"

"No. From now on, call me Beverly."

BREAKING RATTAIL COMBS

I tested Renee's phone for long distance by calling Norma.

"I was getting worried about you! How are you? You were supposed to call me as soon as your plane landed."

"Sorry, I was too busy trying to kill myself."

"That bad?"

"Worse. My sister is pretending like having me over here is the best thing ever, and Beverly—"

Just the sight of me brought a glimmer of sadness to her eyes that was much easier to ignore in New York. "Well, Beverly acts the same as always when I'm in a room, so I guess that's comforting."

"Would it make you feel better if I told you how much I miss you?"

I started to grab a piece of my weave and twist it around my pinky finger, but remembered it was gone. I settled for scratching my head and said I missed her, too.

"I could make some arrangements in my schedule to come down there in a couple of weeks."

"Elizabeth is due in a couple of weeks. You can't do that—"

"I know, but I *want* to. Besides, I haven't been in Houston in years. I can visit my family."

"Isn't all your family up there waiting for that baby to pop?"

"Yes. But I still have other family in Houston. Some cousins that need visiting."

We both knew that her suggestion was empty and would never come to pass, yet I continued to talk as if it could become real. "That would be great if you could, Norma. Man, I wish you were here right now."

"Well, at least we can talk on the phone. You can call me every day, okay?"

"Yes. Believe me, I'll probably have to."

She laughed. "Call me tomorrow, okay?"

"Sure."

I hung up.

I must have forgotten to close my curtains the night before, because I woke up to the sun blinding me and someone beating on my bedroom door. I was still dressed in my clothes from yesterday and walked like a wino to open the door. Beverly stood there, fully clothed in a black St. John pantsuit, a small strand of pearls around her neck and her face made up and lips stained her trademark cherry red. Her hand was raised in a fist as she prepared to knock on my door again. When I opened the door, she put her hand down and smoothed her perfectly coiffed silver hair.

"Henry had a cancellation this morning so he's willing to squeeze you in now instead of this afternoon." She ran her eyes over my short hair that I'm sure was all over my head and said that she had explained how difficult my situation was and he still was willing to take me on as a client.

"I don't have any money."

"We know that, dear. Isn't that why you're staying with us? Renee has offered to pay for it, along with a few other things you desperately need. I've sacrificed my Friday morning for this, so be ready in ten minutes."

She turned on her heel and walked down the hall.

I closed my door and searched through my luggage and pulled out the only thing that didn't need ironing: a pair of jeans and a long-sleeve blue tunic. I always thought that if I ever moved that I would have tons of clothes, but after selling all my designer pieces and pricey handbags and purses, my wardrobe better fit a suburban housewife than a trendy twenty-nine-year-old. I threw on some flats, washed my face, brushed my teeth, and *attempted* to comb through my hair. After breaking two rattail combs I gave up and threw a New York Yankees baseball hat on my head. I couldn't believe I was leaving the house like this. A few months ago, my skin only touched clothes with four digits on the price tag. Now I looked like some of the people who used to wash my clothes. I shuddered.

Beverly took in my outfit and smiled.

"What?"

"I didn't say anything."

I crossed my hands over my chest. "I saw the way you looked at me."

"Why, for goodness sake, Mariah, does everything have to be such a battle with you?" Her face fell, and the sadness returned.

I let my arms hang by my sides. "No, I just—"

"Come on, let's go."

She grabbed a pair of keys off the wrought iron table as we left the apartment. "Renee made you a set of keys."

"That was nice of her."

She shrugged as I followed her to the elevator and we were silent as we reached the parking garage. It was hard to follow my mother's quick steps; she ran-walked everywhere and I was breathless by the time we reached the SUV. She stood near the passenger door, waiting.

"Well?" she asked, after a few seconds, the faint tone of irritation in her voice.

"What?"

"Open the door."

"I don't have the keys."

"I just gave you a pair of keys, Mariah."

"Renee made me a copy of the car keys, too?"

"I just told you that."

I fumbled with them and pressed a button, unlocking the car. My mother got in and I followed suit.

"Wouldn't it be better if you drove? I don't know how to get there."

She sighed. "You did have navigation in New York, didn't you? Renee has the salon programmed in. If you press that button," she said, pointing to a button on the wood grain steering wheel, "you can just say the name of the salon and the directions will pop up on the screen. The salon is called Elite Hair."

"Okay," I said, following her directions. She must have assumed I had navigation in the car I never owned, but I decided to let the subject drop. I hadn't driven a car since—well, high school. And even then it was just a couple of rides taking Henrietta to the store. Her Toyota Corolla had nothing on this thing. It took me a couple of turns and yelps of terror from my mother to handle the behemoth, but after a few minutes I got used to turning wide and loved the smooth ride and the feeling of sitting on top of the world. The salon wasn't far and we arrived in minutes at the modern, glass-enclosed salon.

"You have to parallel park," Beverly said.

"Parallel park? In this thing?"

"Oh, come now, you can do it. *Renee* never has a problem with it."

Determined to do better than, or at least just as good as Renee with parking, I accepted my mother's challenge with vigor. Too much vigor when I heard my mother shout, "Stop!" and heard the loud crunch of metal on metal.

"You backed into someone!" Beverly shouted, getting out of the car to inspect the damage.

I jumped out, too, which was mistake number two, considering I didn't put the car in park. I jumped back in when I realized what I'd done and shifted the car in park, but not before slamming into the silver BMW parked in front of us.

"What is wrong with you?" Beverly screamed, coming around front. "Don't you know how to drive?"

"I do, it just took me a while to get used to it."

"You caused damage to *both* of these cars, not to mention Renee's car. She trusted you!"

"I'm sorry," I mumbled, standing back to look at the damage. And damage it was.

The silver BMW had a damaged bumper and broken taillight, and the car behind us, a white Mercedes, was smashed in the front with scratches of black paint. The Escalade was in pretty good shape, nothing a good mechanic couldn't buff out, but it still was enough damage that I didn't want to explain to my sister. Especially my first day behind the wheel.

"We need to find the owners of these cars," Beverly said.

"How?"

"Well, they're probably customers of the salon, we'll just go in and ask who was driving what—"

"What did you do to my car?" a lady screamed, silver foils dancing around her head, her body draped in a white robe with gold embroidered letters that said "Elite Hair."

"We saw the whole thing, why did you back up so far?" She stood close to Beverly, biting her fist as she struggled to stifle a scream when she saw her Mercedes.

"John is going to kill me!"

"I'm sorry," I mumbled again. Beverly pulled out her wallet and started exchanging information with the woman. She told her how I wasn't from here and wasn't used to driving a luxury vehicle. After a few minutes the woman's anger dissipated and they were laughing like old high school buddies. Beverly's quick thinking came in handy; I didn't have a Texas driver's license or insurance in my name and the last thing I needed was to talk to a policeman.

"We deeply apologize," Beverly said. "Do you know who owns this car? We need to give them our information."

The lady seemed to calm down and told her who she thought it might belonged to. She gave me another hard glare, told me to be careful and walked back into the salon. My mother turned to face me, and I stepped back from the anger in her eyes.

"Tell me, Mariah, is this a preview of what your visit is to entail?"

She paused for a long time as if I was supposed to answer. When I realized I was I just shook my head.

"I have never been so embarrassed in all my life. When we walk in here let me handle the car and you handle your hair appointment. Or do you think you'll screw that up, too?" She didn't expect an answer to that one as she turned her back to me and entered the salon.

SO NAPPY

I walked into the salon and was blinded by white. Everything was white—from the bleached wood floors to the white leather salon furniture, to the white silk upholstered chairs in the waiting area—even the customers. I followed Beverly to a white desk and she introduced me to the thin receptionist. She gave me the once-over and dismissed me to the waiting area. I sat down while my mother trolled the salon and found the owner of the silver BMW parked out front. I felt out of place in the white crispness of the salon, like an octopus that inked itself or a Sharpie marker that escaped from its top. I felt my blackness purely and succinctly.

"Oh, my God," a woman said suddenly, and I knew Beverly had found who she was looking for. She led the woman outside to survey the damage, but not without sending me daggers across the room. I slunk lower in my chair, wishing I was invisible, but sticking out like a Dalmatian's spots. I was offered water or herbal tea and declined both. I was just ready to get the whole thing over and done with. A young woman handed me a white robe and escorted me to Henry's styling chair. His station seemed to float on air. It was made of clear acrylic and had shelves that held a few beauty tools. Everything else was kept hidden in a white chest of drawers near his floor-length, frameless mirror.

"Please remove the baseball cap," he said in a tone of utter disgust.

"Sorry, I forgot I had it on." I took it off and saw my hair in the mirror. It had taken the shape of the cap and looked like I was trying to pop popcorn on the stove on my head. He ran his fingers through it and shook his head.

"Your hair is dry. Very, very dry," he said, his pale hands separating my strands. "Are you trying to go natural?"

"No, I—"

"Then why is your hair so nappy?"

The cardinal sin that any white person could make is calling a black woman's hair nappy. It was like using the N-word; if you weren't black, you couldn't use it. What was Beverly thinking by taking me to a salon that didn't do black hair? Her hair was soft and bouncy, she could go anywhere. But me? I needed a stylist from the Motherland, someone who understood *my* roots as much as *their* nappy roots. This man couldn't help me. But after causing not *one*, but *two* accidents, I was too embarrassed to leave. I sat in his chair and listened to him tell me why my hair was so *ugly,* as he called it.

"I am going to relax your hair and then give you a trendy short haircut—"

"Haircut? I'm having a hard time already with it being this short. Are you sure we have to go shorter?"

"Do you trust me?" he asked, his pale blue eyes piercing mine through the mirror.

I wanted to shout no and hightail it out of there, but I simply nodded like an obedient first-grader.

"Good," he said patting my shoulder. "You have to trust me, or why would you be here?" He laughed to himself and then called his willowy, redheaded assistant to apply my relaxer.

I kept chanting in my head that a free hairstyle is better than no hairstyle, but I somehow felt like a laboratory experiment instead of a spoiled client. Beverly approached as my relaxer sat for a couple of minutes, telling me that Renee was on her way to look at the car.

"What did she say?" I asked, ignoring the tingling sensation on my hairline.

"Your sister is much more patient than I am. She wasn't too worried. I, on the other hand, am very upset. But more than that, I'm disappointed that you don't know how to take care of someone's personal belongings."

"It was an accident! I didn't mean to!"

"Was it?" she asked, her eyebrow perched up.

"What's that supposed to mean?"

She ran her hands through her hair. "Nothing, okay? I'm just a little tense from the accident."

"You think I did this on purpose?"

"Of course not, Mariah," she said, sitting down in the chair next to me. She sounded tired, as if just being near me drained all her energy.

"Beverly!" Henry said, walking over to us. She stood and they air-kissed. "Your hair is wonderful, as always. You want a blow-out?"

"You have time?"

"I always have time for my favorite client." He looked down at me.

"You okay?"

I nodded.

"Beverly, you never told me you had another daughter. She looks so, so . . . unlike you," he said.

She looked at me and twisted the strand of pearls around her neck. She slapped his arm playfully. "Of course you remember me telling you about Mariah. She moved to New York."

He seemed confused, then simply shrugged.

"Come with me, darling, and let Jessica shampoo you." He called his redheaded assistant over and she handed Beverly a robe.

"This will be a first, right? Both of us getting dolled up!" Beverly said. She squeezed my arm and followed Jessica to get shampooed.

"Voila," Henry said spinning my chair around so I could see myself in the mirror.

I was baldheaded.

Bald.

The little hair I did have lay like chicken feathers to my scalp; something by the light in his eyes he deemed a grand achievement.

"It's a pixie cut," he explained when words failed me.

"It's short," I stammered, feeling my hair. The texture I'll admit was a little softer, like changing the grade of sandpaper—rough, but a little finer. It didn't fit my face at all; I felt more *African* than African-American.

"I don't know about this," I said, turning my face different angles to see more of my bald head.

He shrugged. "Your mother said you were difficult."

"Let me tell you something about being difficult," I said, snatching the cape of my neck and throwing it to the ground. "I've endured your criticism and your ignorance, but now I've had enough."

He crossed his arms over his chest. "You people are always so dramatic. So come on, sistah," he said, rolling his neck and snapping his fingers side to side, "tell me what's wrong with your hair?"

I looked around the salon and saw a sea of white faces looking back at me, including Beverly's. They were expecting a show, another black woman to act a fool about her hair. But I was nobody's clown. Squaring my shoulders I turned on my heel and walked out.

I walked down the sidewalk a couple of paces, just enough for the faces in that glass-enclosed salon to not see me cry.

"Don't do it," I warned. But the tears wouldn't listen and down they poured. I wiped them fast, but still they came.

"Stop it. Stop it right now." I bit my lip so hard that I tasted blood, and only then would the tears stop.

"Get control of yourself." I took a couple of deep breaths and wiped my face again.

"Mariah?"

I groaned as I saw Renee close the door of a Mercedes and walk toward me.

"You okay?"

I nodded.

"Have you been . . . crying?"

"Of course not!"

"Okay. You want to explain to me what happened?"

I walked her back to her car and told her what happened, leaving out the part about Beverly's challenge. She shook her head at the damage to the other cars and grazed her hand over the scuff marks on her Escalade.

She sighed. "Well, at least you and Mama are okay. I'll call a tow truck and get it towed to the dealership."

"I'm really sorry."

"It's fine. Really. I should have asked how your driving skills were before I gave you the keys."

"I *know* how to drive."

"I know. I wasn't insinuating that. Where's Mama?"

I pointed in the direction of the salon and she went in. I closed my eyes and tried to summon the feeling I had every time I left the salon in New York.

I'd practiced for years to find the wind, so my hair looked bouncy and light and floated behind me. Everyone stopped to tell me how pretty my hair was. In the couple of minutes I had been outside, no one looked at me—except the man who stepped on my toe. After apologizing profusely, he just kept walking. He didn't remark on my hair or me.

Renee came out in a few minutes with Beverly trailing behind her. Her silvery hair was bouncy and caught the slightest summer breeze.

"Tow truck's here," Beverly said. "I'll tell him where the dealership is."

"You look great, by the way," Renee said. "I like your hair."

"I hate it. I'm not used to short hair."

"Really? When we were younger your hair was always short."

"Not by choice."

A few minutes passed and then Renee's SUV was hooked up to the tow truck. We got in Renee's Mercedes, her weekend car, as she called it.

"I really do think you look great," Renee said, looking at me in the back seat. "The short hair accentuates your long neck. You look just like Grace Jones. No, even better, Alek Wek. You know, the supermodel?"

I turned to look out the window.

"You know who I'm talking about, right?"

"Yes."

"So what's wrong with that?"

I know we have worked long and hard in this country for dark women to be considered beautiful, but I wasn't there yet. And I don't think a lot of people were there yet either, they were too busy looking at the Alicia Keys or Beyonce posters. *They* were considered beautiful in Black America. Certainly not Grace Jones. White people thought they were gorgeous, could see past their shiny ebony skin to their fine bone structure, but it reminded me too much of what I looked like in the mirror. And I didn't like it.

"What's wrong with looking like Alek Wek, Mariah? She's gorgeous."

"If you think so."

"Leave her alone," Beverly said. "She had a hard time at the salon."

"Yes, I did. You want to explain why?"

"You didn't like your hair?"

"Why on earth would you take me to a white salon, Beverly? Henry has no clue how to style African-American hair."

"He does a good job with mine."

"Gimme a break, your hair is straighter than Brooke Shields'."

"I thought it would be something nice we could do together."

"Oh, so now you want to bring me to the salon with you? When I was little I begged you to take me shopping with you or to go with you to get your hair done, but all you did was take me to the library or some boring book-store."

"You weren't into all that feminine stuff, Mariah. You liked to read. So I indulged that aspect of your personality."

"Maybe I would have liked being made up, too."

She turned around to face me. "Is that what I'm going to be doing this whole time you're down here? Apologizing for every little thing I do? I'm sorry, Mariah, okay? Are you happy now?"

She clicked on the radio to stop me from answering.

No, I wasn't happy. I planned to question her on why she never mentioned she had another daughter to Henry, but I was tired of being the bad guy. I leaned back in my seat and closed my eyes.

CHIPS AND QUESO

After following the tow truck and getting everything handled with her car Renee asked if we wanted to get something to eat.

At the mention of food, my stomach growled in anticipation of being fed. In all the rushing this morning I had skipped breakfast.

Renee laughed. "I take that as a yes."

"If you don't mind, I'll just go home," Beverly said.

"Aww, Mama, come on. It'll be like old times when we used to get our hair done and grab something to eat afterward."

My jaw clenched and I turned away. *She never took me out to eat . . .*

"No, really, you girls have fun."

We all climbed back into the car and drove Beverly back to the condo. "You girls have a good time," she said, getting out of the car.

Renee rolled down the window while I got out and sat in the passenger seat.

"You sure you don't want to change your mind?" Renee asked.

She looked at me, then shook her head. "No, thanks. Maybe next time." She walked toward the front of the building.

"What happened?" Renee asked as she pulled away from her high-rise.

"I told you, I don't like my hair."

"But why'd you have to go off on Mama like that? She was so excited about spending time with you this morning—"

"I'm sure."

"What is with you?"

"Nothing! I'm just still adjusting to everything. A lot has happened and . . ." I trailed off and felt those stupid tears trying to make a comeback. I licked my lips. *Don't even think about it. I'm still bloody from the last time you tried it.*

My threat worked and no tears fell.

I missed New York. I missed the noise, I missed the Indian guy who sold pretzels on Eighteenth Street, I missed walking to work and seeing a couple fight on the sidewalk, or a homeless man screaming at the top of his lungs that the world would end. Now I was back at a place I didn't want to be, in a city that brought back so many painful memories that I felt like crying every second. I rubbed my hand over my hair. My weave was who I was, and losing it felt like losing a foot. I was going through phantom pain, it felt like it was there, but every time the wind blew or when I touched my hair, I realized it was gone, and the knowledge of its absence made my stomach burn.

We drove for several minutes and pulled into a Mexican restaurant that I had never heard of.

"You ready?" she said, taking the keys out the ignition.

"Sure," I said, following her inside the restaurant.

"I figured you would want Mexican. I didn't see you eat anything last night."

Technically she was right, considering I snuck in the kitchen at two in the morning and stuffed my face with beef fajitas until my stomach swelled like a watermelon.

"That's true," I said, as we followed the hostess to a table that screamed of a bad Southwestern designer. She told us our waitress would be with us shortly as she handed us our menus and took our drink order.

"Don't you think it's a little early to be drinking?" Renee asked after I told the hostess that I wanted a margarita.

"It's past noon. It's lunchtime. What's wrong with that?"

"Nothing, I guess. I just don't like to drink."

"At all? No alcohol?"

"No."

"After everything that's happened to me today, I think I deserve a little liquor."

"Maybe it's the liquor that caused what happened today," she mumbled.

"What?"

"Mama says you were acting funny today. Were you drinking? Is that what caused the accident?"

"No! Man, Renee, you should know better than to ask me that—"

"That's the problem, Mariah. I don't *know* you at all."

We were silent as a young gentleman named Tony approached with my margarita and Renee's Diet Coke with lime. She ordered us chips and queso to start and then she ordered chicken enchiladas for her meal.

"And you," he asked, his dark hair falling into his eyes.

"I'll have the Tex-Mex platter," I said.

"Very good," he said. "Most people split it, but you look like the kind of woman who can handle the whole thing."

He walked away before I could say something witty back and I looked back at Renee, who was stifling a laugh.

"What?"

"Nothing. It's just . . . it's good having you back home. I've missed you."

I took a sip of my margarita and nodded. I didn't want to be reminded of Renee missing me. When her husband died last year, I'd flown down for the funeral but left the next day. Without saying goodbye. Sure, I could have called and checked on her, but I didn't. And I dodged all her phone calls, feeling guilty by the minute for her trying to reach out to me when I should have been the one who reached out to her. But I couldn't do it. She reminded me of everything I wanted to be. Everything I had—my weight, my hair, my looks, took work or money. Everything she had didn't cost her a thing. A natural beauty, Beverly called her.

"So, what else has been going on with you? Besides, you know, the obvious?"

"Nothing, really."

"You don't have a boyfriend? Nobody back home that's missing you?"

"I can definitely say that no one is missing me back home."

"What about your friend Norma?"

"Oh, yeah, well, she misses me. But she's married and pregnant. She's having a baby girl," I said, more sadness in my voice than I liked.

"That's a good thing, right?"

"Oh, yeah. She's going to be a great mother. She's coming to visit soon."

"That would be nice. We could all get together and have a girls' night! That would be so much fun."

I got the impression that Renee didn't have many female friends and asked her about it.

She shrugged. "I have acquaintances, you know, people I can go shopping with and go to the movies with. Nobody really close. Since Peter's death I haven't felt like doing much," she said, tearing pieces off her paper napkin.

Renee got married at twenty-one. I was a junior at NYU. I balked at the idea of being her maid of honor, but finally relented and walked down the aisle in a pink fitted gown that made me look like a piece of cotton candy on a burnt stick. Peter was a decent enough man; at fifty-six he still looked young enough to have fun. Beverly was proud that all her hard work paid off; she sat in the front row, crying like a baby, as if her world would end when Renee got married. I never thought Peter's death affected Renee—I always thought that she married him for his money. And money is what she had; Peter had been worth millions, and, without a prenup, all that money landed in Renee's lap. Not that I would have noticed—she never offered me a dime and I never asked for one. Until now.

"Well, maybe you should try to start having some fun. What have you been doing all day? Beverly mentioned some kind of volunteer work?"

She shrugged. "It's nothing. I go around and talk to high schools about the dangers of underage drinking."

"I guess getting a real job is something you don't have to worry about."

"What do you mean, getting a real job?"

"Oh, come on, Renee. You volunteer because you're bored, not because you have to or anything."

"I do it because I like it and I'm good at it."

"Shopping is something you're good at. If they paid you to do that, then you'd be a millionaire. Oh, I forgot, you already are one."

Renee stopped eating. "I'm going to ask you one more time, Mariah, what's eating you? You've had an attitude since you got off the plane. I've tried to ignore it, tried to look past it, but it's getting really old."

"You would have an attitude too if you lost your job and had to go around looking like Sinead O' Conner. I miss my hair, my career, my life!" I sank down in my chair. "This isn't how things were supposed to turn out."

"You think you're the only one going through change here? My husband died last year. And I know what you think, I know what everybody thought—I married Peter for the money. But I loved him. And it's hard now to start over."

"Sorry."

She picked up her fork and started eating again.

"I'm really sorry, okay? Sometimes I forget about your . . . about Peter. I'm sorry. And I'll try to fix my attitude."

"With Mama, too?"

"Now you're pushing it," I said taking a sip of my margarita. "Her stylist didn't even know I existed before today."

"Henry has a short attention span. He only hears what he wants to hear."

"Still, that bothered me. Being back in Houston makes me feel like I'm ten years old all over again." I rubbed my hands over the nape of my neck and bristled at the thought of my weave being gone.

"Mama treated us both differently. You don't think it bothered me when we were younger that she pushed you so hard for an education? She never pushed me to do homework. She always used me for her shopping or makeup tips. I would have liked to come home with an 'A' every once in a while. But in the end, she's still my mama. And she did the best she could by us."

We sat silent for a while, both of us eating fast to avoid more conversation.

"I'm speaking at Druid Monday. You want to come?" Renee asked.

"Sure. What else do I have going on?"

She smiled.

PRIDE

Renee surprised me by pulling up into a Sprint store and letting me pick out a new cell phone, which I begrudgingly accepted. She picked out the newest Blackberry, complete with touch screen and everything.

"I don't think I need all this," I said, although my hands were shaking at the mere thought of having an old friend back. My cell phone was often glued to my ear in New York, and it broke my heart to have to end my service. Now I felt like I was part of human civilization again.

"Sure you do. It's really neat; I just bought Mama one last week. We'll take it," she said to the overworked sales clerk.

"Renee, are you sure?" I asked, cringing at the price. "I really don't need all this."

"You need a phone, Mariah. Just relax, okay? While you're staying with me I plan on taking care of you."

I didn't want her taking care of me. I wanted to take care of myself. The sooner I found a job, the better.

"Thanks for the phone," I said as we walked back to the car.

"No problem," she said, starting the car and maneuvering back into the heavy afternoon traffic.

"And I'm really sorry about the car," I said in a small voice.

"Again, no problem. As long as you weren't hurt."

"I hope you don't think I'm going to just lounge around the house all day. I plan on looking for a job soon."

"I know. But why don't you take a break for a little while? You've been working non-stop for twelve years. It won't kill you to take some time off. On my dime, of course."

"I'm not a mooch."

"Did I say you were?"

I couldn't imagine a day not going to work. What would I do all day if I didn't work? Sit at home and watch TV. I shuddered. The thought of watching daytime television made my skin crawl.

Renee seemed to sense my hesitation. "Let's say you were looking for a job. What would you want to do?"

"I want to see if I can do something I'm experienced in. I graduated with a degree in journalism and I haven't done any *real* journalism. While I have this chance I need to get my feet wet and go back to my roots. I'd like to see if any newspapers are hiring."

"I understand, but why don't you hold off for a month? Take this time to find out what you really want to do."

"I guess."

"And if you need anything, just ask."

"Why didn't you loan me enough money so I could keep my apartment and stay in New York?"

"Whoa, that came from nowhere. Okay, since we're going there, why didn't you ever *invite* me to New York so I could *see* this fabulous apartment of yours?"

"Touché."

"You never asked me for money, Mariah. But if you had asked, you know I would have given it to you. You just let your pride get in the way."

"Sometimes, pride is all a girl has left."

DOOR CHIMES

Before we left the parking lot, Renee stopped to get gas.

"You need something?" she asked, clicking off the ignition to go inside to pay.

"No, I'm—" And that's when I saw it. The words—*Beauty Supply*— glowing in red letters next door to the gas station.

"Hello?" Renee said, waving her hand in front of my face. "Do you need something or not?"

"Oh, I'm sorry. No, I'm good." I got out of the car. "You mind if I go in that store real quick and look around?" I asked, pointing to the Beauty Supply.

She shrugged. "That's fine."

We went our separate ways and I pulled open the door and heard a chime go off to alert the owners another customer had entered.

"Hello," a small Asian man said. A woman, who I assumed was his wife, was kneeling, stocking a shelf full of beauty products. She threw me a limp smile, then put her head back to her work.

"Can I help you?" he asked, his accent thick as an elephant's belly.

"Um . . . can I look at some of your hair?"

He smiled and then stepped up behind a platform where rows upon rows of hair weave went up to the ceiling.

"What kind?"

"Indian Remy. Jet black."

He pulled a silver package of hair and opened it for my inspection.

"Good hair," he said. "The best."

"Yes, I know," I said, running my fingers through the silky strands. I sighed and tried to remember the feeling of it in my head. It wasn't the brand I used—Tameka ordered my hair online—but it was close enough.

"You want it?" he asked, sliding the hair from my hands.

"Wait." I pulled the hair back and kept running my hands through it.

"Ma'am, are you ready to pay? I have other customers."

"Yes. I mean . . . no. I don't have any money . . ."

He shook his head and slid the fine, Indian hair back into its protective plastic covering. I snatched it back from him.

"I'm not finished looking."

He held on to the hair and we began a tug of war over a package of hair weave.

"Ma'am, you have money?"

"No," I said, holding on to the hair for dear life.

"Then. Let. Go."

His wife stood up behind me and said something in Korean. "Call police," she said finally, her English broken and heavy.

Just let go, a voice said inside me. *Just let go of it.*

"Mariah!"

Renee's voice brought me back to reality and I let go of the hair. He stumbled backwards and then regained his balance.

"Get out of here, crazy woman! Get out of my store!"

"Mariah, what's going on?"

"You heard the man, Renee. Let's get out of here."

I rushed past her, and pulled the door open to go outside, that stupid chime ringing like alarms in my ears.

She followed me. "What was going on in there? Were you trying to steal a bag of hair?"

"No," I said, standing next to her car. She unlocked it and I got in, resisting the urge to cry for the second time today.

"Then what were you doing?"

"I was just looking at it, okay? That's all."

She threw me a weird look, but said nothing as she peeled out of the parking lot.

CHICKEN HEAD

When we arrived back at the house Beverly was gone. Renee reminded me that today was Friday.

"She still does that?" When we were younger, Beverly used to volunteer her services every Friday to teach dance to underprivileged kids. I couldn't believe she still kept that up.

"Yep, she still teaches. You want to come down and watch her?"

I shook my head no. I started down the hall to my room, needing to unpack my meager possessions. I stop when Renee calls my name.

"You turning in?"

"No, but I need to get some unpacking done." Her face fell and I asked, "Is that a problem?"

"No, but I thought we could chill together in the living room, maybe rent a movie? We have video-on-demand with our cable."

"Not tonight. Maybe tomorrow?"

She nodded. "Well, have a nice night then."

I walked down the hall into my room and immediately went to my bathroom to glance at my bald head again.

He scalped me. I was bald as a newborn baby.

Yeah, I had a few strands on my head, but it was so *short*. With everything that I had lost, my career, my apartment and my *life*—nothing hurt worse than losing my weave. I felt the nape of my neck and closed my eyes, remembering the long tresses that flowed past my neck down my back in luscious curls. I used to roll it, hot curl it, flat-iron it—what was I supposed to do with my hair now? I picked up a few strands and grimaced when I saw they were barely an inch long. *I could just ask Renee to buy me a wig, or help me find a hairstylist that could hook up a weave . . .*

I shook my head. It was bad enough that I had to ask for money, food, a place to stay. I couldn't ask for one more thing, even if it meant I walked around like a chicken head. I knew my hair would only stay as flat as it was if I wrapped it up in a satin scarf. I went back in my room and searched my luggage for something to wrap my hair with at night, then remembered that I hadn't packed such a thing; I hadn't needed anything like that before.

I walked back to the living room to ask Renee if I could borrow one of hers.

"A wrap?"

"You know," I asked, "one of those things you wrap your hair with at night so it stays flat?"

"Oh, you mean a head scarf. Mama wears them sometimes. But she does hers for fashion mostly. Go check in her closet."

I walked down the hall opposite to my room. "Are you sure it's okay?"

Renee waved me off, too engrossed in an episode of *Iron Chef* to pay attention to me. I continued to walk down the hall and pushed her door open. *Her room smells like her.* Fresh and clean like expensive scented soap and baby powder. It was decorated in different ranges of violet and lavender, with vases of white hydrangeas spotted all over the room. I quickly went to her organized closet with its glossy white shelves and drawers with blown-glass knobs. I saw a silk blue paisley scarf playing peek-a-boo out of the drawers and I pulled it out and wrapped it around my neck. I looked up at all the hat boxes that I were stacked on top of each other, and couldn't help but smile. This was one of the best parts of the beauty pageants that Renee and I used to put on: trying on Beverly's outrageous hats. They were huge creations that shielded her face from the sun, and came in every color of the rainbow. Some were decorated with fruit, flowers, or feathers and we felt like little queens roaming the house with her hats on. She wasn't a religious woman, so I never understood why she had so many, but we loved playing with them, regardless if she wore them or not.

I saw a hat box that was decorated with pink and green flowers that I remembered playing with.

"The pink hat," I breathed.

It was my favorite hat to play with growing up. It was a baby pink straw hat, light as air in my hands. I reached out on my tiptoes and put my hands underneath the box, trying to be as careful as possible. The box teetered on my fingertips and came crashing to the floor. The lid slid open, revealing its contents.

Old papers and envelopes scattered on the floor beneath my feet.

Guess I found your love box, I thought while I bent down to pick up the letters. Amid the letters were newspaper clippings from Texas State. I picked one up and read the wrinkled page. It was a big picture of a young man, grinning wide into the camera, holding a trophy. The headline read:

Paul Stevens Wins Meet, On the Way to State!

Paul Stevens won today's track meet against Georgetown. When asked what drives him to succeed, he says, "Everything in life, I go all the way. That's the only way to live." We have to agree with him. Congratulations, Paul!

I smiled looking at the photo. Mama showed it to me several times when I pestered her about my father. Even in the black and white photograph you could see my father's complexion was dark; you couldn't see the outline of his face against the night sky. I put the paper back in the box and what I found next made my heart seize.

"Everything okay?" Renee asked, her footsteps coming my way.

I stuffed the manila envelope in my jeans and pulled my shirt down to hide it. I was throwing the rest of the papers in the hatbox when she came into the closet.

"Did you find it?" she asked.

"Yeah," I said, waving the blue scarf in front of me like I was asking for surrender. I stood on tiptoe and put the box back where I found it. "I was just looking at the hat I used to play with all the time—remember when we were younger? Yeah, I was just looking at it."

"The pink one? I remember that one. You used to love that hat. I'm surprised that she still has it."

"Well, she does. I was just looking at it. The hat, I mean. Nothing else."

"Sorry I was so short with you before—I don't like to be disrupted watching my show. What's wrong?" she asked, searching my face.

"Nothing."

"You sure? You look like you've seen a ghost."

"What? Huh? Oh, I was just thinking how I used to have a closet something like this. A closet full of clothes. Just got me thinking about all the stuff I used to have."

She smiled at me.

"Let's go shopping for some new outfits! We could make a whole day of it."

"We'll see," I said, walking out of Beverly's bedroom. Clothes were the furthest thing on my mind. Could she have lied all these years? The writing was clear as day, *irreconcilable differences.* Beverly filed for divorce a month after I was born. Why would she have to do that if my father was dead? *The dead don't need divorces . . .*

JUST A THEORY

I went to my bedroom and locked the door behind me. I shoved my clothes off the bed and sat down, pulling out the envelope with the divorce papers inside. I looked them over carefully, line by line. Beverly filed for divorce on May 5, 1980. Almost a month to the day after my birth. I looked at Paul's signature on the divorce decree, a scrawl that resembled fine chicken scratch.

Why hadn't Beverly told me that they divorced before he died? Why all the secrets? I grabbed the phone on my nightstand and called the one person who might help me find the answers.

Norma picked up on the second ring. "Hey," she said, groggy, "I forgot about the three-hour time difference."

"Sorry, did I wake you?"

"No. It must be good, though, if you have to call so late. What's up?"

"So I'm in Beverly's closet, right—"

"For what?"

"Never mind that. I'm in her closet and I find an envelope with her divorce papers inside. Divorce papers from my father."

"How did you just stumble across that? Were you snooping?"

"No, just listen, it gets better. So they're dated a month after I was born."

"So?"

"So? Beverly told me that Paul *died* a month after I was born. Dead people don't get divorced."

"Interesting. But he still could have croaked after the divorce."

"But why lie about it? Why not tell me that you were divorced when he died?"

"People lie for all kinds of silly things, Mariah. Maybe your mom was embarrassed about the divorce, maybe she didn't want you to know that she wasn't in love with him when he died—"

I snorted. "It's still not a reason to lie. Do you know I only have one picture of him? One. That's not right. She never wants to talk about him. She cries every time I bring him up—I'm starting to think she did all that on purpose."

"Everybody grieves in different ways."

"It doesn't sound like grief to me. She lied to me."

"Technically she didn't lie. She just didn't tell you."

"That's still a lie of omission."

"Okay, somebody's been watching a lot of *Law & Order*."

"Look, you always said it was weird that I couldn't ask questions about my dad. Back me up here, wouldn't you be angry?"

She yawned. "Probably. Okay, tomorrow morning just ask her about it."

"Just flat out?"

"Flat out."

"That could be a problem."

"Why?"

I told her the story of how I found the divorce papers. She laughed. "I knew you were snooping."

"But you see the reason I can't flat out ask her."

"Well, you're going to have to figure out how to bring the subject up. *Without upsetting her.* If she starts crying, you'll never get the goods."

"All right. I'll figure something out."

"Good. Can I go back to bed now? I'm sleeping for two."

"I thought it was eating for two?"

"Same thing."

DIVORCE

Norma was wrong. The next morning, it seemed more plausible that Beverly *would* lie about something like that. Anyone could be capable of lying. I showered quickly, eager to get the day started. I didn't sleep at all last night, I just kept thinking of all the stories Beverly told me about Paul. She described his funeral so clearly—down to the outfit she had worn.

I toweled off and got dressed in dark blue jeans and simple yellow cardigan. I brushed my hair, feeling more like a boy by the minute, and walked into the kitchen. Beverly was in the kitchen pouring herself a cup of coffee. She was fully made up, as she was every morning. I said hello as I waited patiently for her to finish with the coffee pot.

"Good morning," she said, returning the pot to its warm holder. I grabbed a mug from a cabinet and poured myself a cup, not adding any sugar or cream.

"Did you sleep well?" I asked, not caring if sarcasm leaked into my voice.

"Yes," she said, sitting down on a barstool that didn't look like it was anything more than decoration. "I slept quite well."

"I didn't think you got much sleep."

"No, I sleep fine most nights."

"Do you ever miss Anthony?"

Her eyebrow quirked up. "Of course I do."

"It's been—"

"Five years," she said.

"Wow. I forgot how long it's been."

"Why the sudden interest in Anthony? You were barely that interested when he was alive."

I shrugged. "I'm glad that Renee got to know her father. Not all of us can be so fortunate."

Her hands flew to her throat and played with the strand of pearls around her neck. "I'm sorry."

"Why would you be sorry? You didn't have anything to do with my father dying."

"No, but . . ." She looked away. "I wish things had turned out differently for you."

"I do, too." I took another sip of my coffee. "When was the last time you visited Grandpa?"

She coughed. "It's been years. Why?"

"I haven't seen him in years, either. I was thinking of visiting him now that I'm down here."

"Why are you curious about visiting your grandfather? You never seemed that concerned about him before."

"And that needs to change. I think I'll take a ride out there and visit him."

"No," Beverly said, slamming her coffee mug so hard on the granite, I thought she cracked it. "He's an old man, and he isn't right in the head. Leave him alone."

"Why are you getting so upset?"

"I'm not getting upset. I'm just saying that he's full of old stories. Sometimes he doesn't make any sense. He's over seventy now and he deserves some peace. I don't think it's a good idea."

"I'm going," I said, daring her to try to stop me. *You're hiding something, Beverly. Why? What are you afraid that I will find out?*

We stared at each other for a few minutes and she looked down.

"Fine. I could never tell you anything, you were always so headstrong. Just don't come home upset about all the stories he puts in your head."

She picked up her coffee and slid off the stool in one quick motion.

"Beverly, did you divorce my father?"

She stopped, her back to me. Never turning around, she threw over her shoulder, "You've heard the story a million times, Mariah. I'm not re-hashing it again for you. Your father died."

"I know that part. I'm talking about before he died. You sure you didn't get a divorce then?"

She turned then. "Why are you asking all these questions all of a sudden? Is there something you want to ask me? Because if it is, stop dancing around and ask."

"I thought I did just ask you."

"Okay, what did you ask me?"

"A divorce. Did you get one?"

"No," she said as she left the kitchen.

OFF-LIMITS

Renee came into the kitchen a few minutes after Beverly left and helped herself to a cup of coffee.

"Good morning," she said.

I nodded.

"Mama was real excited about the three of us going shopping; now all of a sudden she doesn't want to go. You want to explain that to me?"

"I have no idea."

"What did you say to her this morning? I thought you were going to fix your attitude—"

"My attitude is fixed. This is just my winning personality shining through."

She sighed. "She was crying."

I said nothing, just took another sip of my coffee.

"You don't care, do you? You don't care how much you hurt her?"

"Did you ever stop to think that maybe she's the one doing the hurting?"

"How has she hurt you? Explain that to me."

"She lied."

"About what?"

I started to tell Renee everything. But then that would mean she would think I was snooping around in Beverly's room, something I was *definitely* not doing.

"Nothing. You wouldn't believe me if I told you, so let's drop it."

She sighed. "You hungry? I could whip us up something to eat. Bacon and eggs, maybe?"

"No thanks. I'll just have some toast."

"Toast it is."

I watched her get the bread from the stainless steel bread box and slide it into the toaster oven.

"Is this the kind of wife you were? Doting?"

"Excuse me?"

"I could have made the toast myself."

"I know, but I like doing it."

"I can see that."

A few seconds later and a soft ding said the toast was ready. She grabbed the slices, slathered a thin spread of butter on them, and then placed the toast on a saucer and handed it to me.

"You make it sound like a sin to take care of your man. Yes, I doted on Peter but he doted on me, too. Marriage is a partnership, something you need to learn."

"Thank you for enlightening me on why I don't have a man."

"The sad part is that you've fooled yourself into thinking that you don't even want a man. But you're lonely. And you can't fool yourself into thinking you're not."

I stood. "I just lost my appetite."

Beverly came rushing back into the kitchen, her eyes red from crying. She stood for a moment looking at me, her arms crossed over her chest.

"Where is it?"

"Where's what?"

"Don't play dumb, Mariah. I knew for you to be asking all these questions that you had to have been snooping in my bedroom." She turned and looked at Renee. "I told you before she came down here that my room is off-limits. I don't want *anyone* in my room!"

"Mama, calm down. She just asked me for a head scarf and I told her that she could go in your room and find one."

"Well, that was just a lie for her to go digging around in my things. Where is it?"

"Where's what?" Renee asked. "What are you two talking about?"

"My divorce papers."

"Divorce papers? From who?"

"My father," I said.

"Mama, I thought that he died—"

"He did die!" she shouted. "I just didn't want you girls to know that I divorced him first, okay?" Tears streamed down her face. "I didn't want anyone to know what I did, how much I hurt him by leaving—" She stopped and snatched a paper towel from the kitchen counter and wiped her face.

My throat clenched. "I'm sorry. I thought . . . I don't know what I thought. I just wish you had told me. When I ask you about him, you never said anything about getting a divorce."

"I was embarrassed! I didn't want you to know about it! Some things are just for me, Mariah!" she said, beating her chest. "For my eyes only! Haven't you ever heard that expression?"

"Yes, but . . ." I looked down. "I'm sorry."

"I want those papers back. Now."

I left the kitchen and went into my bedroom. The folder was sitting on top of my dresser and I picked it up and walked back into the kitchen. Beverly was crying on Renee's shoulder while Renee rubbed her back and glared at me.

"Here."

Beverly turned and snatched them from me. She opened them to make sure all the papers were inside.

"They're all there. And for the record I didn't go in your room to snoop. I really did need something to wrap my hair."

"Well, I hope you found everything you were looking for." She turned on her heel and left.

THE INVITATION

"So that's why you were jumping on Mama's case?" Renee asked me. After the debacle in the kitchen I slunk back to my bedroom to hide.

"Yes," I said, sitting on my bed.

"And you used the excuse of needing a head scarf to look around?"

"I didn't snoop! That information sort of fell in my hands."

"Sure it did. Is that why you came to Houston? So you could learn more about your father?"

"You know why I came to Houston, Renee."

She sat on the bed with me. "Why are you so angry?"

I opened my mouth, expecting a witty defense to come out on why I'm not angry, but nothing escaped my lips. Was I angry? Bitter, and a little burnt out, sure, but angry? I shook my head. "I'm not angry, I'm just . . . frustrated." I lay back on the bed. I closed my eyes and pretended my weave was around my head, circling me like a paper fan. "This isn't me."

"What?"

"This," I said, waving my hands around the room. "In New York, I would walk in a room, and heads would turn. People noticed me. But here," I sighed. "I'm invisible."

"People notice you here, too. You just stopped paying attention."

I sat up. "Yesterday when I left the salon I didn't get one compliment. Not one."

"So?"

"So? Do you know how many compliments I would get before I even left the salon? Total strangers would tell me how much they loved my hair."

"So you need validation from complete strangers to tell you that your hair is pretty?"

"Don't make it sound like that! I'm just saying—"

"I hear what you're saying. I've heard everything you said. If you hate your hair all that much, Mariah, why didn't you ask me for the money to get you a decent weave? There are plenty of stylists here that could hook you up."

There it was. The invitation I'd been waiting for. All I had to do was say yes. Say yes, give me the thousand bucks for my weave, not to mention the weekly touch-ups and maintenance. *What are you waiting for? Say it! Tell her okay! No. Not without the test first.*

"I couldn't do that, it's too expensive."

I waited for her to chime in and say, "It's no trouble. Money is no object. How much do you need?"

And I waited.

And waited.

Finally I choked out, "I'm really starting to adjust to this new look."

She smiled. "Good. You look really pretty that way."

I smiled back to hide my disappointment. Well, let's hope it did.

"Come on, get ready."

"For what?"

"We're going shopping, remember? Mama's still doesn't want to go, but we still can."

So I could get clothes on her dime, but not hair? I nodded and told her I'd be ready in a couple of minutes.

Renee was always the one who tried. When we were little, she always tried to make me feel included, tried to make a part of the activities she and Beverly shared.

"Come on, Renee, you ready? The mall closes soon."

"But Mariah wants to come with us, don't you, Mariah?"

"Mariah has a history exam she needs to study for. Don't you Mariah?"

"Yes, ma'am."

"I'm going to quiz you when we get back."

Just once I wanted to see what it felt like to go shopping with Beverly, besides the big trip we took every year before school started. She never asked me, never even thought to ask me. So I pretended that I couldn't be bothered and stuck my nose further into the world Judy Blume created. But when they would come home from shopping I would look over the top of my book and see a rainbow of colors in Renee's hands. Purple skirts, floral pink dresses, turquoise shorts.

"Come look what I got for you," Beverly would say. Looking into my bag of clothes held about as much as excitement as eating oatmeal for breakfast. Black, grays, browns, beiges—all the color of dirt.

"Beverly, why do you always buy me stuff that isn't colorful?" I held up one of Renee's lemon-yellow sweaters. "See, this is what I'm talking about. Why can't I wear this?"

She frowned. "You and Renee have different coloring. Those colors look better on your skin tone," she said, nodding at the bag of clothes on the floor.

"So I'm too black to wear yellow?"

She snatched the sweater from my hands. "Why do you insist on being so dramatic? Did I say you were too dark to wear it?"

"No, but—"

"I *said* that these colors look better on you," she said, handing me a pair of khaki shorts. "See?"

I didn't see. I simply nodded and went back to my book while Renee tried on dozens and dozens of clothes in front of Beverly.

"Gorgeous, baby! You look gorgeous."

"Thanks, Mama."

"Here," Beverly said, handing Renee a soft pink dress. "Try this one on."

After enduring all I could take, I would stomp into the bathroom and slam the door. I would wrap a bath towel around my head, changing my short locks to long strands of royal blue cotton. Instantly I was transformed into Mariah Carey and balled my hand as a microphone and sang "Emotions" as loud as I could, my voice breaking at all the wrong places.

It was easier that way, to create my own world to become someone else. In this world, my hair was long, my skin was light and I could wear whatever color my heart desired.

I never insisted on tagging along with them on their shopping sprees. The older I got the more distant I became. Eventually I found my own circle of friends where straight A's and 4.0 grade point averages were more important than my dark skin and short, nappy hair. Soon I stopped caring where Renee and Beverly went, because I had places of my own to go to.

"Do you want to go with me and Mama to the store?"

"No, I'm going out with some friends."

"You want to go to the movies?"

"No, I already made plans."

I knew I was hurting Renee. Her face would seem to fall in on itself, like a flower that needed water. But like I said, it was easier to be away from her. It's easy to be second best when first place isn't around. You almost feel just as good, like you can stand on your own.

I hurt her by pulling away from her, and thus cemented the bond that she and Beverly had. And eventually she stopped asking me to go places, stopped including me in her life. And even though I knew it was my fault, knew that this is what I'd asked for, I was hurt when she moved on without me.

SHOPPING SPREE

A surge of adrenaline flooded me as we arrived at the Galleria. I hadn't been shopping in months and I almost forgot the intense pleasure that shopping gave me—the rush of trying on outfits regardless of price and leaving specialty shops with bags upon bags of expensive clothes.

"You ready?" she asked as we entered Neiman Marcus, the air conditioning sending goose bumps on my skin.

"You bet," I said. We scoured the store, finding crazy amounts of clothes to try on, laughing like schoolchildren at some of the ridiculous creations we tried on. Two hours later I finally settled on several blouses and jeans with a pair of comfortable Prada flats. Renee bought two scarves and a supple brown leather Bottega Voneta bag. We would have kept going but we still hadn't eaten anything, so we walked the mall and indulged in two slices of pizza. "Yum," Renee said, mozzarella sliding across her chin.

"I know, I was starving," I said, taking a huge bite.

She wiped her chin with a napkin and took a gulp of her Coke. "So what else did you have planned today?"

"Nothing much." I originally wanted to see Grandpa to ask him questions about my father. But now after the showdown with Beverly in the kitchen, there was no need for the questions. *Do you hear yourself, girl? You should want to visit him because he's your grandfather, not trying to pry questions out of him. Where's your respect?* Guilt made my mouth go dry and I drowned it with Diet Coke.

"You made it sound like it was a big deal, and now it's nothing? What's really going on?"

"I thought it would be good to visit Grandpa. I haven't seen him in ages."

"That sounds nice. He would love that. How long has it been?"

I shrugged, but I knew it had been since I graduated high school. Eleven years is a long time.

She pulled her cell phone out her purse.

"Who are you calling?"

"Mama. She would love to come with us."

"No!" I said, snatching her phone from her before she could dial.

"What's wrong with you?"

"Nothing. It's just that we've been having such a great day. I feel uncomfortable with her around."

"All right," she said giving me a weird look. "But we'll have to go tomorrow. They stop having visitors after five and it's already four. We'll never make it there in time."

"Tomorrow? Are you sure?"

"I'm positive. Why are you so eager to go all of a sudden? You waited this long, you can wait another day, right?"

"Sure."

"Good," Renee said. "Want to go see that new Tyler Perry movie?"

BONDED

It felt like Renee had crammed in years of catching up in one day. After the movie we went to dinner and finally we were on the elevator back to her home—tired and spent.

"Where have you two been?" Beverly demanded as soon as we walked into the door.

"I told you, Mama, we went shopping—"

"That was this morning," Beverly snapped. "Where were you all afternoon and evening?" she said, her gaze fixed on Renee.

"I called you a couple of times, Mama. We went shopping and then to eat—"

"I was hungry. Why didn't you ask me if I wanted something to eat?"

Renee looked at me.

"Oh, I get it. Mariah didn't want to include me, did she?"

"I'm standing right here."

She finally turned her attention to me. "I'm aware of where you are, Mariah. How many times are you going to disrupt things? I made it perfectly clear that you would only be allowed back if you could behave yourself—"

"Behave myself? I'm not a two-year-old."

"Well, you certainly act like one. You can't take care of yourself, you had to move back home and mooch off your sister," she said, waving her hand over my shopping bags.

"You live here, too, Mama. So what does that make you?"

She stepped back as if slapped.

"Renee, I will not have this girl talk to me in such a manner—"

"Enough. From both of you," she said, looking at me. "Like I said, Mama, I told you where I was going. You didn't seem to mind. I needed to bond with my sister, and there's nothing wrong with that."

"I see," she said. "Well, I'm glad you two have *bonded*. I'm going to bed." She stalked off, her silk robe fluttering in her wake.

"Sorry about that," she said. "You know how Mama can be."

"Oh yes, I know how *Beverly* is."

Okay, so I deserved that. After this morning's debacle I fully expected Beverly's tongue lashing. I went in my room and called Norma, ready to give her another earful.

"Hello?" she answered, her mouth sounding full.

"Girl, what are you eating?"

"Mariah?"

"Yes, it's me. What do you have stuffed in your mouth?"

"Cheese fries. It seems I'm always hungry at night. Are you ever coming back?" she asked, her tone wistful.

I wanted to say yes. If I closed my eyes I was still there—the smell, the noise, the people. But most of all I missed my independence. Since college, I took care of myself. Staying with Renee did not feel like home. And I don't think it ever would.

"I don't know," I sighed. "Maybe."

"What about the baby shower next week? You said you'd try to come back for that."

"I know, Norma, but things have been really hectic here. I don't think I'll be able to pay for it."

"You don't think your sister will give you the money to fly out here? It's just for one weekend."

I considered it, and then shook my head. "No, I'm already on her back enough as it is. If I do go I need to finance it on my own. My unemployment stops this month, so now I'm officially broke. Sorry, I think I'm going to miss it. But don't worry, as soon as I get a job I'll be out there, okay?"

She sighed. "I guess that will have to be enough. Are you even looking for a job?"

"No." I told her about Renee's suggestion that I take a break for a little while.

"That's good. We both know that job was driving you a little crazy. Do you miss it?"

"I miss the independence of making my own money and having my own place. But the job? Surprisingly, no."

"Wait a minute, did you just describe working at *Spirit* as having a job? Not too long ago it was your *career*, remember?"

"The longer I stay unemployed, the more I realize that they're the same thing. I wasn't fulfilled at *Spirit*. The thing I liked the most was bossing Cassidy around and feeling important. But looking back, it was doing me more harm than good."

"What about schmoozing with the literary elite? Don't tell me you don't miss that."

"I can't lie, I do miss that. I guess I'll have to admire them the way I used to—by reading their books."

"You're really not coming back?" Norma asked in a wistful tone.

I felt tears trying to break free and I closed my eyes shut, squeezing them together so hard that not even an atom could squeeze by.

"I don't think so."

The pause on the phone told me that I wasn't the only one trying not to cry.

"Okay then," Norma said, her voice shaky. "How long is this vacation going to last? What are you planning to do?"

"You know, for the first time in my life, I don't know."

Having a plan had always worked for me. Following a schedule, having routines, that's what made me happy. At least I thought it did. Now, the days stretched before me like the ocean, and a part of me was terrified that I didn't know my next step.

Studying as hard as I did in high school prepared me for college. College prepared me for my career. But being unemployed, what did that prepare me for? What other lesson was being in Houston preparing me for? I opened my journal and wrote:

What am I supposed to be learning from all this? What?

I've heard all that gibberish that there's a lesson in everything, but this feels more like I'm being punished. For bad behavior? I'll admit that I haven't always acted nicely, but where has being nice gotten anybody?

I thought about Renee. She was genuinely nice, and not one of those people who faked being nice just because someone was watching. Nice would be a word that described her. But where had it gotten her? She was rich, yes, but that wasn't because she was nice.

Maybe her being nice doesn't have anything to do with what she wants out of life. Maybe it's about how she wants her life to be.

GOOD TIMES

Sunday morning rolled around and I couldn't stand one more minute of inactivity. I didn't have time to get much exercise in New York, but all the walking I did, and the fact I had an ulcer that induced vomiting, kept my weight down. But my ulcer was on good behavior lately, and my Maalox bottle was half-full—something that never happened towards the end of the month. This also meant that some of my size 4 clothes were starting to feel tight, and after being scalped I couldn't be fat, too. I threw on a pair of sweatpants and a tank top and went to the kitchen to ask Renee if I could borrow a pair of sneakers.

"For what?" she asked, flipping over what looked like a blueberry pancake.

"I want to go running."

"Sounds great. We have an amazing gym here."

"I think I want to try doing it outside."

"In this heat? You'll be a puddle of sweat in five seconds."

I crossed my hands over my chest. "Still, I'd like to try."

She shrugged. "Check in my closet. I know I have a few pairs in there. Don't bother returning them. Just take whichever one you want."

"Thanks," I said, heading to her bedroom. I opened her door and shook my head. Her bed was unmade, her pristine white comforter tossed on the floor. I walked into her closet and stood there for a minute, my eyes trying to adjust to the mess before me. Shoes, clothes— everything lay on a heap on the floor. The clothes that were hung up were awkwardly on wire hangers, one sleeve on, the other tilted to the floor. I clawed through the mess, and pulled the only pair of sneakers I could find, a brown pair with Coach's distinctive logo splayed across the shoe. I sat on the floor and put them on and walked back toward the front of the condo to the door.

"See you later," I said to Renee.

"Don't melt."

Getting off the elevator I nodded at the doorman and headed outside. A burst of heat hit me so hard, I lost my breath. I shook it off and started running, heading to the walking trail that surrounds Renee's building.

Five minutes later I was back in the condo, soaking wet from sweat. My hair had puffed up into a teeny-weeny Afro and my legs felt like licorice.

"Back so soon?" Renee asked.

"Shut up."

After a shower and laying my hair down with gel, I was in the kitchen eating the blueberry pancakes Renee fixed.

"These are good. Homemade?"

"But of course."

"Where's Beverly?"

"Mama sleeps late on Sundays. You don't remember that?"

I shrugged and inhaled another mouthful of pancakes. "I guess I forgot."

"You don't remember the sign she made and put on her door every Sunday?"

I laughed from the memory. Renee and I used to sit on the floor outside her room and write notes on big pieces of construction paper, then slide them under Beverly's door. Most Sundays she would walk out like a zombie and slip on the paper on her floor. She never completely fell, just stumbled around like a drunk. She'd yell at us every Sunday morning, and never remembered to look down the following Sunday.

"What do you have planned today?" I asked.

"I wanted to just lie around and rent movies."

"Sounds good to me."

Renee squealed in delight, and, after finishing my pancakes, we headed to the living room. I was tense for a few minutes after eating so many pancakes, but my stomach sent no pain, and I felt the tension leave my shoulders. We laughed our heads off at the new Vince Vaughn movie, and then watched DVDs of all of *The Hills* like two Valley girls. It was the first time I'd really relaxed since I got to Houston. I have to admit, lying on the couch with Renee on the floor near me was soothing.

I thought that Beverly would pop out of her room around lunch. But she hadn't left her room all day. Renee went in there occasionally, sometimes bringing her water or food on a tray, but other than that I didn't hear a peep from her. After yesterday's tussle, it felt good.

"We used to do this all the time when we were little," Renee said. I was running her long hair between my fingers, pretending I owned it.

"Huh?"

"We used to watch TV with you lying on the sofa and me like this on the floor. And you used to touch my hair." She turned to look at me. "Remember?"

The memory came flooding back. We used to sneak in the living room and watch *Good Times* or *Sanford and Son*.

"I do remember now," I said. "Man, I wonder how I forgot that."

She shrugged. "I can't believe how much you forgot. When you moved to New York it's like you created a different life for yourself."

"Well, duh. That's what people are supposed to do when they move away. Time for them to spread their wings and be independent."

"I'm not talking about independence. I'm talking about how you shut me out of your life. It's like I didn't exist anymore."

I groaned. "Do you really want to get into this right now? I thought we were having fun—"

"We are. I just want to know why you didn't visit. Or call."

"I did! Remember when Peter—"

"Yes, I remember when Peter died and how you flew down here and stayed for what? An hour after the funeral? Don't you know that's the hardest time for a family? After the funeral?"

I didn't know because I hadn't lost anyone.

"Really, Renee, did you need me there? You had Beverly—"

"It wasn't the same. And yes, since you brought it up, I *did* need you there."

I sighed. "I'm sorry, okay? Sorry I wasn't there for you. But I'm here now. Can't we just drop all that stuff?"

"You're only here because you *have* to be, not because you *want* to be. If it was up to you, your next visit down here would have been at Mama's funeral. Or mine."

"That's not true!" Even as I said it, I knew her statement had a touch of truth in it. Would I have come back to Houston for any other reason?

"I would have come back if Beverly re-married. Or if you had."

She shook her head. "You see? You come back for *events*. But even then it's not a real visit. We never talk anymore . . ."

"We're talking now," I said. I sighed again and rubbed the nape of my neck, still shocked to not feel my weave on my shoulders. "Look, since you feel like dredging up stuff from the past, why aren't we at Grandpa's? I told you yesterday I wanted to visit him."

"I don't know, I guess I forgot."

"And when I mentioned it this morning, I guess it slipped your mind then, too?"

She stood up and stretched. "Just forget I brought it up." She walked to the kitchen and I followed her.

"Oh, no, you're not going to get off that easy. Why?"

She looked in the refrigerator, the stainless steel door like a wall between us. "You want a sandwich? I'm hungry."

"No, I don't want a sandwich."

"Suit yourself," she said, pulling out ingredients and setting them on the counters. I closed the door and watched her cut up a tomato.

"You can try to ignore me, Renee, but I'm not going to let the subject drop."

She stopped chopping. "Fine. I'll take you to go see him. It's not like I was preventing you from driving . . ."

I raised an eyebrow and she shook her head and continued.

"Although . . . I can understand your apprehension after the accident the other day. I didn't want you to see him yet because I don't want you stirring up stuff about Mama."

"I know. But I really just want to visit him. I'm not going to ask him anything about my father."

"Ask who about your father?" Beverly asked.

I didn't even hear her walk up, so the sound of her voice made me jump. Bare feet on hardwood floors would do that to you.

"Ask who about your father?" Beverly asked again, returning an empty glass to the sink.

"Nothing. I wanted to visit Grandpa tomorrow."

Beverly crossed her arms over chest. "What is it that you would like to ask him that you don't feel comfortable asking me?"

Why did my parents divorce? Did Beverly really love my father? All those questions and more swirled through my brain. Instead I said, "Nothing now. You caught the end of our conversation. I was telling Renee how bad I felt about yesterday. I'm sorry."

Beverly uncrossed her arms and exhaled. She pulled me toward her and held me in her arms. It was the second time that being in her arms brought tears to my eyes. I blinked them back and felt the familiar burn deep in my stomach. I pulled away.

"You all right?"

I smiled and rubbed my stomach. "I'm fine. Just pigged out a little too much. I think I'll turn in."

"It's only 1:00! You're tired?" Renee asked.

I kept rubbing my stomach and nodded. "Just going to take a quick nap," I said to both of them as I walked to my bedroom.

"Don't forget, you're coming with me tomorrow!"

I nodded, and race-walked down the hall to my bedroom. After closing the door I ran to my bathroom and threw up violently into the toilet. I flushed undigested food down and sat there on the cold, travertine floors. After the feeling of nausea subsided, I crawled to my nightstand and opened my bottle of Maalox, swallowing it like water. I grabbed my journal and pen and wrote:

Have I really been away so long that my mother's touch makes me cry like a silly little girl? I hate the way she makes me feel—all clingy and needy. Me, needy? No way. And I hate the way I just lie around all the time. Renee keeps telling me to relax, but it feels lazy to me. I don't know what to do with myself. What do you do when you have all the time in the world? I hate change. As weird as it sounds, throwing up just now made me feel better. That was the closest thing to a routine that I've done this past week. How sad.

NOT A CLUE

Hearing someone knock on my door was not a regular occurrence when I lived in New York. Norma had a key, and the only other knocking would normally be Chinese takeout. So you can imagine how nice I was to Renee when I found out she was the culprit behind the knocking.

"What?"

"Sorry," she looked down at my white socks. "You're not ready. Are you still coming?"

"Where?"

"I told you I'm speaking at Druid today. Remember?"

"Oh, yeah."

She looked at me. "So . . ."

"Oh. Oh, you want me to come with you?"

"What other reason would I be knocking on your door?" She looked down at her watch. "Can you be ready in ten minutes?"

I rubbed my hands through my hair, which I'm sure was standing up all over my head. I tied it down with the scarf every night, but somehow the thing managed to slip off, so I woke up with bed head every morning.

"I'll try."

She nodded. "I'll wait for you downstairs."

Fifteen minutes later I walked off the elevator to meet Renee in the lobby. She stood when she saw me.

"I thought you said ten minutes?"

"Do you see this hair?" I said, pointing to my head. My hair was brushed back and slicked with pomade. Well, I wish it was slick. Puffy would be a more appropriate word.

"It looks fine to me."

"You would say that. You know I look a hot mess."

"You're fine. Come on, we're going to be late."

I followed Renee to her Mercedes and got into the passenger seat. "I can tell this is going to be a bad day," I said as I buckled up. I ran my hands through my hair and burst into tears.

"Oh, my goodness, Mariah are you okay?"

I couldn't answer. I pounded my thighs with my fists, bit my lips, but nothing would stop the tears from falling. I couldn't stop them.

"What's wrong?" Renee asked, putting her hand on my shoulder.

I jumped back. "Don't touch me! I'm fine. I'm just fine," I choked out as the tears kept flowing. *Mariah, get a hold of yourself. You are a strong black woman, and strong black women don't cry! Now pull it together.* But the more I tried to rein it in, the more the tears flowed.

Renee pulled me into her arms. "It's okay. Let it go. Cry, Mariah. It's okay to cry."

I went limp in her arms. All sorts of sounds came from me, grunts, howls, and groans. I just kept crying. I sat up finally and wiped her shoulder. "Sorry."

"It's okay. It'll dry by the time we get to the school. Now tell me, what brought this on?"

"My hair."

"Your hair? You're crying because you don't like your hair?"

"No, I'm crying because I *hate* my hair. There's a big difference."

Renee laughed.

"You think this is funny?"

"I think it's downright hilarious."

I wiped my wet face and opened her glove compartment looking for a napkin. There wasn't any.

"Here," she said, handing me a tissue from her purse.

I wiped my face and blew my nose. I pulled the visor down to check my appearance, but got one look at my hair and slapped it closed.

"I should've known you would think this was funny. You don't know what's it like to walk around with nappy, short hair. You have good hair."

Renee pointed to her head. "This is good hair?"

"Don't play dumb, Renee. You know exactly who got blessed with good hair and who got stuck with the nickname Cotton Ball. You know I struggled with my complexion for years. That's one thing I can't change. But I refuse to be dark and nappy. I can't have two burdens on me."

"Burdens? Do you hear yourself?"

"Yes, I hear myself! I don't care about being politically correct. It's just you and me in this car. You like being the lighter sister, the pretty one. You like the fact that I'm in

Houston, staying with you, needing your help. You get off on this. And you know what else? I'm starting to believe the real reason why you won't offer to put some weave in my head is because you're afraid I'll steal your shine."

"What?"

"You heard me. Let's face it, Renee, you may have all the looks in the family, but I got blessed with all the brains. If I get my weave back, you'll feel threatened by me. 'Cause with my weave I'll have it all."

Tears started welling up in Renee's eyes. "Is that what you think of me?"

My stomach began to burn and I pressed my hands to it. I didn't answer.

"Is that what you think of me, Mariah?"

"Yes."

She nodded and started the drive to our old high school.

"You are a mean, ungrateful bully."

"What?"

"You heard me. I'm sorry about your hair, Mariah. I am. But I'm not going to apologize for how I look. This is how God made me. And if I were you I wouldn't apologize for how I looked, either."

"I didn't—"

"Let me finish!" Renee shouted. She stopped at a red light. "You think you got all the smarts in the family, but if you're so smart you would have figured out that it's not society telling you that you're not good enough—you're telling yourself you're not good enough. I'm sick of people thinking I think I'm better than them because my skin is lighter or because my hair is longer. So they try to talk about me, call me names, tell me how stuck-up I am, or that I think I'm all that. But you know what? *They* think I'm all that. So they try to get me feeling bad about myself. In that twisted mind of theirs, they think I'm better than them. And that's stupid. And so are you."

The light changed to green and she wiped the tears that were under her chin. "You know the real reason I didn't offer to buy your weave?"

"Why?"

"Because you become that person. You become the person that thinks she's better than everyone, that stomps on anyone who seems beneath her. You're evil with that weave, Mariah."

Evil? Ouch. That was harsh.

I swallowed the lump in my throat and continued to rub my burning belly.

"So what if I am? I like being that way. It's better to be the one doing the damage instead of the one receiving it."

"It's the same and you know it. You can feel however you want to feel about your hair. But I'm not responsible for what God gave you. You better learn to appreciate it. A lot of women would kill to have hair like yours."

"Whatever." I clicked on the radio and turned the volume up to let her know that I was finished talking.

"I know you didn't." She clicked it back off. "This is my car. Don't touch my radio. If you don't want to talk just say so."

"I'm done talking," I said, acting more like my shoe size than my age.

"Fine."

It's funny; when you're young, everything looks big to you. When I was a student at Druid High, everything was bigger, the halls were longer, the teachers intimidating. But as I followed Renee into the library where a few students were gathered, I was surprised at how small everything seemed. Renee walked to the front of the small circle of students while I took a seat in the back and slurped my latte.

She shook someone's hand and he introduced her to the class.

"Students, this is Renee Johnson. She's the last speaker in our drug and alcohol program, and she's going to share her story on how she beat her addiction to alcohol."

I choked on my latte and started coughing. One of the students had to slap my back to get me to stop, and finally I let out a strangled whisper that I was okay. Renee? An alcoholic?

"Good morning, students. Thanks, David, for the introduction. You wouldn't believe that my dependence on alcohol started right here at Druid. I was always getting made fun of, constantly teased. I didn't have many friends, and the other girls here made life seem unbearable."

A few students chuckled.

"No really, I got it pretty bad. Some of my classmates started a vicious rumor that I was HIV positive."

A girl raised her hand.

"Yes?"

"You're really pretty. Those girls were probably jealous that you were getting all the guys."

"In hindsight I see that now, but that's pretty hard to explain to a sixteen-year-old. The teasing was bad. One evening after dinner at home, I cleared the dishes. I carried them all into the kitchen and noticed my father had left his brandy glass on the table. It was still half-full. I took a sip, and I remember how it burned my throat. But I drained his glass. Soon I was sneaking into his liquor cabinet and drinking and adding tea to make all his liquor bottles feel full. Then I started paying our maid to buy my alcohol."

I couldn't believe this. Renee? A drinking problem? How could I have missed that?

Another hand went up.

"Yes, sir, in the purple shirt?"

"How did you keep getting away with it? When did your parents find out?"

"I think my father suspected something right away. He had to notice that someone was drinking his stuff. But he never said a word. I drank pretty much through my entire junior and senior year of high school."

"Did you go to college?"

"No. After I graduated from high school, I stayed home. I kept drinking, and a lot of the times I would black out from having drunk so much alcohol. At a party I drank so much that I woke up in a hospital. They said I had alcohol poisoning."

"Did you stop?"

Renee laughed. "I wish. Things just got worse. By this time my parents knew I had a problem, so they tried to get me to do all sorts of treatment programs. But I refused."

"Why couldn't they make you go?"

"I was eighteen. I was an adult. By law they couldn't make me do anything."

"So what happened next?"

"When I drank I felt popular and cool. I was invited to tons of parties—mostly because I provided all the alcohol. It was at one of these parties that I got so wasted and was out of my mind. I convinced myself that I could drive home. So I did."

"None of your friends tried to stop you?"

"They were all drunk, too, so they thought me driving was a great idea. But I got in an accident. I was okay, but I was pretty banged up. I hurt the other driver—broke his leg in two places."

"Did he sue you?"

"Worse. He married me."

They all laughed.

I remember faintly about Beverly telling me about Renee's accident. I didn't know that's how she met Peter, though. Why didn't I know that?

"Did you stop drinking when you got married?"

"I tried, but I didn't stop. I hid it from him, but soon he noticed how much I drank. He tried to help me, even tried an intervention. I don't have many friends, so it looked pretty pathetic that it was only my parents there."

My stomach began to tremble.

"My father died shortly after and I really began to hit bottom. I stopped trying to hide my drinking from Peter and . . . well, things got really bad."

"What made you stop?"

"I got pregnant."

My heart seized. A baby.

I could hear the tears behind Renee's voice, but not one tear fell from her eyes. "I did pretty well for the first month. Went cold turkey. Not one drink. But then I slipped up and started drinking again."

"Even when you knew you were pregnant?"

Renee nodded.

"Did your husband leave you?"

"No. He stayed. Even after I lost the baby."

Sharp intakes of breath filled the room, followed by silence.

"After that miscarriage, that was it. I haven't had a drink since."

"Did you try to have more kids?"

"Yes."

"How many do you have?"

"None. I've had four miscarriages."

"You think it's because you drank?"

She shrugged. "I'll never know. But to be honest, I do think I put so much stuff in my body that I can't carry a child."

"Did you adopt?"

"No. My husband died—"

"Did you relapse?"

"I thought I would. But no, I'm still clean. Not a drop of alcohol."

The students clapped.

Another student raised their hand.

"Yes?"

"Why didn't you talk to someone before your drinking got so out of hand?"

Renee's eyes locked with mine. "I didn't have anybody to talk to."

After Renee finished talking to the group of students, I walked out of the library and down the hall to the girls' restroom. I rubbed my stomach, opened the door to the stall and knelt down on the toilet and threw up. I wiped sweat from my brow and flushed. I stayed on the floor near the toilet and for the second time that day, cried.

A few minutes later I heard Renee calling my name.

"I'm in here," I said, the urge to vomit again coming back. I swallowed, then threw up. Renee pushed open the stall to see me in all my glory.

"Are you okay?" she asked, stooping down near me.

"No. No, I'm not okay. Why didn't you tell me, Renee?" I wiped tears from my eyes. She left the stall and returned with a moistened paper towel. She patted my forehead.

"Like I said, I tried to tell you. But you were so wrapped up in yourself, you didn't pay attention. Eventually I stopped trying to tell you. I hoped that you would catch on by noticing how different I was acting. But you never talked to me. I thought you were so busy at school . . . I finally figured out that you didn't *want* to talk to me."

"I'm so sorry, Renee." I fell into her arms and she rubbed my back. "I didn't know about the drinking and about . . . the babies."

I could feel her stiffen, but she continued to rub my back.

"I'm a horrible sister." I waited for her to deny it, to ease my guilty conscience by telling me that I just made a mistake. But she said nothing and just continued to rub my back.

"Are you feeling better?" she asked finally.

I nodded. "I have an ulcer. Sometimes I get a little nauseated."

"Maybe you need to get that checked out."

I waved my hand and stood up. I walked to the sink and rinsed out my mouth with water. "I'll be fine."

She followed me to the sink and we both looked at ourselves in the mirror. Renee was beautiful with her brown eyes with flecks of green, her long, wavy brown hair and her light skin with a sprinkle of freckles across her nose and cheeks. And I was the complete opposite. But did being opposite of her mean that I was ugly? Why did I think long hair and light skin meant beautiful?

Renee put her hand on my shoulder. "You weren't the best sister to me. But maybe now that you're home, you can make it up to me."

Home. Was I home? I didn't know. But I turned to my sister and gave her the tightest hug I could muster, hoping she felt the love I was giving her in my arms as I felt the forgiveness she was giving me in hers.

WILLIAM KNIGHT

I think losing my job can give me a second chance. At loving Renee more and forgiving my mother for the small things that she's done to me in the past. So what if she didn't take me shopping with her, or trips to the spa? Who was the one who sat with me and helped me paint all those Styrofoam balls to resemble planets? Beverly. Who helped me study all those words so I could win District XI spelling bee? Beverly. And who was the one who paid for the tutor so my SATs were a breeze for me? Beverly. Beverly ensured that I would have the best education possible. Yes, she was upset that I didn't accept going to Yale, but she got over it and never made me feel bad about it. I could do better by her.

I closed my journal and slipped it under a dish towel when I saw Renee walk into the kitchen.

"Good morning."

"Morning," she said. "You're dressed and ready? Wow."

"I know. I didn't want another day of someone knocking on my bedroom door."

"You excited about seeing Grandpa?"

"I am."

"You're not fooling anybody, you know. I saw you writing. Why would you try to hide it?"

I pulled my journal from underneath the blue dish towel. "I don't know. I feel sort of silly still writing in a journal."

"That was your thing when we were growing up. That and reading, of course. You couldn't keep your nose out of a book back then."

I nodded and drank a sip of my coffee.

"I'm starting to know why you didn't call me, but why didn't you ever check up on Grandpa? He really missed you."

I sighed. The whole time I'd been in Houston, all I'd learned was how messed up I was. How I'm such a bad person. It's bad enough being a bad sister, but I didn't need any more reminders of why I was a bad granddaughter, too.

"I know I've messed up with you guys. I should have been there. I had my priorities all mixed up—"

"You didn't even have us *as* a priority."

"I'm sorry. I'm really trying here, Renee. Cut me some slack."

She opened her mouth to say something and then closed it. "I'm going to get ready. I'll be out in a couple of minutes."

When she left I opened my journal and wrote:

How many times can a person say they're sorry for it to be true? A hundred times? A thousand? Is that the lesson that I'm learning? To learn to apologize? Well, I've learned it. I'm sick of doing it. I never claimed to be perfect. I know I let a lot of people down. Problem is, I never knew they were depending on me in the first place.

Oak Forest Nursing Home was in the Woodlands, a suburban city on the outskirts of Houston. It looked like a Spanish estate with its stucco walls and its red Spanish tiled roof and expansive rolling grounds. We walked into the two-story foyer, and I gazed up at the wrought-iron chandeliers and stone floor and felt like I was in a mansion, not a nursing home. Renee nodded at the woman sitting at an oak table and let her know that we were here to see William Knight.

"Of course," she said. "Would you like to visit him in his room?"

"Yes. Then we'll take him for a walk around the grounds."

"Nice morning for it. He would love that." She pointed down the hall and I followed Renee to his room.

William Knight, better known as Grandpa, was always smart; his mind was clear as fresh spring water. I hoped he would be the same way as I saw him several years ago; it would be heartbreaking to see him without all his mental faculties. Renee knocked on his door and I heard his gruff voice. "Come in," he said.

We entered the room and found Grandpa hunched over a desk. Wood shavings lay around his feet as he whittled a piece of wood into what I was sure would be some kind of animal. Several of his wood creatures were around his room, shiny and bright with paint. Morning sun filled his room and glinted off his mahogany-stained furniture. He looked up at us and smiled, his teeth artificially perfect. His hair was white, which spoke of his seventy years, but still full. His light skin was touched with hints of grey, and I felt my heart sting me. *I should have visited more often.*

"Cotton Ball?" he asked, standing. His back was bent at the shoulders, like he was carrying something heavy. The curlicues of wood fell to the floor as he walked to me.

"Yes," I replied, going toward him and reaching out for a hug. I always felt more secure at my grandparents' house; their love was given in large doses and I felt full, not starving with the crumbs that my mother doled out. In his arms I felt safe and protected. He smelled the same, like wood and clean soap.

"It's good to see you, Cotton Ball," he said, his hands on my face. "You look so pretty with that short hair, like a model."

I reached up to smooth my hair, feeling self-conscious.

"Thanks."

"My goodness, you sure did turn out to be a looker."

Was I? I smiled at his kindness; he always knew how to make a woman feel good. That's probably how he charmed his wife, Porsche. He'd told me the story millions of times, of how he saw her walking the hallways at high school and knew with a certainty that she was going to be his wife. And he didn't hesitate to tell her so. She laughed at him, not taking him seriously, but every day he would be waiting for her after school to walk her home. Their love blossomed and grew as the dirt road they walked on became paved, and the seasons changed. They were married the next year, and she got pregnant shortly after with their first child. That child was still-born, and so were three others. Porsche had several miscarriages, and thought she would never have children. Finally, in her twenty-eighth year of life she gave birth to Beverly, her one and only child. I knew he missed his wife terribly—Porsche died years ago from complications from diabetes—but a day didn't pass when she wasn't thought of.

He walked over to Renee and hugged her with as much warmth as he'd given me, and turned to look at me again.

"So what brings you to Houston? And don't say you came all the way down here to visit me. Grandpa can always tell when you're lying."

"I live here. For now, anyway," I added.

"You don't say? Why?"

"Well—"

"She got tired of the cold weather in New York. Wanted to come back to Houston where the weather is warmer." Renee winked at me, and I was thankful for her rescuing me.

"Well, I never could stand cold weather. That makes sense, Cotton Ball."

"Grandpa, you want to talk a walk outside for a little while?" Renee asked.

"That would be nice," he said, shuffling in between us. He stood in the middle of us, and we hooked our arms through his. "Let's go, ladies. Boy, all the fellas here are sure going to be jealous of me walking around with two models on my arms. Wait until they get a load of this!"

We laughed and walked slowly out of his room, with him stopping every few seconds, introducing me to everyone. I felt special.

We finally got outside and sat on a bench near the entrance, watching the morning breeze go through the tops of trees, making them dance.

"This is nice," I said after a few minutes of silence.

"Sure is. Porsche used to love to sit outside all the time on the porch. Didn't matter if it was too hot or not, she just wanted to sit outside. Said she had to get the ceiling off her head."

"Same with Mama. She likes to get outside a lot, too," Renee said.

"Yeah, back in the day we had trouble keeping your Mama *inside* the house. Always was too busy outside chasing boys." He shook his head. "Me and Porsche tried to get that girl to calm down, but she thought she knew better than us. Even after the divorce she kept on with the boys. Or men, I should say. Paul tried to hold out hope for her, but when she married Anthony I think that was the final straw. He tried for years to win her back—"

My stomach quivered. "Grandpa, how could Paul try to win her back? He died before Beverly remarried."

He turned away.

"Didn't he, Grandpa?"

"I'm getting tired. I think I want to go back to my room now."

"Grandpa—"

"Mariah, that's enough. He's tired." Renee stood and helped Grandpa up. "You coming?" she asked.

"Yeah, yeah." I stood and laced my arm through his and we walked back to his room. His gait seemed weaker now; his body was hunched over so much, I think all he could see was his shoes. Renee kept throwing me dirty looks, but I ignored her, intent on getting Grandpa to his room to ask him more questions.

We got to his room and sat him back down in his chair, and he picked up his knife and piece of wood and started whittling away, just as he had when we first came.

"Grandpa—"

"You girls can come back this weekend if you want. Saturday. And come alone. I don't want your Mama coming, messing things up."

"And then you'll tell me? Tell me about my father?"

He paused for a moment, and then continued shaving away wood. "Come back Saturday, baby."

"Grandpa . . ."

"Saturday," he yelled, then started coughing. When I approached, he put his hand up to signal he was all right. After a moment, he stopped coughing. "Come back Saturday. It's time," he mumbled. Although he could have said, "About time," or "I have the time," I wasn't sure. I nodded and gave him a hug and we left.

I could feel Renee's anger before I even asked her what's wrong.

"You just came over here to ask him questions."

"No, I didn't. I really missed him."

"Yeah, right. That's why you called him all the time and came down to visit every blue moon. Boy, sure sounds like you missed him."

"Well, I did. And I didn't even have to ask him anything; he slipped up with the whole Paul thing—"

"Slipped up? You act like everyone's keeping secrets from you. He's seventy years old, Mariah. His memory isn't exactly what it used to be."

"It seems crystal clear to me."

"You're using him. You don't care anything about him—"

"Don't go there, Mariah. I love that man. I just need to know the truth."

"You *do* know the truth. You just don't want to believe it. Your father died—"

"Maybe."

"Oh, come on! So now you're thinking he's alive? Gimme a break, Mariah, even Mama couldn't pull that one. Please tell me that's not what you're thinking."

I didn't answer.

She rolled her eyes at me. "I can't believe that she would lie about something like that. Not Mama. She wouldn't have made that up."

"Well, something's not right. You can feel it, too, can't you? That's why you're so upset."

"I'm not upset. But if I was, it would be because you keep making this thing an issue."

"It is."

"Drop it, Mariah!"

"No!"

We stood in the parking lot, a few feet from her car, both of us in a stare-down that neither of us wanted to lose. Finally, she looked down. "If Mama is lying about this, Mariah, you're not the only one who loses. I lose, too."

"I'm sorry. But you need to understand that I have to do this. For me."

"That's all you ever did care about. Fine. Keep digging. If Paul is still alive, he won't be a *dead* father, he'll be a *bad* father for not being there for you all these years. Do you really want that?"

My pace slowed. I hadn't thought of that. If Paul was alive, why wouldn't he have tried to contact me? This idea was crazy. The more I thought about it, about the more I wanted to dismiss it, but I couldn't. Could Beverly have lied all these years? Could there be a man out there with the same blood as mine in his veins?

"I don't know, but I'm ready to find out."

ANSWERS

It seemed like Saturday would never come, but finally it dragged itself here. I was up early that day and showered and dressed as if it was an Olympic sport. I still would have lost the gold medal because Renee and Beverly were already in the kitchen eating. It seemed the kitchen was where we always met, and so I often tried to stay in my room.

"Good morning," I said, pouring myself a cup of coffee.

"I made your plate already. It's on the counter. You might have to heat it up," Renee said.

I thanked her and slid the plate of eggs, bacon, and grits into the microwave. Beverly had yet to acknowledge my presence. She was too engrossed in the newspaper to even look up. If she wanted to play that game, that was fine by me. I was not going to kiss her butt to get a response. When I was younger, I spoke to her first. I used to wrap myself around her legs so she couldn't walk, just so she would look at me. Not anymore. If she wanted to talk, she knew where I was.

I took the hot plate out of the microwave and sat at the small table in the breakfast nook. I saw Renee nudge Beverly, but she wouldn't look up.

"Renee, are we still going today?"

"Going? Going where?"

"To the store. Remember?" We both agreed that we wouldn't mention going to Grandpa's so Beverly wouldn't try to tag along.

She looked at Beverly and then looked back at me. "Mama wants to go too," she said, so low I had to strain to hear her. She shrugged her shoulders as if to say she was sorry and then slid off the stool she was sitting on.

"I'm going to finish getting ready. I'll be back in five minutes."

Without Renee in the room, the silence was even more deafening. Every scrape my fork made across my plate was magnified, and the snap of Beverly's newspaper sounded like a thousand drums.

"I need to keep an eye on you," she said. I couldn't see her face, it was hiding behind an advertisement for Macy's "Red Apple" sale, but her tone told me plenty. Told me that I wasn't wanted, wasn't needed. Told me to stop stirring up mess.

"Why? What are you afraid of, Mama?" I got her attention then as the newspaper crept down her face, revealing her icy eyes.

"I'm not afraid of anything, I just don't want you making my *father* upset," she said, the word "father" especially hurtful because I didn't have one.

"*Your* father won't be upset. But I think I have every right to visit *my* grandfather."

"Of course you can visit him. He just tires easily, and a lot of questions wear him out."

She smiled at me then, and walked over to me at the breakfast table. She ran her fingers through her soft hair and then reached out to touch my shoulder, stopped, then finally rested her hand on top of mine. After a few moments she removed her hand.

"I had hoped that we could get along."

"So did I."

"Why? Why do you think it's so hard for us?"

Because you don't love me enough. It was on the tip of my tongue, like a lyric from a song that had been forgotten then remembered. I wanted to blurt it out, but couldn't—I couldn't tell her why we would never get along. Instead I replied with an "I don't know."

"Well, Renee and I have such a wonderful relationship. I want the same for you. But it's different with us. We had it rocky from the start, as if it wasn't meant for me to be your mother. I look at you and I'm haunted by bad memories, by nightmares. It's hard," she said, looking away from me.

"I'm sorry," I said, apologizing again for something that was not my fault.

She stood. "I am trying, Mariah. I know you may not feel it, but I'm trying to be better. Just remember how hard I had it with you, how you make me feel. Try to be a little compassionate, okay?"

I simply nodded, and she left the room. The knot in my throat expanded and I cried silent tears into my breakfast.

The drive to the nursing home was about as comfortable as sitting on a chair of needles.

Finally, we were out of the car and headed upstairs to Grandpa's room.

"Come in," he said from behind his thick oak door.

Beverly blew out a ragged breath as she fingered the pearl necklace at her throat. *She is nervous*, I thought. *Why?*

We walked into the room to see Grandpa seated in a chair near the window, looking out. He stood and hugged Renee and I, then looked at Beverly for a long time. Finally, he patted her on the shoulder.

"Good to see you, Beverly."

"And you, too, Daddy."

"What brings you by today?"

"I have to have a reason to visit my father?"

"For you? Yes."

She grimaced and then smiled. "I wanted to see how you were doing."

"I'm sure Renee keeps you abreast of everything that goes on with me. Now if you don't mind, I'd like to talk to my two girls."

"Daddy, are you sure?"

"Absolutely. Why don't you walk around and get some air? I'll be out in a minute," he said, waving her off.

Her eyes glanced in my direction and I knew I would be blamed for her early dismissal. She turned on her heel and left.

"Well, come on, girls, sit down," he said, pointing to a pair of wingback chairs in the corner across from his bed. "Now tell me, young lady, why is it that you haven't kept in touch?" he asked, his light brown eyes looking in my direction.

"I'm sorry, Grandpa—"

"I know you're sorry. What I want to know is what or who could have kept you so busy in New York that you couldn't come down and visit an old man?"

"I should have done better," I said, my voice low from the guilt I was feeling. I felt bad that I hadn't done better by him, worse still that I used to be his favorite. I doubted that now with Renee's weekly visits. Grandpa used to be all mine, and now I had lost him to Renee.

"Well, when you know better, do better. I hope you'll be back in Houston for good?"

"I don't know."

"Let's hope that you do. I didn't like you being in New York all by yourself." He saw me open my mouth to protest and he put his hand up, stopping me. "I'm not saying that you're not a grown woman, but I still worry about you. And that won't ever go away."

"I'm glad."

"You and your mother getting along better?"

I looked at Renee and hesitated.

"Once you cross that door there are no secrets in this room, Mariah. Renee's a big girl, and it's a simple question."

"No, we aren't getting along. I think it's because of what happened—when she was younger? I need to know what *really* happened."

"About Paul."

"Yes," I said. "I found the divorce papers. All these years Beverly hasn't mentioned anything about a divorce, so why hide it? Why didn't she tell me that they were divorced?"

His silver eyebrow went up when I said "divorce," but otherwise he sat and stared at me, waiting for me to continue.

"I've always felt that the reason she treated me so differently was because of how Daddy died, and how he treated her. I know I look like him and remind her all the time of what she lost—"

"This is ridiculous, Mariah," Renee said. "Why are you out here hounding him about something that happened years ago?"

"Because I think he's still alive. My father. A real man out there that could love me instead of the ghost I've imagined all these years. Is that why you asked me to come back today? I need to know, Grandpa. I need to know if it's true. Is he alive?"

He looked at me so long, I didn't think he would answer, but he finally found his voice. "Have you ever seen your mama dance?"

I nodded.

"She looked like an angel when she danced. I knew she was going somewhere with her life. I used to complain about the expense for all her dance stuff, but when I saw her dance, I got chills all over me. Beverly was the prettiest little thing that me and Porsche could hope for. And she knew it, too, always flaunting her long hair and those pretty eyes. Problem was she wasn't the only one who thought she was pretty; I had to fight off all kinds little boys after a piece of your mama. But one boy stole her heart. Paul Stevens, your father. They snuck and got married a couple of days before her graduation. I couldn't believe it when she told us. Moved to Memphis to stay with him and his mama—that's where your Daddy is from. Porsche almost fainted with shock, her baby girl—a wife. Then to top it all off, three months later we hear she's pregnant. Porsche was happy, she was like that, could let things go in an instant. I couldn't. I was still too disappointed that your mama didn't go to dance school like we always planned. And then with a baby on the way, she would never go back. I stopped speaking to her after that. I never liked your father. I couldn't stand the way he took away Beverly's dream. She was too young for marriage. Marriage is hard enough on two mature adults. But two kids? And with a baby? They didn't stand a chance. She came to her senses and got that divorce."

"Did you make her?"

"Beverly was grown. She told me so all the time. No, I didn't make her get a divorce, but I did let her know what kind of man she fell in love with. She made the decision to leave all by herself, and I was happy that she did."

"Was there an accident, Grandpa? Is that how my father died?"

He sighed. "There was an accident. But other than a few scrapes and bruises your father came out fine."

"Is he still alive?"

As if on cue my mother burst in the room. "We're leaving," she said. She went up to Grandpa and said something in his ears that made him sink from shame.

"You started this," she said.

"I'm trying to fix it—"

"Like you did back then? You trying to turn my kids against me, when all of this is your fault in the first place. I'm warning you, Daddy, stay out of my life—"

"Why won't you let me help? I just want to help . . ."

"You've done enough helping. Get up," she said to me, her voice dangerous.

I ignored her, and knelt down in front of him. "Finish telling me."

"Get *up*, Mariah," Beverly said, pulling on my elbow to raise me from the floor. She was surprisingly strong, and I had to struggle to stay kneeling as I waved her off.

"Tell me, Grandpa, *please*, I need to know. Tell me the truth."

Unshed tears danced in his eyes as he looked up at Beverly, and then back to me.

"I'm sorry, Cotton Ball. Your Mama's right. Maybe it is time for you to go."

"Why?" I said, standing, my hands tight fists balled at my sides. "Why are you *doing* this?" I asked, my face inches from my mother's.

"You better back up," she said. Her voice was strong, but her bottom lip quivered.

Renee pulled me back. "Not here," she said.

She walked over and gave Grandpa a hug, and I followed suit. He held me so tight it forced the tears that were at the brink to come forward. "You're a smart girl," he said. "And you'll find the answers. And when you do, I'll be here. I'll always be here, okay?"

I nodded and pulled away from him reluctantly.

LABOR PAINS

I refused to get in the car with them; I was too angry. I called a cab while they waited next to me for it to arrive. The air between us was full of secrets, and I was so tired from trying to get answers that I wanted to ball up and cry. It was enough already. I was a big girl, why was everyone hiding it from me?

I knew Renee was concerned for my safety, so she waited for my cab to arrive. Beverly just wanted to make sure I wouldn't go back in and talk to Grandpa. The cab pulled up and I jumped in, ready to get away from them.

"Where to?" the cabbie asked.

Anywhere would be better than here. But Grandpa was right, I am smart. And smart girls hang out at smart places.

"Downtown library, please."

He nodded and took off so fast it took me a few seconds to buckle up.

This ends today. Whatever this is, whatever Beverly was hiding, it ends today. If Paul was out there, then I deserved as much love as Renee. I deserved to know if someone out there had longed to hold me as much as I longed to hold them.

The library had gone through a renovation since the last time I'd been there. Gone were the worn red carpets and outdated brick entryway. It was replaced with a sleek and shiny interior worth its cards in bragging rights. I must have looked lost, because a woman with a badge on the breast pocket of her jacket approached and asked if I needed any help.

"Yes, I'm doing some research and I need to find a death certificate."

"That shouldn't be a problem. Do you have the person's full name?"

"Yes."

"All right, follow me," she said as I followed her to wall of computers. Her long braids dangled down her back and I tried to look away for fear of crying about my missing weave.

"What date do you need specifically?"

"The summer of 1979. More specifically, July. I tried to do it at home, but it wouldn't let me get past 1985."

"Our database is more extensive. We shouldn't have a problem." Her fingers clicked over the keyboard. "There, 1979. Use the mouse to pick what month you need. If you need to print something, it'll come out on printer seven, just behind you. Think you got it?"

"I do. Thanks."

She smiled and left me to do my business. I hoisted myself on the stool in front of me and clicked on the month of July. Scanning for several minutes I found nothing. An hour passed, and still nothing. How hard could it be to find one measly little death certificate?

"Ma'am?" I said, waving my hand to the woman who had helped me before, like a kindergarten student who needs a restroom break.

"Yes?"

"I can't find what I'm looking for. Are you sure that if I have the date the person died, and their name, I'll find their death certificate? Because nothing's coming up."

"Let me try," she said. I slid off the stool and let her have a go.

"Hmm. I see what you mean . . . Nothing's coming up. You sure this guy is dead?"

"I used to be."

"Pardon?"

"No, I'm not sure."

"Well, he might still be living. If you get his social then you can do a background check on him. They do it all the time online."

"Is it free?"

"No, but the results don't take long."

"What do you think?"

"About getting the background check?"

"About trying to find out the truth. I mean, you work here, so you know all about this stuff, right? If I can't find a death certificate, then it means he's still alive, right?"

"Or he could have died on a different day. You sure you got all your facts straight?"

I shook my head, and blinked back tears. "No. I don't think I'll ever get all the facts straight."

She put her hand on my shoulder. "You okay? You want me to call someone?"

I heard the buzz of my cell phone and started to ignore it, then decided against it.

"No need," I said, as I answered the phone.

"Which is weirder, being in labor and calling you, or being in labor with a full face of makeup?" Norma asked.

"Norma! You're in labor?" I mouthed, *I'm okay*, to her and she walked away, helping someone else who was in need.

"Yep. Don't panic, I'm just in the beginning phase. I thought if I called you now you could be here to hold my daughter."

"Oh, my goodness, Norma, you're going to be a mama! How does it feel?"

"Besides the overwhelming urge to take a dump? Pretty good."

"You are *so* gross."

"Well, what do you say? I need you here."

"Norma, I don't think I can. I in the middle of some things . . ."

"Well, when do you think you can make it? And don't lie and say it's about money—I'll pay for your ticket."

I sighed. "I promise the first chance I get I'll be out there."

"I guess I'll take what I can get. Hold on a sec—"

After a few grunts and deep breathing she was back on the phone, albeit a little breathless.

"Sorry, contraction."

"You sure you should be on the phone?"

"Yes, I'm sure. Since you're not here I had to take the next best thing. I'm by myself until Chris gets here, so talk to me, calm me down."

"What do you want to talk about?"

"Anything!"

"Well, I'm at the library right now. Still digging for more information about my father."

"That's what's keeping you from visiting?"

"Kind of."

She sighed. "Find anything?"

"No. I was looking for his death certificate, but I can't find it."

"Is that bad?"

"It's just another thing that makes me believe he's out there somewhere. Why am I going through so much fuss? If he is alive, he didn't even want me in the first place. He never contacted me."

"You're making a fuss because you want to know the truth. And I agree something sounds fishy with all this, but maybe it's because you're missing key information. Maybe you have the wrong date—"

"Maybe. I just need to get—"

"Ouch!"

"Norma, are you okay?"

"Maybe the phone isn't the smartest thing to do right now. Call you when this girl is born."

She hung up before I could say good bye, but I was thrilled to know she was bringing life into the world.

My phone rang again and I ignored the annoyed stares of everyone and picked it up, expecting it to be Norma again.

"Baby popped out that fast?"

"Baby? What baby?"

"Sorry, Renee, I thought you were Norma."

"She's having her baby? Already? That's fast."

"Yeah, seems like it. Is she with you?" I asked, knowing full well we both knew who *she* was.

"I just dropped her off at home. Where are you? I'm coming to get you."

"I'm at the library downtown. I'll be waiting out front."

Thirty minutes later I was buckled up in the passenger seat on the way back to see Grandpa.

"I can't believe I'm doing this," Renee said.

"You're doing this because you feel the same way I feel. You know something isn't right."

"Even if what you're saying is true, it doesn't make any sense for Mama to lie about something like that. She was really upset this morning. She didn't talk to me the whole ride home."

"Well, she's going to blow a blood vessel when she learns that we're going back to visit Grandpa."

"I shouldn't be getting in the middle of this."

"You're already in the middle, Renee."

"Why can't you just let dead dogs lie? Why do you need to keep digging? It won't change anything."

"It changes *everything*. I can't believe you even said that. You're just afraid of what Beverly's going to do. If you were in my place and Beverly had lied to you all your life, you know you'd be making like one of those people on *CSI*. I need to know if my father is alive. If he is . . ."

"Then what?"

"Then I want to meet him."

She shook her head. "I'm trying to understand, but—"

"You could never understand what it feels like to be a mistake, Renee. To walk into a room and to have your mother's eyes glaze with regret at your presence. No, you wouldn't understand anything I'm going through, you're too busy being the princess."

"Princess? Is that what you think of me? That I'm a spoiled princess?"

"If the shoe fits."

"You don't know me at all," she said, her voice a few notches above a whisper. "You're going to find out everything you want, Mariah. I know what it feels like to search for peace, for answers. I hope you find it."

When we came back to Grandpa's room, he was sitting in the corner reading a book, sunlight pouring in and turning his silver hair blinding white.

"Back so soon?" he asked without looking up.

"Finish," I said, sitting in the chair across from him. Renee stood near me.

He sighed and closed his book, not keeping his page. He closed his eyes for a long time, and, when he opened them, fresh tears were there.

"Paul Stevens is alive and kicking."

I blew out a ragged breath, not even realizing that I was holding my breath until then. Renee seemed to crumple into the chair next to me, her eyes wide.

"Why?"

Tears filled his eyes and he looked away.

"The day Paul got into the accident he was driving back to Houston to see your mama. The accident stalled him, but he still managed to get to the house. I saw him first and I knew that Beverly would feel sorry for him because he was all banged up and go back to him. I couldn't let that happen. So I blocked him from seeing her."

I stood up. "How could you do that? How could all of you lie like this to me? I came to your house crying about not having a father, and you let me believe he was dead when all along he was out there. How could you do this?"

Grandpa stood and tried to reach out for me, but I pulled away. His shoulders seemed to slump lower. "I'm sorry, Cotton Ball. I know it wasn't right, but you have to understand that Paul was no good for your mama—"

"You lied to me."

I turned to Renee. "Did you know about this, too?"

"What? No! I had no idea about any of this!"

"You're Mama's best friend. There are no secrets between you! If you were in on this, too, just tell me!"

"No!" Renee shouted. "I didn't know!"

A nurse came in and told us that we had to lower our voices. I sat back down and hugged my knees to my stomach and rocked back and forth, feeling my stomach sending the first waves of pain.

"You lied," I said again, tears running down my face.

"I didn't know what else to do . . ."

"You could have told the truth!"

"I should have. But the lie became too big, bigger than me. I didn't know how to tell you. I didn't want you to look at me the way you're looking at me now. Please, Mariah—" He tried to touch my hand, but I jerked away.

"Who came up with the lie?"

He paused and then said, in a voice so low that I had to strain to hear him, "I did."

"You? The lie came from you?"

"I suggested it. I didn't want Paul in your life, so I told Beverly to tell you that. I never thought she would actually follow up on it, but she did."

"Did he ever try to come back for me?"

"He tried, but—"

"Let me guess, you blocked him from coming by and calling? Grandpa, I can't believe this!"

He started coughing and Renee got him to sit back down. She gave him some water and finally his throat closed.

"I think this is enough," she said.

"How could you guys have done this? I had a father all these years and you stole that from me. You're nothing but a thief."

"Oh, baby. You have to understand—"

"Understand what? That my grandfather is a liar? And so is Beverly? The only person who probably would tell me the truth is my father."

"You don't know that man, Mariah. I know I was wrong, but at the time—"

"At the time you felt like you were doing right. What you did had no right in it, Grandpa." I had to bite down on my knuckles to prevent myself from screaming. *How could he do this?*

"I need to get out of here," I said. I looked over at Renee, slumped over in her chair like a bag of wet flour. "Let's go."

"Beverly did the best thing she knew how to do at the time. We all did. Porsche was the only one who couldn't stand it. She wanted to tell you, but she died before she could. She made me promise that I wouldn't hold the secret. That I would tell you when the time was right."

"I'm thirty years old. When were you going to find the right time? Forget it," I said when he opened his mouth to talk. "I don't want to know. I can't listen to any more of this. I need to get out of here." I walked out of Grandpa's room, ignoring his calls for me not to leave. I stepped outside and into Houston's heat, another thing that slapped me in the face.

He was alive. My father is alive. Why all the deceit, all the lies? Now I had to get the answers from the one woman who I feared wouldn't give me a straight answer.

GOOD AS DEAD

"What are you going to do now?"

"You know what I'm doing. Take me home," I said, getting into Renee's car.

"You want to talk to Mama, don't you? Grandpa said she made a mistake . . ."

"Lying about the death of my father is more than just a mistake, Renee. You can't justify her actions. At some point you need to see how wrong she is for what she did."

"I know she's wrong. But so was Grandpa. You can't put all the blame at her feet."

"You wanna bet?"

She pulled away from the nursing home and headed back toward her condo.

"This is all just a big misunderstanding. Mama will set things straight."

"You just don't want her to be wrong."

"She's already wrong. I just want you to listen to her side of things. That's all."

Twenty minutes later I was walking into Renee's condo, determined to get answers from Beverly. She was sitting on the couch working on her delicate embroidery when I stormed in. She looked up at us and smiled, but then frowned when she saw the anger in my eyes.

"What's wrong?" she asked. She stood up and reached for me, but I pulled away from her.

"I'll tell you what's wrong, Beverly. When exactly were you planning to tell me that my father is alive?"

Her hands flew to her throat and started wringing the pearls that lay there. "He told you."

"You bet he told me. How could you lie to me like that? All these years?"

"Baby, please listen—"

"No, you listen. I cried in my bed almost every night wishing I could have a father. And you saw me and did nothing. You could have stopped my pain."

"I didn't know what to do, I'd already lied for so long, I didn't know how to fix it—"

"You tell the truth!"

Beverly stood back at the forcefulness of my words.

"I know that. I do. But things got out of control so fast, I didn't know how to tell you—"

"Would you have *ever* told me? You would have sat on this secret your whole life if it wasn't for Grandpa."

"You know your grandfather isn't the saint you make him out to be. He's one of the reasons I divorced Paul in the first place."

I crossed my arms over my chest. "Go on."

"I told you girls how I was brought up. I was raised like the two of you were—private schools, designer clothes—I had it all. But my parents were so strict with me, they never let me go anywhere or do anything."

"Grandpa said that you were fast with the boys. Is that true?"

She laughed and her hands went up to her necklace again. "He thought so. But I wasn't. Most of those boys were just my friends, nothing more. But he couldn't see that. He was so afraid that I was going to mess up and get pregnant and not go to school like we all talked about. But then I met Paul."

"How?"

"Paul and some friends came down to Houston for their spring break. He was a freshman in college. We met at Galveston Beach. We started dating, and when I introduced him to my parents, Daddy flipped out. He didn't want me dating, and he thought Paul was after my money. But Paul didn't even know that I had money, not until then, of course. I was so in love with Paul, I couldn't see straight. He asked me to marry him, and we eloped. When your grandfather found out he threatened to cut me off, but I didn't care. We moved to Memphis and we stayed with his mother, Gloria."

"Go on," I said when she stopped talking.

"You have to understand the way I was brought up, Mariah. I had everything done for me. I was accustomed to a certain way of life. To say that Paul had nothing was an understatement. His uncle owned a shoe repair shop and he worked there. I worked part time at a grocery store. A grocery store, can you imagine?"

"Oh, the horror," I said flatly.

"For me it was. Gloria never liked me, and she punished me by making me hang clothes on the line to dry, or scrubbing floors and washing dishes—"

"So she made you work?"

"It was more than work—"

"No, Beverly. That sounds like work. And let me guess, your gentle spirit couldn't handle the strain of real married life and you went back home to Daddy?"

"Not at first. I really tried to stick it out. Like I said, I was in love with Paul and I thought his love would be enough—"

"But it wasn't, was it?"

She shook her head. "I started thinking of everything I'd given up to be with him, my family, my education, dancing. I'd been accepted to the Alvin Ailey School, but I passed it up because of him. So I started thinking that I didn't have to give up everything. I could have him *and* I could still dance. But by then it was too late. I was pregnant with you."

"So I'm the reason you stopped dancing?" I said it like a question, but I knew the answer. My stomach churned and I rubbed it to get it to quiet down.

"By that time I was bitter and unhappy. Paul and I argued almost every day, and it didn't help that his mother was there in his corner for most of the arguments. I couldn't take it anymore and I left," she said, quietly. "I called home and my father met me at the bus station."

"You were still pregnant?"

She nodded. "I had you the next week. Paul didn't even show up," she said bitterly.

"But Grandpa said he blocked him from seeing you—"

"I know, but I didn't find that out until years later. He told me after my mother died. You were three at the time and by then I already . . ." She hung her head.

"You already had started lying."

"I felt like he was dead to me! He didn't try to see me, to see you. I was devastated. So when my father said I should tell you Paul was dead, I agreed. It was easier that way."

"For who?"

"I know now what I did was wrong, but I was in so much pain. By the time I found out that he loved me and did try to meet me, it was too late. I was married to Anthony, Renee was here and I had made a new life for myself. I couldn't go back."

"Did Anthony know?"

She shook her head. "No one knew." She sighed. "The truth is, I'm glad you know. But I wish I would have had the strength to tell you. For years I tried to tell you, and he stopped me, telling me how much I would hurt you if I told you the truth. Now he has the audacity to tell you, and he looks like an angel while I look like . . ." She ran her hand through her hair. "Fine. You would think bad of me no matter how this turned out. I'm glad Daddy told you. I'm tired of the lies and the secrets. I know you came here for the truth and now you have it. I know what I did was wrong, but to me Paul was as good as dead."

"Good as dead is not the same as *being* dead, Beverly. You cheated me," I said. "Cheated me from a chance to have a father—"

"I didn't cheat you! You had Anthony—"

"He wasn't my father. I was tolerated around Anthony, not loved."

"That's not true. He loved you."

I shook my head. "How could you do this?"

She just stood there, her hands playing with the pearls around her neck.

"Answer me," I screamed, snatching her hands away from her precious pearls. The necklace broke and her pearls hit the floor and danced around us. She went to the floor and tried to pick them up; her hands trembled as she collected the bouncing pearls around her.

"You're pathetic," I said.

She looked up at me. "Paul gave me this necklace."

My stomach burned, but I held her gaze.

"I did the best I could with you."

"I know. And that's the part that's sad."

If truth is beauty,
How come no one has their hair done in the library?
—Lily Tomlin

SLEEPING UNDER BRIDGES

I had a dream that I choked Beverly to death that night. I sounded like an animal, strangled screams and grunts coming from my mouth as I tried to kill my mother.

I woke up and was relieved that I was dreaming, but mad that I hadn't harmed her in some way. She needed to be punished.

I always thought that if someone said something hurtful to me that I would react and give them a few choice words. But I hadn't. I had my chance with Beverly and I just left the room like a loser in a bullfight. I didn't know what to feel.

Renee came in my room and sat on my bed. I felt numb inside, it's like something in me clicked off. She rubbed my feet underneath the covers and said, "I'm sorry." Those two words felt like salve to my wounds, and I curled up into a ball and burst into tears. She hugged me, rocked me like a baby and smoothed my puffy hair, telling me over and over that everything would be okay.

"You're leaving?" Renee asked, watching me toss my belongings in a black duffel bag.

"Yep."

"Where are you going?"

"Don't know, don't care. I can't stay another day here. I need to leave."

She sat on my bed and watched me, her face still puffy and red from our cry fest earlier.

"Mama's really upset."

"Good," I said, throwing a few sets of pajamas in my bag.

"She's staying in a hotel."

"So?"

"So you don't have to leave."

"Is she coming back?"

She didn't answer.

"Exactly," I said, zipping my bag closed.

"Don't leave."

"I'm not staying here."

"Where are you going?" she asked again.

I didn't have a clue. I didn't have a dollar to my name, but I would sleep under a bridge before I would stay here another day.

"I don't know. Probably back to New York."

"Can I go with you?" she asked, her voice small.

I looked at her.

"Why?"

"I don't think you should be alone right now."

I shook my head. "Wrong answer."

"All right, fine, I want to go, okay? I want to go wherever you go right now. Besides, I'm the one with the money, remember? You need money to get to New York."

She made a good point.

"How quick can you get packed?"

⚊⚊

Too quick, I thought as we wheeled out of the parking garage toward the airport.

"This is going to be fun. You're sure Norma is expecting us?"

"She's expecting me, but she'll love to have you, too. We'll have to get a hotel, of course. She won't have room for us with the new baby."

"I can't believe we're doing this—just up and leaving. We're having an adventure," she said. I looked at her and she was bouncing up and down in her seat.

"Excuse me if I don't share your level of excitement— my mother's been lying to me for thirty years."

"Sorry," she said.

"I should have hit her."

"Why? What would that have solved?"

"Nothing. But I bet I'd feel better right now."

"She made a mistake—"

"That wasn't a mistake, Renee. That was a crime."

"She was afraid—"

"Look, I agreed that you could come, but not if you're going to defend her the whole time. She was wrong. And she needs to make it right."

"I'm trying to make you feel better."

"You can't make me feel better! You can't fix every-thing, Renee."

"Sorry."

Two hours later I was sitting in first class, courtesy of my rich sister, my head back on the leather headrest, a glass of champagne in my hand.

"A girl could get used to this."

"Tell me about it," Renee said, looking out the window.

"What do you mean? You have money. You could travel like this all the time. You *are* used to living like this."

"I should be. Mama tells me all the time that I need to travel more, spend more money. But I'm not used to being rich."

I gave her a look.

"Okay, of being *this* rich."

I drink another sip of champagne.

"Did you love him?"

She kept looking out the window. "Truthfully? Not at first. But I did grow to love him. People thought it was a marriage of convenience. He was rich and I'm—"

"Beautiful," I said, finishing her sentence for her. And she was breathtaking. Her waist-length hair was in a messy ponytail, her cheeks were flushed from all the excitement of the day and her eyes sparkled. She didn't even notice all the male passengers drooling over her, she was too busy looking out the window. But I noticed. I felt myself shrinking again, becoming invisible, turning right back into Cotton Ball. No one noticed me, no eyes glanced my way.

"If you say so. He was nice to me," she whispered. "And he didn't have to be, but he was. He was kind and gentle. We grew to be good friends. I miss him," she said, her voice soft and wistful. I knew she was back with him, going back in time, reliving memories.

"What's it like?"

"What?"

"Being in love."

She closed her eyes. "It feels like . . . you know that feeling you get when you watch Mama dance?"

I nodded.

"It feels like that. You get goose bumps and get tingly all over . . . Yeah, that's what love is like."

"Excuse me while I throw up."

She shrugged. "You asked. Tell me something, why is it that you're asking me? Why haven't you been in love before?"

"No time, I guess. I wanted to launch my career first."

"And now?"

I sighed. "Now I'm sad that I never got that tingly feeling."

"We both need to get back out there."

"That's the least of my problems, Renee."

"Maybe it would be nice to have someone to share your problems with."

"Maybe."

"Mama really liked Peter. I hope that she would like whoever else I brought home."

"Why do you care?"

She looked down.

"You don't understand, Mama has this way of doing things. I couldn't date someone she doesn't approve of."

"What about what *you* want to do?"

She turned to look out the window again. "I don't know what I'd do without Mama."

"Try living in my shoes for a while. You'd do just fine. I swear, Renee, you irritate me sometimes. You're too old to still be acting like this. Cut the cord already."

"It's hard to not need her opinion—"

I groaned.

"I would think after today you would see how warped Beverly's opinion is. Her opinion doesn't matter, Renee. If you don't see that then you're as stupid as you are pretty."

"You don't like me." Her voice was flat as paper, devoid of emotion.

I didn't comfort her with a lie. I just sat next to her, silence filling us like water in a sponge.

"It's sad that you don't. That you don't even try to like me. I know you love me—"

"I do." I say. And I do. She's my sister. I *have* to love her.

"I know you do. But liking someone—that goes deeper. If you like someone you would hang out with them even if they weren't blood, even if they weren't family. And I would. I would hang out with you even if we weren't family. But you wouldn't. I would not be the kind of woman that you would like. And that's sad. Because I really like you. You being home, us hanging out—it's the most fun I've had in a really long time."

I didn't reply. Today had been too much hurt and I didn't want to imagine hurting Renee. Pain is pain, even if it's not intentional. I didn't want to hear about it.

"Sorry I called you stupid. I didn't mean it."

"Of course you did, Mariah. But I forgive you anyway."

She closed her eyes and I followed suit, thankful for the reprieve.

BABY MONKEY

I was home. The wind caught my breath as soon as I pushed open the glass door leaving the airport. I waved for a cab, and the young man jumped out and grabbed Renee's bags while I watched.

If I had my weave, he would be jumping on my bags, too.

After her bags were stowed away in the trunk, he lifted my bag and threw it in, slamming the trunk closed. "Where to?" he asked, his eyes glued to Renee. She glanced at me and I told him the hospital Norma was in. He seemed annoyed by my voice, and after a sharp reprimand he started driving.

I'd called Norma as soon as our plane landed, and she screamed with delight when I told her I was in town. I needed to hear someone who loved me unconditionally. It felt good to be loved.

"Don't you think we should check into a hotel first? Maybe rent a car or something?"

"You're right. I'm not thinking straight. Omni Hotel, please," I said to the driver. He nodded, sneaking peeks at Renee the whole time. The Omni was in my old neighborhood, and I needed to see something familiar right about now. He pulled up in front of the hotel and we grabbed our bags and checked in, Renee waving her black American Express card out of her wallet, not noticing how the clerk's eyes perked up and his voice got two octaves higher.

"You want to share rooms, right?" Renee asked. I didn't, but I didn't feel right suggesting different rooms since she was paying for everything.

"Fine by me."

We checked in and opened the door to our suite. The room was modern, yet homey enough that it didn't feel like a hotel.

"Do you think I have time for a quick shower?" Renee asked, pulling her luggage on top of her bed. I didn't plan on taking a shower, but since Renee was taking one, I couldn't go around as the dirty sister. Broke, black, and ugly, yes, but definitely not dirty.

"Sure, just be quick. I'll jump in when you finish."

"I'll be out in five," she said.

When the bathroom door closed and I heard the burst of the shower start, I laid across the bed and cried again. Thankful that I remembered to bring my journal, I pulled it out and wrote:

I'm not working, and don't have a dollar to my name.

My hair is a complete disaster.

I'm completely alone and haven't had one successful relationship.

I haven't accomplished anything worthwhile since being born twenty-nine years ago.

Things would have been different if I knew about my father. Maybe I wouldn't have turned out so screwed up.

The more I thought about my life, the sadder I became.

I heard the shower shut off and I wiped my eyes, not wanting Renee to see me cry again. I threw my journal back in my luggage.

"It's all yours," she said, wearing a thick, white terry cloth robe and towel-drying her long hair. My hair was so short that a square of toilet paper could dry it. I went into the bathroom, undressed and started my own shower. The tears came again, and I let them come, not sure if my face was wet with tears or the water. I've always felt that a shower was a woman's best friend, her own personal place to cry. After several minutes, I got out and towel dried myself. I looked in the mirror and reeled back in horror at my hair. I forgot to tie it down, so it was wet. Wet hair is never a black woman's friend. I threw on a robe and walked into the room to see if Renee had any styling products I could borrow. In the rush, I hadn't brought a thing with me.

"Sure," she said, handing me a silver, high-gloss tube of gel. "I use this to control the frizz in my hair."

"Thanks," I said. I walked back into the bathroom and squeezed a gob of it into my hair and smoothed it down. The top layer of my hair was sleek and shiny, but I could feel the layers underneath rising from my scalp, making my hair swell up like a pregnant woman's feet. "It will have to do," I muttered to myself as I walked back to the bedroom.

"Here you go," I said, throwing the gel back to Renee. She was already dressed in a pair of grey slacks and matching grey cardigan. I threw on a pair of jeans and black sweater. Not exactly my former self, but still not too bad.

"You look like a model going out on a casting call," Renee said.

"You must be delusional. I look like a baby monkey with my hair like this."

She laughed. "You have funny ways to describe yourself. I think you look great."

"Well, that's nice of you to say . . ."

"Why don't you feel pretty?"

"I do feel pretty."

"No, you don't. You're always saying negative things about yourself."

"I've had a pretty rough day today, Renee. I don't feel like getting into a big deep discussion about my self-esteem."

"I wasn't trying . . ." She shook her head. "All right, I'm sorry. Should you call Norma first, or should we head to the hospital now?"

"Let's just go. I'm ready to see a familiar face."

Renee's lips turned down, and I realized my mistake.

I sighed, frustrated with hurting her feelings, but more frustrated that I had to apologize every five minutes.

"Sorry. You're face is nice, too—"

"I know what you meant. Let's go. I haven't seen Norma in years."

~~

Saying Norma had a big family was like saying an elephant was big. She had a huge family, and when we finally made it to her room, we had to squeeze into it. I recognized several members of her family and went around the hospital room, giving hugs to everyone and introducing Renee to the people she didn't know. Renee stood in the corner of the room, and shook hands while I went up to see my best friend—the new mom.

"You're here," she said, grabbing my hand. Her face was flushed and her long hair lay across her pillow like a rainbow over her head. She squeezed my hand and my eyes watered.

"What's wrong?" she asked.

"Nothing," I said, shaking my head. I wouldn't dare tell her my story yet, not when I was here to see her newborn daughter. I shook my head and willed back tears. "Nothing's wrong," I added, more for my sake than for hers.

"You're lying. Something's up."

"Later," I said, giving her a kiss on her cheek. "Where is she?"

"She's in the nursery. Chris is sitting with her."

"Good. I'll go down and see her in a minute. How are you feeling?" I asked, sitting on the edge of her bed.

"Besides the fact that my vagina feels like a balloon? Perfect. She's so beautiful, Mariah. She has my eyes and Chris's mouth. She's too perfect. We named her Elizabeth Mariah."

"That's beautiful," I said. I was beyond flattered that she gave the baby my name, especially after looking at how big her family was. "You didn't have to do that."

"I wanted to. You're my best friend, it's the least I could do."

"You look happy," I said. And she did. Her brown eyes glowed and she couldn't stop smiling. Most of the time her bright mood was infectious, but not today. No matter what, I couldn't get her happiness to rub off on me.

"Tell me," she said, rubbing my arm. "What is it? What happened?"

I shook my head. "Soon. Right now I want to see that darling girl of yours."

"I'm leaving tomorrow. How long do you plan on staying in New York?"

I shrugged. "I'm not on a schedule."

"So you'll come by the house tomorrow?"

"Of course." I stood. "I want to see the baby." I nodded at Renee. "We'll be back."

We left the room and took the elevator to the ninth floor, to the nursery. We signed in with the clerk, and waited for Chris to escort us to the nursery. The security in a maternity ward was tighter than Janet Jackson's abs, so we couldn't see the baby without a parent present. He came through the heavy steel doors and I hugged and congratulated him. I introduced him to Renee and he led us to the nursery—a proud papa showing us his daughter for the first time. His gait suggested that he hadn't slept well in several days, and I wondered if all parents knew what lay in store for them when they decided to have a family—the sleepless nights, the responsibility of taking care of a new life. It was a lot to take in a short period of time. He stopped in front of a large window and we peered at a multitude of babies—some crying, some sleeping—just a room of nothing but precious life.

"There she is," he said, pointing at a small white crib on the far side of the room. "There's my Elizabeth."

Her head was covered in a thick cap of dark hair. She yawned and pursed her red lips in a slight grin as if she could sense us watching her and was putting on a show just for us.

"She's beautiful."

"Wait until you hold her," he said. "Come on."

I followed him into the room but noticed that Renee hadn't budged.

"You're not coming?" I asked.

She shook her head. "No, I'll just wait for you here."

"You sure?"

"Positive. I'll go back and wait up front." She walked away before I could say anything else.

I followed Chris into the nursery and almost tiptoed to her crib, not wanting to make a sound. He nodded at one of the nurses and then picked her up so smoothly that it looked like he'd been doing it for years.

"You're good at that," I said.

"I've had a couple of hours to practice. I was scared to pick her up at first, but now . . ." he looked down at his daughter. "Now I can't seem to put her down. You ready?" he asked, positioning her to slide her into my arms.

I opened my arms and was holding my best friend's baby. *Little Elizabeth.*

Tears sprang into my eyes for the billionth time today as I cradled her in my arms. I began to rock her. *How could something so foreign to me become so natural?*

"Look who's talking. You're a pro at this," he said.

"No, but I want to be." I looked up at him. "How does it feel?"

"I can't describe it. But I can say that I never felt this kind of love for anyone before. Who knew something this small would cause the biggest change? I'd give my life for her," he said, stroking her soft hair.

Did my father feel the same way when he saw me? Did Paul even get a *chance* to see me? I looked at Chris peering down at his daughter with so much love in his eyes, and I wondered if my father had ever looked at me like that.

STILLBORN

"Why'd you leave like that? Why didn't you want to see the baby?"

We were back in our hotel. After going back to say good bye to Norma and her family, and promising that I would see her tomorrow, Renee and I rode back to the hotel in silence. Her mood was off ever since we went to the hospital and I wanted to know why.

"Have you forgotten already?"

In all the craziness, I had. "I'm sorry. I didn't realize—"

"It doesn't matter."

"It does matter. I should have remembered that you have kids—"

She blanched and her face crumpled in like a fist in pie dough.

"Sorry, *had* kids."

"People think getting over a miscarriage is easy. But three? That's impossible. Kids I can deal with, but babies? It's too hard."

"I'm really sorry."

"It's fine," she said as she pulled the comforter off her bed and laid down.

"Really, Renee, why didn't you—"

"Call you? Tell you? Get real, Mariah, you wouldn't have cared. The times I did call you with news, you rushed me off the phone like I was a bill collector."

"I didn't—"

She gave me a look and I quieted.

Well, maybe I had.

"You were in school and starting your big career. You couldn't be bothered by your younger sister. You always looked down on my choices in life, like being a wife was such a bad thing. I made my choice to marry young. I wanted to have a big family."

"*You* didn't make that choice. Beverly made that choice for you."

"Mama has been a big influence on my life, but I didn't marry Peter just because Mama said so."

"Since we were little girls Beverly groomed you to be a wife. She knew that your light skin and long hair afforded you certain privileges—"

"Privileges? You think being light-skinned and having long hair is a privilege?"

I patted my hair and looked down at my hands, the color of freshly stained ebony. "Well, it certainly makes your life easier."

"You think Mama pushed me to marry him? I *wanted* to marry him. I wanted to be a wife and mother more than anything."

Tears sprung into her eyes and she blinked them back. "You think you have all the answers about everything, Mariah. But I *chose* my life. And I'd do it all over again."

I was too mad at Beverly to let the matter drop. "Just admit that Beverly *made* you want that. Just like she trained me to be career-oriented because she felt I was too ugly to get a man."

"That's not true."

"Yes, it is. It's not fair, but it's the truth."

"You never understood me. It was always about you growing up. You never could look past yourself and see that I had problems, too. Yes, a light-skinned girl can have problems."

"Not like me," I muttered.

"You want to keep acting like you got the short end of the stick all the time. You like playing the victim. Yes, Mama took me shopping with her and taught me all about fashion, but not once did she read to me at night, or check over my homework. Growing up I wanted that, and she didn't give it to me. But I finally had to let that go."

"I can't," I said through clenched teeth. "I'm so angry it hurts."

"Your anger is only hurting yourself." She sighed. "I know these have been a tough couple of days for you, but did you ever stop to think how I felt about all this? If Mama lied to you, she lied to me. I'm hurting, too."

"Sorry," I said again.

"Stop saying you're sorry all the time. You're not sorry. You just feel bad. And that's fine. But you're not the only one dealing with stuff, Mariah. The world doesn't revolve around you."

She clicked her lamp off near her bed, and the room was flooded with darkness. I could hear her turning over, her back to me.

"The babies I lost? The first two were boys, and the last one was a girl. I was going to name her Mariah," she said.

The next morning I woke up before Renee. I showered and was getting dressed when she rolled over and looked at me.

"You're heading to Norma's?"

"Yes. You want to go?"

She shook her head and yawned. "No. I'll just stay here."

"You're going to stay inside all day? You don't want to walk around and see this beautiful city of mine?"

"Not by myself. How long will you be gone?"

I shrugged. "Don't know. You never know. When I hang out with Norma I tend to lose track of time. But I'll try to be back by this evening. We'll have dinner together, okay?"

She nodded. "That sounds great."

I grabbed my purse. "Try to get outside. It really is a nice day."

"I'll try," she said.

I left the room eager to walk around my old city, eager for fresh air. The wind hit my face and I took in a deep breath of car fumes and dirt.

Oh, to be home.

I saw a reflection of myself in the shiny window I passed by and stopped. I was different now. Not just physically, but mentally as well. *I have a father,* I thought. I held my stomach in anticipation of pain, but nothing happened.

⟊⟊

Norma's house was loud and crowded, filled with three generations of women all telling her the best ways to be a mother. I walked in and greeted everyone, giving her mother and grandmother a hug.

"Where's the new mom?" I asked Chris as he cooked what looked like pancakes on the stove.

"She's in the nursery feeding Elizabeth."

"A little late for pancakes, huh?"

He shrugged. "That's what everyone wanted. It gives me a chance to be away from all the estrogen in the house."

I laughed and headed to my old room, which was now decorated in pastel shades of pink and green for the baby. Norma was sitting in a wooden rocking chair with celadon green padding, a quilt thrown over her bare feet. She was still wearing her robe, and her hair looked greasy and limp over her swollen face.

"Well, there you are," I whispered, walking in to give her a kiss on the cheek. She was switching the baby from one breast to the other, and I got an eyeful of her swollen breasts. Her nipples had taken the size and shape of dinner plates, with blue and green veins coursing through.

"Thanks for the peep show," I said, sitting down on the ottoman near her. I made fake gagging noises and she slapped me on the knee.

"Let's see what your breasts look like when you have a baby tugging and pulling on them."

"That's why I'm bottle feeding."

"That's what they all say," she said, finally getting her daughter to suckle. She swiped her hair behind her ear and looked at me. "So, how are you doing?"

I opened my mouth to answer, but quickly closed it. My lip trembled and I burst into tears.

"Hey, hey, what's going on?"

I wiped tears that had crept down my chin. "My whole life has been a lie. *Is* a lie."

"What do you mean?"

"Beverly lied. My father is alive. She lied about the whole thing."

"Whoa, slow down, cowboy. Start from the beginning."

I did. I caught her up to the part where I broke Beverly's pearl necklace.

"Wow."

"Wow? I tell you my father's alive and all you can say is, Wow?"

"I'm sorry. All this took me by surprise. It's pretty unbelievable."

"Tell me about it."

She sighed and looked down at Elizabeth. "When I look at her, all I think about is how I hope I don't screw her up. But in the end, we all do. One way or another we say something that will hurt our children. I know Beverly is wrong—"

"Of course she's wrong—"

Norma put her hand up. "But your grandfather was wrong, too. She had a partner in all this. The hormones your body releases can make you do some crazy things."

I got up. "Why is everyone on her side? I'm the one that's messed up here. I'm the one who missed out on getting to know her father. Me, not her. I'm sick of hearing about what she went through."

"Sit down, okay? I just brought that up so you could get some clarity, to see her side of things. If you did, maybe you could move on."

I sat back down, my foot tapping on her hardwood floor. After a warning glance I stopped tapping and dug my heels into the floor.

"Chris is in your kitchen right now, making everybody pancakes. Pancakes. What if my father wanted to make me pancakes? What if he wanted to read to me at night? What if he could have told me not to pay attention to what people say about my hair, that I'm beautiful anyway?"

"But he didn't. He wasn't there. I know that's a crappy thing to say, but he wasn't. Yes, you were cheated. Yes, you were wronged. But what does that change? You can't rewind time and become five years old again. You're an adult, and adults make hard decisions about their lives all the time. I know you're not ready yet, but soon you're going to have to let that go."

Swiping tears from my eyes, I whispered, "I don't know if I can."

Norma gently slipped Elizabeth off her breast and placed her over her shoulder to burp her. After a few seconds she put her back in her arms. "Here," she said, reaching over to hand me her beautiful baby. I reached out and grabbed her and nestled her in my arms.

"What if your father is out there somewhere, wishing he could have held you like that? What if he's thinking about all the missed chances with you, and how he wasn't there for you? Too much regret can make you bitter, Mariah."

I stroked Elizabeth's face.

"Think about the bright future you have ahead of you—"

"Oh, let me see, the one where I have no job, no man, I'm bald as an eagle, and my mother is a compulsive liar? That bright future?"

"No, I was thinking of the future where you have the time to think about what you really want to do with your life instead of working yourself so hard that you have a hole in your stomach. The future where you have time for a man, and can stop hiding behind all that weave and let people see the real you. The future where you realize your mother is flawed and imperfect like all mothers. I'm talking about *that* future."

I nodded and continued to cry as I held Elizabeth. She yawned and stretched and opened her eyes for a sliver of a moment. In that tiny second I saw my future. And dark as I was, it looked bright.

"I'm going to find my father."

Beauty draws us with a single hair.
—Alexander Pope

DIFFERENT, BUT BEAUTIFUL

I felt numb on my walk back to the hotel. Norma's baby girl, Renee's miscarriages, Beverly's lies were like wet ink on my mind. Renee's family wanted me to stay for dinner, but the house was congested enough as it was. One more person might make it explode. When I entered our hotel room Renee was sitting in front of the TV Indian-style.

"It's on commercial, so you can talk."

"What's on commercial?"

"Only the best show in the world, *Iron Chef.* So how was she?"

"Norma seemed great. Her family was over there, so it was a little crowded, but it was nice."

"Did you tell her?"

I nodded.

"What did she say?"

"I want to meet him."

"Your father? Whoa," she said, standing up and clicking off the TV.

"Your show—"

"It was a rerun. Come on, you promised me dinner. Show me around this fabulous city that you call home."

"Where do you want to go?"

"Anywhere. I've been stuck in this hotel room for hours. I need to see the sun, what's left of it, anyway."

"All right, I know a couple places. Let's go."

She was already dressed in a cornflower blue cardigan and dark designer jeans. She slipped on a pair of silver ballet flats and announced she was ready.

"Sorry I couldn't see the baby," she said as we walked to the elevator.

"You made the best decision for you."

We remained quiet as we walked into the elevator and waited for it to descend into the lobby.

"Where are we going?" Renee asked, following me outside, the setting sun giving her light skin an amber glow.

"It's a surprise," I said, grabbing her hand, taking her back to the days when we were small children.

We strolled through Manhattan, me pointing to my old apartment building, my old job, my old life. She pointed at all the boutiques and shops that she wanted to cruise in the next day. After an hour we both were hungry, and I found one of my favorite cafés for us to eat in.

"It feels weird to eat outside this time of year. In Houston we would be sweating and slapping at mosquitoes."

"I remember."

Our waiter approached, a pale-skinned, redheaded young man with the aura of Conan O'Brien.

"What would you beautiful ladies like to drink?" he asked, handing both of us menus.

"I'll just have a glass of water. With lemon."

"I'll have a glass of white wine," I said. I looked at Renee. "Is that okay? That won't—"

She waved her hand. "Have whatever you want. I'll be fine."

"I'll change that to water."

"Good choice," he said, walking away.

"You didn't have to do that. I can handle being around alcohol."

"I know. Still." I shrugged. "Don't want to tempt you. How have you been doing with that?"

"My alcohol addiction?" She laughed. "You can say it out loud, Mariah, it's okay. Fine. Some days the urge is really strong, and some days not."

"I'm so sorry I wasn't there for you."

"Stop apologizing! I feel like you've been doing that ever since you came home. I'm fine. Now anyway."

The waiter came and brought our water and we ordered. A chicken Caesar salad for me, a gourmet hamburger for Renee.

A soft breeze blew, and Renee's hair fluttered in the wind. A pang of loss hit me so hard I had to look away.

"I can see why you didn't want to come home," Renee said. "New York is a beautiful city. Different, but beautiful."

"I want to talk to you about that. I stayed here, in New York, because it was easier for me not to see you. I think you know how jealous I am of you. Of the way you look."

"Why?"

"Why? I can't believe you're asking me that. Look around."

A dozen or more men were eyeing her.

"You're beautiful. You're loved. Your hair is long, your skin is light. You have everything I want. Everyone looks at you, they notice you." I looked around again at the men staring at her. "Even now, people are drooling over your beauty."

"You're beautiful, too," she said. Because she had to, not because it was true.

"Not like you. I'll never be pretty like you."

"We're two different people; our beauty is different. You have a long graceful neck, glowing skin—"

"Dark skin," I added.

"What is so wrong with having dark skin?"

I laughed. "You can't be that ignorant, Renee. Beverly praised your light skin and long hair. I got called Midnight and Burnt Cookie—"

"Those were kids at school. Not Mama."

"I know. It's just that growing up I felt that Mama was ashamed of me. She always asked your opinion on outfits, like my opinion didn't matter. She always took you shopping with her, never me. Me, she told to read a book."

"And look at how your life turned out. You went to college. You made something of yourself. All my accomplishments were tied into Peter. You have a great life, Mariah."

I shook my head. "It ain't so great."

"Well, maybe not now. You're in a weird place now, but still overall, you have a pretty good life. I wish I could go back and start over. I wouldn't have started drinking; I wouldn't have gotten married so young . . ." She sighed.

"I would have done a lot of things differently. I'll probably always go through life going through this 'what if?' stage. But then I would be wasting my life now. No, I'm not a mother—" Her throat caught, and I reached across the table and grabbed her hand. "In the back of my mind, I always will think that I poisoned my body with alcohol, so no life can survive in my womb."

"That's not true, you don't know that."

"Some things you just know, okay?" She blew out a ragged breath. "You can't go back, Mariah. You can't live like that. You won't be living at all."

Our food arrived and I dropped her hand. We didn't talk; the only noise was the scrape of my fork against my plate and Renee's chewing. The silence was like antiseptic on our wounds, healing us from past grievances. For the first time, Renee felt like my sister.

"What did you do all day?"

"Nothing really, talked to Mama—"

I dropped my fork. *I had spoken too soon.* "Her? Why did you have to call her?"

"She wanted to know where we were."

"And you told her?"

She nodded.

"Why would you do that?"

"Look, I know Mama is wrong. She is. She hurt me, too, with all her deceit, and I needed to clear the air with her."

I rolled my eyes.

"She's worried about you."

"She should be."

"She wanted to know how you were handling things."

I picked up my fork and moved the Romaine lettuce around on my plate. "What did you tell her?"

"I told her that you were devastated, but were coping okay."

"Devastated is right. Why do you need to call her all the time?"

"She's my friend. My only friend. Do you know how sad that is? That your mother is your only friend? I cherish her and resent her at the same time. But like it or not, she's all I've got."

This time she grabbed my hand. "But now that's changed. Now I have my big sister looking out for me."

CIRCLE OF LIFE

We ordered our dessert to go—fudge brownies thick as bricks topped with homemade caramel and vanilla ice cream. We ran, ignoring the crazed glances from strangers, eager to get to our hotel room before it melted. We laughed like kids as we ate our brownies and ice cream soup.

"I'm having fun," Renee said, licking the back of her spoon. We were both lying across her bed on our stomachs, our legs up in the air.

"I am, too." And I was, which was a surprise.

"So, tell me a secret."

I rolled my eyes. "You really are trying to make this thing into a big slumber party, aren't you?"

"Well, it is. We just need to throw on pajamas. Go on," she said, nudging my arm. "Tell me a secret. I'll tell if you tell."

I sighed. "All right, let me think." I licked the back of my spoon and said, "I haven't seen my real hair since high school."

"No, try again. That's not a secret."

"Okay, well . . . I pluck all the hairs off my big toe."

"Gross! You're supposed to be telling me a secret, *not* describing your beauty routine."

"That is a secret! You didn't know, did you?"

"No, but—"

"Okay, so I told a secret."

"Come on, that doesn't count. I want a real secret!"

I sighed again, hoping she could sense my displeasure. "All right, if you really want to know, I tell everybody that I dump all my boyfriends, but the truth is they dump me."

"Really? How many have you had?"

"Three."

"And all three of them have dumped you?"

I nodded. "And get this, they all tell me the same thing. They all say that I'm 'boring,'" I said, making air quotes with my fingers.

She kept eating her ice cream without looking at me.

"Can you believe those jokers? They say I'm too rigid, not flexible, and not fun! What a bunch of losers."

Renee kept eating her ice cream.

"What? You don't think they . . . You think I'm not fun?"

"Well . . ."

"I don't believe this! I am the queen of fun!"

"Okay, name something you've done fun in the last couple of weeks."

"The last couple of weeks don't count because I was stressed about being unemployed."

"Okay then, the last couple of months."

"Same thing."

"All right then, when you thought your job was secure. When was the last time you had fun?"

I bit into a piece of brownie and thought back. What about when . . . no, that didn't count, that was work-related. Surely when I went . . . no, that was for the job, too. Was I that pathetic that I can't remember the last time I laughed, let alone had fun? I slowly came to the realization that my evening with Renee was the most fun I'd had in a long time.

"I don't remember," I said sadly.

She smiled at me. "Well, if it's any consolation, our trip here has been anything but boring."

I laughed.

"And look, that's the second time you've laughed tonight! That's a record."

"Thanks."

She nudged my shoulder again.

"All right, Dr. Phil, what's your secret?" I was through with her analyzing me. Now it was her turn.

She paused for a minute, then said, "I wish we had the same father. I hated when we were younger and you introduced me as your half-sister."

"That bothers you?"

She nodded. "You haven't done it since being back, but still . . ."

"Okay.. I'll start calling you my sister. We don't look anything alike, so people will figure it out on their own . . . What are you doing?"

She was off the bed and throwing the remains of her brownie in the trash.

"You just did it again. I'm aware of how we look in the mirror. You act like my skin color gives me some kind of power over you—"

"It does. I've seen with my own eyes how your skin color and wavy hair is like a magic wand that gives you everything you want. I love you, Renee. And I appreciate everything you've done for me, but we have different fathers. That makes us half-sisters. It is what it is."

"I'm well aware of what it is. But you act like you don't want to claim me sometimes."

"I do, Renee. A lot of times I just said it so people wouldn't ask questions. If I introduced you as my half-sister I wouldn't get all the stares. It just made things easier for me."

"All right. I forgive you," she said teasingly, sitting back on the bed.

"Well, it's about time somebody forgave me. I've committed more mistakes this past week then in my whole life." I ate another spoon of my brownie. "I want to leave tomorrow. I need to get started about my father."

"You really are going through with this, aren't you?"

"I have to. Wouldn't you?"

"Yes." She nudged my arm again. "I'm proud of you."

"Don't be. I'm beyond scared."

"That's normal. At least you're still going to meet him. Can I ask a favor?"

I held my breath and nodded.

"Can we leave tomorrow night? You were teasing me by showing me all those shops and not letting me go inside any of them. I want to get some shopping done."

I laughed. "Whew. I thought you were going to tell me something else in my childhood that I did wrong."

She hit my arm again.

"I know I'm black, but if you keep hitting me you're going to leave a mark."

Now it was her turn to laugh.

"But that's fine," I said. "That will give me a chance to say goodbye to Norma."

"I want to go with you."

"You sure?" I asked.

She nodded.

"Did you really want to be a mother?"

"More than anything."

"You will."

"I know. I know I'll get another chance. It's just hard, you know?"

"I can imagine." I grabbed her hand. "I know I haven't been there for you before, but I'm here for you now. Sis."

She tightened her grasp in my hand. "Thank you."

Is this what it could have been like growing up? Having fun conversations and eating so much junk food that you think you'll be sick, but surprisingly find yourself feeling fine? And I do feel fine. No, better than fine.

I wrote as I sat on top of the closed toilet seat in the bathroom, Renee's snoring creeping in under the crack in the door.

I missed out not only on having a father, but on having a sister. Who can I blame for that one? Only myself. This trip has been more eye-opening than I wanted. So far I've learned that I'm a selfish, boring, mean bully that loves to intimidate people who I think are inferior. But that's not me at all. Not the me I want to be, anyway.

Renee slept during the plane ride back to Houston. The way she marathon shopped from store to store, she had me tired—and this was coming from someone who felt they *invented* marathon shopping.

Saying goodbye to Norma was hard. She cried as she hugged me—so tight that she squeezed tears out of my eyes.

"You're going to get the love you've been searching for your whole life."

"You think so?" I asked into her hair.

"I know so. He's going to love you, Mariah. Just like I love you."

"What if he doesn't?"

We broke apart and she held my face in her hands. "Trust me. He has to love you."

Has to love me.

I looked over at Renee and hoped I was making the right decision.

Houston's heat slammed into me like a car accident.

"Man, it's hot," I said, slinging my bag into the back-seat of the rental.

"I can't believe that a Toyota Camry was the only car they had left," Renee whined, getting into the driver's seat.

"So sorry, princess, all the Bentleys were rented out."

"Shut up," she said, starting the ignition. "Where to?"

"Grandpa's, right?" We both decided before we left New York that I should start with Grandpa for information about my father.

She shook her head.

"I need to go home first."

"Well, take me to Grandpa's first."

"No."

"What?"

"I've been talking to Mama—"

"*Your* mama."

"She wants to see you—"

"I'm jumping out this car, Renee. Don't pull this on me."

"You need to talk to her. She might have more information than Grandpa."

"I'm not talking to her," I said, my teeth clenched, my hands turning to fists.

"Relax," she said, touching my shoulder.

I flinched. "I can't believe you're doing this."

"Do you trust me?"

"No."

"Well, too bad. We're going anyway."

"I *don't* want to see her."

"Do you want to meet your father?"

"Yes."

"Then you need to talk to her. She's the one that has the information you need."

"I can't believe it's come to this."

"The circle of life."

I turned away from her and faced the window.

"Don't be upset."

"Shut up."

The rest of the trip was in silence.

HAT BOX

She was sitting outside when we arrived.

Her back was to us as she was overlooking the patio.

"I'm going to my room."

Renee snatched my bag from my hands. "No, you're not. Go," she said, pointing outside to Beverly's direction.

I glared at her.

Her face softened. "Please. I promise this will help."

She nudged me, and I walked toward her, willing my legs to freeze. They wouldn't, they worked like my brain told them, and I was standing on the patio, hot wind blowing my face. Not my hair, I might add. I pulled out a chair from the iron patio set, making a harsh scraping sound against the concrete. I sat down and waited for her to turn around, but she was more interested in Houston's skyline than in me. As usual.

Several minutes passed and she turned around to face me. Her nose was red and swollen, and her eyes were watery.

"I look pretty bad, don't I?"

I didn't say anything.

She sat down across from me. Her face lacked the foundation and blush that usually sat on her skin, and her hair was flat and lifeless, without all the Texas volume and bounce it usually had. I noticed the small lines around her eyes and mouth for the first time. Her shoulders were hunched and her expression was drawn. There was a hat box on the table, covered with faded pink roses. I kept my focus on it, refusing to look at her. If I looked at her eyes, drained and dead, then I would apologize, like I always did, for being born. I wouldn't do that again.

"Renee says you want to meet your father."

"Yes."

She slid the box to me.

"What's this?"

"Look in it."

I opened the box and saw a mass of crumpled papers. I picked one up and smoothed its edges and read it.

Why don't you call? Is it something I've done or said? Whatever it is we can work it out. Please don't be scared . . .

"My father wrote these? To you?"

"Yes."

"Why are you—"

"I thought this would help."

"How?"

She reached her hands to me across the table, but I pulled away. She sighed. "This is all I have to give you."

"You could have told me the truth. You shouldn't have lied—"

She put her hand up. "I know you hate me right now. But read these letters before you pass judgment."

She stood up.

"That's it? That's the big speech?" I stood and faced her. "That's the big forgiveness speech? You lie about my father being dead and you think a box full of letters is going to fix it?" I shook my head. "You are so lazy—always wanting someone else to fix everything for you. This isn't enough," I said, standing.

"What do you want from me? *Blood?* I've racked my brain trying to figure out how to fix this, but honestly I don't know if I can. I have done my *best* with you. Ever since you were a little girl you've wanted an excuse to hate me. So now you have an excuse. So HATE me," she screamed, spittle flying from her mouth.

"Be careful for what you wish for." I grabbed the box and left the room.

What can I do to get you back? I've begged and still nothing. Marriage is hard, don't let ours end this way. I love you. I need you. Please come home. I know things are hard with my mama, so I've saved enough for us to get our own place. Please come back. I'll take care of you and the baby. Your father told me that we had a girl. Did you still name her Mariah?

Love, Paul

I want to see my daughter, Beverly. I know me and you can't be together, but why would you block me from seeing my daughter? I love her. She needs a father in her life. Don't let what happened to us mess her up. Please contact me.

Love, Paul

A knock on the door stopped me from digging further into the box and retrieving another letter. I knew it was Renee, and told her to come in.

"I take it things didn't go well?"

I shrugged. "What did you expect?"

She sighed. "I thought you two would patch things up."

"Some things can't be patched up." I patted the spot next to me on the bed and she sat down.

"What are you reading?"

I handed her one of the letters.

"This is dated over twenty years ago. You think he still lives here?"

"Let's hope so."

Renee started reading aloud:

"Beverly,
You pushed for this divorce. Well, I won't stop you. I thought your father was always behind your silence, but know that I see it in writing that you don't love me—"

She stopped reading and looked at me. I nodded and she continued.

"The court ordered me to pay child support, and even though you refused, I'm a man and I take care of my responsibilities."

She pulled a check out of the envelope.

"It's made out to Mama. Two hundred and twenty seven dollars?"

"Must have been child support."

"You think he sent a check—"

I nodded.

"Every month?"

"I haven't looked through the whole box, but I think so."

"Oh, Mariah—"

"Don't look at me like that."

"Like what?"

"Like you pity me."

"I don't pity you, Mariah, I was just . . ." She shook her head. "Never mind. What are you going to do now?"

"Isn't it obvious?"

"You're going to find him." She sighed. "Oh boy." She flicked over the envelope, and read the address aloud: "5217 Herkimer Lane, Memphis, Tennessee."

"Well, Memphis, here we come."

BEYONCE OR HALLE?

Beverly was staying in a hotel until we left for Memphis, which I was thankful for. I was glad of her tears, but also felt guilty, like I always did when she cried.

We planned on leaving first thing tomorrow morning, but Renee wanted to run a couple of errands first. Like a dummy, I tagged along.

"Where are we going?" I asked as we pulled into a shopping center. "You didn't buy enough stuff at the mall?"

"This isn't for me, this is for you. Come on, get out."

I followed her out of the car and saw her heading to a hair salon. *Weaves 'R' Us* was emblazoned on the sign out front.

"Renee, I know you—"

"Well I couldn't let you meet your father not looking your best." She smiled as she pulled the heavy glass door open and I walked into the best scent in the world. Hair spray and burnt hair. Heaven.

Renee walked to the receptionist and checked me in while I looked at the walls that were full of all their before and after pictures. From the photos I could see that their weaves were virtually undetectable, and looked real enough that you could run your hands through them.

"Okay, you're all set," Renee said, turning to face me. "Your stylist's name is Kasandra, and she's ready for you.

I told them to do whatever you ask for. I have some more running around to do before our trip. So I'll come back in a few hours."

I pulled her tight in my arms, crushing her to me. "Thank you so much."

"Okay. Okay, calm down," she said, patting my back so I would let her go. I did finally.

"Remember it's just hair, okay?"

I nodded and reached out to hug her again, but she ducked out of the door. She waved goodbye through the glass doors and was gone.

"Mariah?"

"Yes?"

"I'm Kasandra. I'll be doing your hair today. Come follow me to my station."

She was pleasant looking. Pretty enough to not be called ugly, yet average enough to be forgettable. I sat down in her black hydraulic chair.

"Your sister mentioned that you would probably prefer a weave?" she asked, as she ran her hands through my frizzy hair.

"Umm . . ."

"Don't worry, you're in good hands. I lot of people are nervous about getting their first weaves. You want to look through some books first?"

I nodded and she reached under her station and pulled out several hair magazines. "Take your time and look through these. Would you like something to drink?"

"Water would be fine."

She skipped away, and I started flipping through the pages, seeing Beyonce, Alicia Keys, Gabrielle Union—all with their perfectly coiffed long hair. I flipped another page and saw a picture of Halle Berry winning her Oscar. Her short hair was delicately spiked and feathery, and accented her features. I looked in the mirror above her station.

I had the same heart-shaped face as hers, some of the same petite features. How had I not noticed before?

Probably because it was hidden under a mountain of weave.

I kept flipping between the two pages. Beyonce or Halle? Halle or Beyonce?

"Here's your water," Kasandra said, handing me a cold bottle. "Did you decide?"

"I want this one."

Kasandra smiled.

"Good choice."

⌐

"You look great!" Renee screamed when she came to pick me up. "I love it!"

I touched my hair. "I love it, too."

Kasandra darkened my hair to a shiny black, and it was tapered low around the sides, with soft spikes in the crown. She kept my bangs short and they were wisped to the side; "So everyone can see those big brown eyes," Kasandra said. I have to admit I looked good. Better than good, I was fierce.

I pushed open the door of the salon and a gust of wind blew and not a hair moved. And for the first time, it was okay.

Hair style is the final tip off whether or not a woman truly knows herself.
    —Hubert de Givenchy
        Vogue, July 1985

CAFFEINE-FILLED KANGAROOS

Should my coming to see him be a surprise? Or should I call him and let him know that the daughter he's never seen is on her way?

I bit the end of the pen, then wrote:

I thought it would have taken longer to find his telephone number, but technology makes everything easier, and when I typed his address into Google—bam. His phone number appeared. Renee thinks I should call him. "You'll give him a heart attack!" she said. But calling him would give him a chance to say he didn't want me to come.

I shook my head.

Okay, I doubt that he would tell me no, but still I just . . .

I stared at the ceiling. What do you say on the phone to the father you've never met? "Hey Dad, it's me, your daughter. How you doing?" Or "Hey, remember the child that you never got to see? Well, hey, that's me." I shook my head again.

Truth is, I don't believe he really wanted to see me. How could someone stay away for thirty years? No one was stopping him, why didn't he try harder to see me? I've only had the stomach to read five of the letters. Every time I start reading my stomach burns and I get so angry at Beverly for blocking his love out of my life. Maybe if my father was around, I would have a man, and a family of

*my own, instead of sitting in the bedroom in my sister's
house. Alone.*

I closed my journal and my eyes, and tried to stop the
whirlwind of thoughts going through my head. I sat up
and rummaged through my suitcase and found my only
picture of Paul. I stared at his face so long, my eyes
blurred. *I'm coming Daddy. I'm coming.*

When Renee arrived two hours later, I was pacing the
living room floor.

"You got the tickets?"

"Better," she said, breathless. "Come downstairs."

"Why?"

"Just come downstairs," she said, grabbing my hand
and dragging me into the elevator.

"What is this all about?"

"You'll see," she said, as we exited the elevator and I
followed through the lobby to the entrance of her
building. She pushed open the glass doors and started
jumping up and down. "What do you think?"

"About what?"

"About this!" she said, pointing to a white BMW convertible. She walked around it like one of those girls on
The Price is Right, her hand gliding over it as she pointed
out all the bells and whistles.

"And it has navigation so you won't get lost."

"*I won't get lost?* Renee, is this car for me?"

"Well, duh! Did you think *I* needed another car?"

My feet started bouncing off the ground and we were hugging each other, both of us jumping up and down like a bunch of caffeine-filled kangaroos. "You bought me a car, you bought me a car!"

"I bought you a car, I bought you a car!"

I stopped jumping and she handed me the keys, and I got in and inhaled that new car scent, ran my hands over the peanut butter leather interior, grabbed the shiny mahogany-stained steering wheel. *I could get used to this . . .*

"I want to take this baby out for a spin. Hop in."

She giggled, and then got in the passenger seat.

"Where to?" I asked.

"How about Memphis?"

"What?"

"I was thinking how fun it would be if we took a road trip, you know? I always wanted to do something like that, especially in a convertible. Sunglasses on, wind blowing through our hair—what do you think?"

She had me until she mentioned the wind in the hair part.

"Nothing's blowing with my new hair cut, Renee. Besides, that's crazy. We can't just go take a road trip."

"Why not? We have the time. Besides, you need to practice driving anyway. What better way to do that than on the open road? We can plan the whole thing, and it'll only take a couple of days—"

"I don't know about this . . ."

"Look, it'll give you time to figure out what to say. Have you thought about that?"

"No . . ."

"Good. Road trip," she shouted, her head back.

"I don't know how long I can be in a car with you."

She hit my arm.

"I'm just playing. Man, Renee, this is a nice car. I've never had my own car. I don't know what to say—"

"Say thank you."

"Thank you."

"Good. Now let's park this baby and plan our trip. I want to leave first thing in the morning."

It took us a few hours and several phone calls to decide on what route to take for our trip. After washing a load of laundry and packing the clothes I would need, I called Norma.

"Hello?" she answered, her voice sounding like the voice of a new mother, tired and haggard.

"Hey, Mama! How are you feeling?"

"How does it *sound* like I'm feeling? She hasn't been sleeping, so I'm up all night. My breasts feel like a dog's chew toy, and I haven't bathed since you left."

"Wow. Sorry."

"Hey, the trials of motherhood. But she smiled at me today."

"Really?"

"Yes. She opened her eyes and gave me a wide tooth-less grin. It's amazing how much I love this little girl."

"Of course you do."

"How is everything with your mother?"

"Beverly? She handed me a box full of letters that my father wrote her. And I found out that she's a compulsive liar."

"All right. But what's your plan? Are you still going to see your father?"

"Yes. Renee bought me a car so—"

"You have a car! Whoo-hoo!"

I pulled the phone away from my ear to save my eardrums. "Calm down or I'll need a hearing aid."

"What kind of car?"

"A BMW," I said, my voice filling with the confidence that a BMW owner has.

"Oooh, la te da, a BMW. I can't believe your sister bought you a car. A BMW at that. You were getting too old to not have a driver's license."

"I have a driver's license. I just don't drive. I didn't need to in New York. In Houston everybody drives."

"So you two are getting along?"

"We are," I said, surprised at my answer. "We've been getting along pretty well."

"You must be if she bought you a car."

"We're taking a road trip to Memphis tomorrow."

"Man, you're really doing this, aren't you?"

I sighed. "Yes. It's time."

"And you don't think calling is the best way to go?"

"No. I'm going to find him, check him out, and then tell him."

"Pretty bold. Not the way I would go, but you never did listen to me."

I laughed. I heard Elizabeth's faint cry and we said our goodbyes. She was going to take care of her baby, and I was on my way to meet my father.

WIND BENEATH MY WINGS

"It'll take us two days to get there," Renee said as she heaved her Louis Vuitton luggage into the trunk.

"How much stuff are you bringing?" I asked.

"You never know how long this reunion could last."

I threw my bags in the trunk and walked over to the passenger side. "Do you mind if I let you drive the first leg? I need to collect my thoughts."

"You want me to drive? I would have thought that you would be chomping at the bit to drive your car."

"I know, but I'm still nervous from wrecking your car. You mind?" I said, handing her my keys. *My keys.* I still couldn't believe it. I had a new car. I slid into the passenger side and inhaled the scent of new leather, and watched as my sister pulled out of the parking garage with ease.

The air outside was still and humid, and we both agreed to keep the top up and run the air conditioner full blast.

"The passenger runs the radio, so crack open one of those new CDs and let's see if we share the same taste in music."

"Well we know we don't after last night," I said. Last night we went to Target to pick up a few toiletries, and she had me laughing at our different tastes in music. She listened to Bette Midler, Celine Dion, and Barbara Streisand, while I enjoyed the cool musings of Eric Benet and Anthony Hamilton.

"What are you saying? You telling me you don't lip sync to 'Wind Beneath My Wings' anymore?"

I laughed at the memory. Beverly was a huge Bette Midler fan, and she blared her music most evenings. The bathroom was near her bedroom, so I would go in there, lock the door, roll a towel over my head, imagining long dark locks trailing my waist, and lip sync "Wind Beneath My Wings" until Renee pounded on the door that she had to pee.

"I remember those days," I said. "But I've grown up and we're going to listen to something more to *my* liking."

"All right, pop something in."

I tore off the plastic covering off Alicia Keys's latest and put the CD in. Her smooth voice and carefree piano playing brought my mood up and eased the terror in my stomach about meeting my father.

I gathered enough from the letters that he wrote Beverly until I was five. After that he simply sent checks. And he still stayed with his mother. What kind of man still stays with his mother at fifty years old?

"What you thinking about over there?" Renee asked, driving the crowded morning freeway with relative ease.

"That you're a good driver. Who taught you?"

"Mama. Don't you remember her taking—" She stopped, and then shook her head.

"You know Beverly didn't teach me anything. I take that back, she taught me how ugly she is inside. She taught me how not to be a mother. If I ever have children I'll never lie to them. They'll always know the truth, good or bad."

"I'm sorry—"

"Stop apologizing for her! You didn't do anything wrong, okay? It was all her."

"I noticed you brought the box."

I looked at it in the backseat. "Yeah?"

"You didn't read all the letters?"

"I read most of them. It's too sad looking at them. Just seeing his handwriting makes me want to cry." I shook my head. "I don't want to talk about it anymore."

"Okay. But you should know there are two sides to every story, Mariah."

"I've heard hers. There is no excuse for what she did to me."

"I agree."

"And I can't believe that you would even suggest that Beverly was right in any way. There was no right in what she did."

"Did you see the way Grandpa reacted to her in the room?"

"I don't remember . . ."

"She had a hard childhood, Mariah."

"However hard her childhood was, she brought it on herself."

"Grandpa barely even spoke to her."

"So?" I asked.

She sighed. "You don't know the half of it."

PECANS

When I think back, visits with Grandpa were some of the best times in my young life. His old house was near the nursing home he was in now. It sat on five acres of land with tall pine trees that overshadowed his massive red brick house. He had a pecan tree in the backyard and Renee and I used to pick pecans from it and bring them inside the house. We raced to see who could crack them open the fastest, and I would always win. I knew the trick with the nutcracker to crack the pecans on the side first so it would reveal the fleshy sweet nut inside.

Grandpa would have Lucille make us homemade vanilla ice cream, which took her hours, but she never complained about the extra duties he assigned her along with her housecleaning. After Grandma died, she grew more like a grandmother to us and less like the help. She always sprinkled the pecans throughout the ice-cream, so generously that we tasted them in every bite.

"This tastes so good, Grandpa," I would say, licking the back of my spoon.

"Mm-hmm," Renee added, ice cream on her chin.

"I'm glad you girls like it," he said, his light brown eyes sparkling.

We would eat until our bellies were full and then eat some more as we watched silly cartoons. I remember falling asleep in his arms, smelling the musky scent of his aftershave.

When Beverly came to pick us up on Sunday afternoons, you could feel the air shift, like a car switching gears. Things were different when she came over. Grandpa's face lost his smile and was replaced with frowns, or worse, he would be devoid of all emotion and nothing Beverly said could evoke a reaction from him.

"Daddy, I'm going to the store, you need anything?"

He shook his head no.

"You sure? I could pick you up some of that ice-cream you like so much—"

"So you're blind as well as stupid, Beverly? You see the girls are eating ice cream, why would I need you to pick some up when they're already eating it? Mine is homemade."

"Oh. Well, I guess I'll stay and have a bowl—"

"I don't think so. Girls, give Grandpa a hug and go in your room and pack your things up. You'll be back next weekend."

"Oh, I didn't tell you? Anthony is taking us out of town. To Disney World. Won't that be fun?"

"Yay!" Renee and I screamed, dancing and prancing around the room. At twelve the fantasy of Disney World couldn't be lost on me. All my hair was back—it was still short, but I had hair finally.

"I'm going to tell them. It's time."

Grandpa's face flushed red and his lips tightened to a thin straight line. "Don't you do that. You'll ruin everything."

"Daddy, it's time—"

His hand slammed down on the counter so hard our bowls jumped.

"I said no! She's too young, it'll devastate her."

"Devastate who?" Renee asked.

Beverly looked down at her, then me.

Her eyes went back to Grandpa. "Look at what you've done. Come on, girls, let's go." She walked out of the room to the protection of her car outside.

Grandpa blew out a ragged breath and looked at us.

"Sorry, girls. Go get your things together."

So my girl is one now. Is she walking yet? Talking? I know you have moved on, but I hope this letter reaches you. Could you at least send a picture?

Sincerely, Paul

I folded the letter back up.

"How many times do you think Mama read those letters?" Renee asked.

I stuffed it back into its envelope.

"I don't know."

"I bet she read them hundreds of times."

"Yeah, well, that shows what kind of heart she has. What kind of person could let someone write to them for years and never respond?"

"Maybe she has a reason—"

"There is no explanation for what she did!" I burst into tears.

Renee let me cry, and after a few minutes I wiped my face and mumbled out an apology for my outburst.

"It's okay."

"These letters. They're really getting to me. Every time I read one, I just want to scream."

Renee pulled over.

"What are you doing?"

"Pulling over so you can scream."

"What? Get back on the road."

She stopped the engine. "I was five months pregnant when I lost my first baby. I had to deliver him, just like a real baby, except he wasn't. He was dead."

She turned to look at me. "I screamed the whole time. I screamed about how unfair it was, I screamed at how my baby should be alive—I just kept screaming."

"Did it help?"

She shook her head. "No. But it was the only time I felt it was appropriate. You only get a few chances in your adult life to scream. This is one of them." She rolled down the windows and let out a scream so loud, I wanted to check her for gunshot wounds. She turned to me. "Now it's your turn."

I didn't think I had it in me. I thought it would take a few times before I could belt it out. But on my first try, I let out a scream so loud that I think Beverly heard me.

Renee nodded. "I thought you never did that before?"

"I haven't."

"It was a good one."

"I guess I needed to do it for a while."

CREASES

"I'm getting hungry. Let's stop and get something to eat," Renee said.

"It's about time. I thought we would never stop."

"We stopped at that gas station an hour ago—"

"Yeah, so I could pee."

"Look, I thought you were eager to see your dad. I was trying to hurry."

"I *am* eager to meet him, I just want to take it easy."

She nodded as she pulled in front of a diner. The tin building had seen better days, but I was hungry and beggars couldn't be choosers.

"Let's go."

I followed her inside the diner and we seated ourselves. A gum-smacking, leather-skinned waitress took our order and we sat there in silence for a few beats. Our food arrived and we ate—I had a tuna melt and Renee had chicken fried steak.

"Bet your husband never would have eaten in a place like this," I said, taking a huge bite out of my sandwich.

"Why do you say that? Because of his money?"

"Of course."

She shook her head. "You didn't know him. He was a kind, gentle man."

"You're right. I didn't know him."

"But you're right. He wouldn't be caught dead in a place like this."

We both laughed.

"What was it like? Being married, I mean."

She sat back in the booth and looked up, as if the gesture would send her back in time.

"Good. Most of the time it was good. Except when Mama got in the way—"

"How did she get in the way?"

"Our honeymoon, for one."

I held my hand up. "Please don't tell me that Beverly came on your honeymoon."

She nodded and I groaned.

"I can't believe it . . ."

"He planned this beautiful trip to Fiji to a gorgeous resort, and she was there at the airport with her bags packed. She felt that I needed a chaperone—"

"You were married!"

"I know, but what was I supposed to do? She was already there."

"You could have told her no."

"I couldn't do that. Mama is all I had. If she thought she needed to come, then she was probably right."

"You're not serious, are you? As pretty as you are, you never got out and hung out with your friends?"

She shrugged. "I told you before I didn't have many friends."

"It sounds like you didn't have *any* friends."

"My best friend was a bottle of vodka."

"Oh. I'm sorry." And I was.

She smiled. "Why? I have a good life. In the end everything worked out." She seemed nervous all of a sudden; realizing she said too much, she grabbed her purse and pulled out some money for the bill, throwing it on the table.

"You ready?"

"Um . . ." I was still trying to finish up the last of my French fries. I picked up a few, ran them through the ketchup on my plate and nodded.

"Why the rush?" I asked, as I followed her out the restaurant into the night air. She yanked open the door and slid behind the wheel.

"There is no rush. Just didn't want to stay in there longer than necessary."

It took us a while to find the hotel that Renee booked, but we finally pulled into the parking lot and dragged ourselves to check in. What is it about sitting down all day that makes you so exhausted? I couldn't wait to jump into the shower, but Renee insisted on going first, so I agreed and laid on the bed until she got out.

I rummaged through the hat box and found a letter that had Grandpa's handwriting on it. It was addressed to my father. I opened it.

Paul,

I admire your tenacity, young man. You've written to her a long time. You wouldn't take my money, either, which I always thought was stupid, but you had your pride, I guess.

Beverly is married to another man, the man she should have married a long time ago.

She has never seen any of your letters, and I hope she never does. So stop writing, you are wasting your time. And as far as your daughter goes, she doesn't even know you exist. You are dead in her eyes, same as mine, and I'm sure, same as Beverly's.

Do not write again.

William

"Renee!" I yelled, climbing off the bed. "Renee, come here!"

"What?" She was in a white bathrobe, her hair wrapped up in a towel. "What is it?"

"Read this," I said, my hands shaking as I handed it to her.

She read it and then met my eyes.

"Beverly didn't see them?"

I shook my head.

"Grandpa?"

"Can you believe it? This story gets crazier with every passing minute."

She sat down on the bed. "So Grandpa blocked the letters?"

"Yeah. Beverly never saw them. He must have felt bad and given them to her later."

"Including the letter that he wrote your father."

I nodded.

"So this changes things—"

I snatched the letter from her. "This changes nothing."

"But Mama didn't know your father was trying to contact her all those years. Maybe—"

"Maybe what? Maybe she wouldn't have lied to me? Maybe she would have let me know my father? That's something a good mother would do, and Beverly is not a good mother."

"You still want to blame her for everything. She lost, too—"

"What did she lose?"

"She was in love with Paul. Maybe she would still be with him if it wasn't for Grandpa's meddling."

"She was a spoiled brat who got scared straight because she had to do a little housework. That is not love. If she loved Paul she would have stayed—"

"She was young."

"She would have stayed!"

Renee crossed her arms over her chest. "Why can't you see the whole story here?"

I bit my lip as I felt hot tears press at the corner of my eyes. "Because if she's not the monster I made her out to be, then who is? Who is to blame for all this?"

"Everybody made a mistake, and then made the mistake bigger by trying to cover it up. Now everybody needs to heal. You, Mama, your father—everybody. Like it or not, she's the only mother you've got. You need to forgive her."

I looked down at the letter, and followed the creases to fold it exactly as I found it. "I'm going to take a shower now."

COMPASSION

The closer we got to Memphis, the emptier my Maalox bottle got. By the time we arrived it was empty.

"You drink that stuff like it's water. Maybe you need to go to the doctor."

I flicked my hand. "I'm fine."

But I wasn't. The trip took us longer than we planned because of my frequent restroom breaks. The whole point of this trip was to meet my father, and now all I wanted to do was turn around.

Our hotel loomed before us, and I gave my keys to the valet, ready to get out of the car again to stretch my legs. I got my bag out of the backseat and trailed after Renee into the Hilton lobby.

"Your reservation was for the suite, yes?" the concierge asked, his voice tinged with an European accent.

"Yes," she said, wagging her credit card in front of him like a piece of meat. He grabbed it and slid it through the machine, and I watched her scribble her signature on the bottom.

We were silent on our trip up the elevator, and when Renee slid our room card into the electronic lock, I dumped my luggage on the floor and flounced on the first bed I saw.

"I take it that's your bed."

"Yep."

"You mind if I jump in the shower?"

"Nope."

It felt like I'd been in more hotels in the past two weeks than in my whole life.

My cell phone vibrated in my pocket and I pulled it out and saw it was Norma.

"Hey."

"You made it safely?"

"Yeah, we're here."

"Have you made contact?"

"Not yet." I sat up and pulled off my shoes. "I'm beat."

"You drove?"

"Some of the way."

"Which means you drove for about an hour."

"Exactly. What are you doing?"

"Feeding Elizabeth."

Flashes of her plate-size nipples entered my mind and I almost gagged into the telephone.

"So when do you make contact?" Norma asked.

"The question is *how* do I make contact? Should I call him first? Or just do the old-fashioned pop-in?"

"I don't know, what does Renee think?"

"I haven't asked her yet. Hey, let me ask you something. Don't you think it's weird that Renee doesn't have any friends?"

"She has your mom."

"I know, but she doesn't have any real friends."

"Beverly's really been there for her. Your sister's been through a lot. It's hard for her to open up to people."

"I guess. Listen, when Renee's husband died, why didn't you tell me you wrote to her?"

"Oh, jeez . . ."

"I'm not mad, I just wanted to know."

"I thought she needed someone to talk to. I just wrote her a couple of letters and called her a few times."

"Why didn't you tell me?" I asked.

"You know how you felt about your family. You would have just gotten upset."

"Yeah, but why didn't you tell me I should have reached out to my sister? You should have reminded me to be there for her."

"I didn't think I needed to remind you. She's your sister. Her husband died. You should have been there."

"Touché. Look, I gotta go."

"Don't be mad, Mariah."

"I'm not. I'm sad. Talk to you later, okay?"

"Love you."

After hanging up, I laid across the bed. Ever since leaving the restaurant yesterday, I was haunted by the fact that Renee's only friend was Beverly. I kept thinking about the past, and wishing I could rewind time and fix it. But I couldn't change my behavior, especially everything I did that horrible day.

The day of Peter's funeral was sunny. One of those days where you want to fly a kite or sit all day on the beach. Instead I was sitting under a tent watching my sister's husband go in the ground.

And I felt nothing.

Sure, I looked sad like everyone else, but I kept glancing at my watch, wandering when I could sneak a peek at my phone to check some e-mails, itching to get out of my dress, this place, this city.

My eyes scanned the crowd, tears on the faces of many. The crowd looked like a Dalmatian's coat—there was an even amount of white and black faces around me. I stopped cold when I saw Beverly's eyes on me; her disapproving glance pierced through me. She knew what I was thinking. She shook her head at me and put her arm around Renee. She didn't have to show such signs of possessiveness, I knew who was loved most.

Renee looked devastated. Her skin was the color of snow, her hair pulled back in a severe bun that made her eyes appear as if she was caught in a wind tunnel. Her face was wet from tears and her nose oozed so much snot that her hand was full of wet tissues. I felt nothing at her loss; I hadn't spent much time with Peter, so I hadn't formed a bond.

But I should have felt sad for Renee. As her sister I should have felt something for her standing there with Beverly and Anthony, the three amigos back together again.

But I didn't. And dare I say it? I felt twinges of pleasure crawl up my lower back as Renee cried. The harder she cried, the more joy I felt until a smile played on my lips. Norma was watching me, and shock was on her face. She knew me better than anyone, and she knew what kind of thoughts existed in that black heart of mine. Shame flooded me and I had to get out of there . . . *Had to be anywhere but here.*

"You don't understand, you didn't grow up like I did—"

"Show a little compassion, Mariah. That's your sister, and she's in pain."

And I tried. Reached deep inside myself and tried to feel compassion, and when that didn't work, tried to feel compassion's distant cousin—pity. But that didn't work, either. It was hard to feel pity for someone who lived a life of luxury and who would inherit millions. No, old feelings of jealousy and unworthiness remained.

"I'm leaving," I whispered to Norma two hours later.

"What? You can't! You need to stay . . ."

"I can't do this. I can't pretend that I care anymore."

And behind me stood my little sister, her face wrenched in a different pain and her eyes filled with fresh tears.

"Oh, Renee," I said, "I didn't mean that—"

"And the Oscar for Supporting Sister, goes to— Mariah Stevens!" She imitated her hand into a microphone and thrust it in my face. "How does it feel, Mariah, to know you won?"

I slapped her hand away. "I got it, Renee. You don't have to make a scene," I said, trying to ignore the glances being thrown our way.

"Oh, I think I can do whatever I want right now. My husband's dead, remember? But you don't care, not that you ever did. So leave."

I wish I could say that I hugged Renee tight and begged for forgiveness. But I was happy that I'd been granted my wish and left with no feelings of remorse.

IT IS WHAT IT IS

"Hey, open up, you know it's me. It's dinnertime." I knocked again and heard her feet shuffling toward the bathroom door. She was dressed in floral silk pajamas and her wet hair was plaited in several braids, making her look like Pollyanna's little sister.

"Can't we just order in?"

"Great, I'm starved," I said.

"What do you want?" She picked up the menu.

"What do they have?"

She threw the menu at me and it landed in my lap. "Look for yourself. I'm not that hungry. I'm just ordering a sandwich."

I scanned the menu and then decided I would have a sandwich, too, and ordered BLT's for both of us. After hanging up the phone, I watched her as she sat on the bed, her legs beneath her Indian-style. She was watching an episode of *Survivor*.

"Can we talk?"

Without turning her head she said, "Is this important enough that I need to press mute?"

"This is important enough that you need to turn it off."

She obeyed and watched me as I sat next to her.

"I know you're nervous about meeting your father, but—"

"Nervous isn't the word for what I'm feeling. I want to talk to you about the other day. When we were at the restaurant? You seemed to freeze up when we talked about your lack of friends."

"It's fine." She patted my knee. "I had a hard time at first, but you get used to the way things are. It's fine now."

"It's not fine. And I'm very sorry for how I've treated you."

"Haven't we had this conversation already?"

"Yes, but . . ." I sighed. "Sometimes when you don't have something you fool yourself into thinking you don't need it. I never had a father, so I tricked myself into thinking it was okay. I convinced myself that I didn't need a father, or any family, for that matter. I was wrong. I need you, Renee. And I'm glad you're here."

Renee looked down. "All my life all I've ever wanted is your friendship. God made us sisters, but it takes *work* to be someone's friend. It's embarrassing to me when someone asks me how you're doing and I don't know. I didn't know you. And for years you thought that was okay."

Her eyes sparkled like diamonds from unshed tears. Seeing her pain was like catching a cold—it was contagious. Tears pricked my eyes.

"You don't have to keep apologizing for the past. It is what it is."

I hugged her and she hugged me just as tight. Pulling away, she wiped my wet cheeks.

"I think I've cried enough for a lifetime."

"Crying is good. Makes you human."

After a fitful night of sleep, I finally sat up in the bed at 6:00 a.m. Tired enough to go back to sleep, but too anxious to close my eyes, I got up and took a shower. I got dressed quickly and was hitting Renee's arm at 6:30.

"Are you serious?" she asked, rolling over, her morning breath making an appearance before her. I stepped back.

"Get ready."

She shook her head. "You're crazy, it's too early." She yawned, causing me to vomit a little in my mouth, and I told her to brush her teeth and get ready. She brushed her teeth but came out the bathroom wearing her night-clothes and lay back in the bed.

"Aww, come on, let's go."

"No way. It's too early."

I sighed and laid down in the bed next to her. "I'm meeting my father today."

She sighed, and I smelled spearmint. All was well in the world.

"You're not going to let a girl sleep, are you?"

"That's the plan."

"You nervous?"

"A little. Excited, mostly."

"So how are you going to make your approach?"

"I'm going to knock on his door and tell him that I'm his daughter."

She laughed. "This isn't some *Lifetime* movie. How are you *really* going to tell him?"

"I'm serious. That's the plan."

She just looked at me, her hazel eyes flashing green.

"You don't like that idea?"

She shrugged. "It's your plan. If you think that's best—"

"I do."

"You don't want to call first?"

"I thought about that." And I had. I was afraid that if I called it would give him a chance to reject me. In person it would be harder for him to do that—he would be looking at his flesh and blood daughter and not just a voice over the telephone. He couldn't reject me once he saw me. I'd practiced making my eyes big and pitiful, like a dog begging for a treat. There was no way he could deny me.

"Trust me, this is the best way," I said.

"All right," she said, closing her eyes.

I gave her a few minutes and tapped her shoulder.

"Go away," she moaned.

"If you get up now it'll give us enough time to get breakfast—"

"Man, you are annoying!" she said, throwing back the covers and standing up. "You better be glad I love you."

SPACE SUIT

The hardest part about not having a father is seeing the people around you who have one.

Seeing Anthony kiss Renee good night.

Seeing him read her bedtime stories or look up from his morning newspaper to tell her that she was pretty—if I hadn't seen these things, maybe I wouldn't know what I was missing out on.

Anthony never attempted to fill the void left in my life by my father's absence. The few times he came in my room to read to me, he raced through the story so fast, I thought I was at an auction.

"Don't ask me to do that again," I heard him say when he closed my bedroom door. "I feel weird enough around that girl. Don't force something that's not there, Beverly."

"You don't love her?"

I could hear his deep sigh through the door. "Of course I do. But she's not my daughter. I'm not her father. We don't have that bond."

Their steps retreated from my door and I strained to hear the rest of their conversation.

Was that all? He didn't feel the same love for me as he did Renee, but that was fine. *I could make him love me.*

And I tried. For the next month or so, *I* was the one who poured his coffee, who folded his newspaper in half, the crease so neat it could be a pair of pants. I complimented him on his ties, sat next to him as he watched the news and commented on President Reagan's diplomacy. All this with a nod from him, or a stiff thank you. No hugs, kisses, or tickles.

That's okay. Just push harder. Love him harder.

When he read to Renee at night, I laid down in the bed next to her, forcing him to kiss my cheek after he kissed hers. When he danced around the house with Renee on his shoulders, I screamed, "My turn!" until he picked me up. Brief as the turn was, I relished the attention. Two weeks later as he was leaving for work, I did the unthinkable—I hugged his knees and told him I loved him. I don't think that was what offended him so, it was the "Daddy" I added at the end. He shrugged me off like a dog and patted my shoulder.

Beverly sat me down for a talk one day. "Why are you getting so touchy with Anthony lately?"

I shrugged.

"He loves you. You don't have to try so hard with him."

"But I was just . . . I thought that I could—"

"Could what? Make him your father? He is *not* your father, Mariah."

"Why can't he just pretend? For me? Why can't he act like he loves me?"

She sighed. "I wish things could be that simple." She wrapped her arms around me and said, "Just give him some space."

"Did he tell you to talk to me?"

"Of course not."

I looked at her. Of course he had. It was written all over her face, the way her hand fingered the pearl necklace that was always around her throat.

"I'll leave him alone."

"I didn't mean not to talk to him—"

"No, I got what you meant. Tell him I won't bother him anymore."

COWS AT LUNCHTIME

"Do you want me to drive?" Renee asked.

I looked down at my hands and saw they were trembling. I folded them in my lap to still them. I tried again to start the car, but my hands shook so badly, I couldn't turn the ignition.

"Yeah, maybe that's a good idea."

We got out and switched seats and I looked at her get-up, high-heeled Christian Louboutin shoes (trust me, I knew), a hot pink YSL sundress. She looked nice.

"I didn't notice how dressed up you were. You look nice."

"Thanks," she said, starting the car. She put her high heel down on the brake to shift into drive, and I heard the distinct sound of a $600 pair of shoes breaking.

"Oh no!" she squealed, looking down at her broken heel. "It's ruined!"

"Let me see." She handed me her right shoe, and I saw her heel hanging on so loose that if I blew on it, it would break. "We can get these fixed. We just need to find a shoe repair."

"A shoe repair?"

"Yes, rich lady. Some of us don't have the luxury of throwing away good shoes, we have to get them repaired. We could do that first, before we find my father. It'll give me time to calm down."

"I still need a pair of shoes in the meantime," Renee whined.

"I have a pair of flip-flops in the trunk. They'll do."

She rolled her eyes and hobbled to the trunk of the car, muttering about how wrong the shoes were with her outfit. She got in the car still grumbling.

"Those must have been your favorite pair."

"They were. It doesn't matter. Let's find this shoe repair." She flicked on the navigation and typed in "shoe repair." Several addresses popped up and we picked Good Day Shoe Repair because it was the closest.

"We should call them and make sure they work on designer shoes."

"Does it matter?" I asked. "You just need a heel repaired. It's not rocket science."

"Yeah, okay . . . you're right." She pulled out of the hotel parking lot and into traffic.

Good Day Shoe Repair was only ten minutes away and we followed the robotic voice of the navigation system until we pulled into the parking lot of a bright orange building that resembled a small house. A group of men loitered out front laughing loudly.

"Will you come in with me?"

"Sure."

She grabbed her shoes and we walked up to the entrance of the store. The men stopped laughing and the air grew thick between us as we passed them. My weave gave me the confidence to stride past groups of ogling men, able to say good morning without breaking a sweat. But without it I was shy as a three-year-old, yearning to hide behind my mother's knees. We entered the store and the smell of varnish and polish hit my nose like bricks. It was crowded, which was a good sign. It meant their work was good—or at least competent.

"Can I help you?" a woman called out. Her mouth twisted around as she smacked her gum, giving her the impression of a cow at lunchtime.

"I need to get my heel repaired," Renee said, walking up to the counter.

"Let me see 'em," the girl said. Renee handed her the heels and the girl whistled.

"This is a nice pair of shoes. I gotta get Mister to sign off on these. Hold on a sec," she said, hopping off a stool, lessening her height by four inches. She went into the back room of the store and we heard voices, and then a tall, dark man followed her out the room. I sucked in a breath. It was him. Renee must have recognized him, too, because her face went pale.

He picked up Renee's shoes and inspected them. "Shoes over a certain price point have to sign a waiver. This is a simple fix, but I'm gonna need to keep them overnight." His voice sounded like a retired jazz singer, throaty smooth and low. He slid a form across the counter for Renee to sign while cow girl handed her a pen. But Renee was like me—frozen in place, unable to move.

"Y'all okay?" the girl asked, her dark penciled-in eyebrows raised in concern.

"Um, yeah, we're okay . . . We're right as rain. Except it's not raining. It's sunny outside—" I would have kept going if Renee hadn't pinched me. She signed the form and I asked the question to make sure . . .

"What's your name?"

"Latisha Banks. People call me Tisha."

"Oh, okay. But I was asking about you," I said, my eyes fluttering to meet his. "What's your name?"

He frowned and then said, "Paul Stevens."

*Experience is a comb
which nature gives us
when we are bald.*
—Proverb

KERMIT THE FROG

"And what's yours, pretty lady?"

"What's my what?"

Renee had to touch me to speak and I sputtered out my name.

"Y'all related?" Latisha asked, giving her gum a loud smack.

"Yes," I said.

"No," he said at the same time.

"Yes?" he asked.

"Yes," I answered.

"I'll give y'all a minute to figure it out," Latisha said, walking away.

"My mother's name is Beverly King. Her maiden name was Beverly Jenkins."

He sucked in a breath and leaned on the counter. "You're my . . . my daughter?"

He was wearing a denim apron filled with black smudges of shoe polish, and he untied it, revealing his thin frame. He came from behind the counter and put both my hands in his.

"You look more beautiful than I imagined."

I smiled.

"Can I?"

I nodded and he pulled me into his arms. He smelled of shoe polish and aftershave.

He pulled me back and looked at my face. "I can't believe this. You're my daughter?"

"Yes."

"She named you Mariah. I still can't believe this," he said, running his hand over his short crop of hair, tinged with gray. "How did you find me?"

"Actually, she gave me a box full of your letters—"

His face darkened. "She had them? I thought—" He shook his head. "Never mind all that, you're here now. And I'm glad."

The pop of gum returned. "It's great that y'all have a reunion, but we got a load of shoes to get finished. And you know we short staffed today," she said.

"All right, Latisha." He looked down at me. "She's right, we're swamped today. I finish in a couple of hours, you mind hanging out here?"

I looked around at all the leering men and shook my head. "That's okay—"

"Hold on a sec." He walked back toward the counter and picked up the phone. With his back to me he had a hushed conversation, and then hung up. He turned back to me and grinned.

"It's all settled. You'll wait for me at home. My mother's there—I almost gave her a heart attack when I told her you were here."

I just nodded, my mouth dry.

He scribbled his address on a piece of paper and I took it, not bothering telling him that I already had his address. "When you leave here make a right, and then two lefts. My house is the second from the corner. You can't miss it, it's painted lime green." He looked down at his watch. "You better hurry. Mama won't answer the door during her soaps. It's almost eleven."

Renee had to nudge me again to speak.

"Okay, thanks. We'll wait for you there."

The shop had been lively when we entered, but it was as quiet as a cemetery when we left.

"I can't believe it . . ."

"Me, either. What if my heel hadn't broken?"

"I guess we would have gone to his house, and still waited for him. Come on, let's get going. I want to meet my grandmother."

We looked at each other and squealed as we raced to the car.

"Paul wasn't lying when he said his house was lime green," Renee said as we pulled up into the cracked, concrete driveway.

"No kidding, looks like Kermit the Frog lives here."

We both laughed.

"You ready?"

I nodded. "Yep. Let's go."

We got out of the car and approached the house. A row of red and white begonias lined the walkway, and I put my hand through the rip in the screen door to knock on the worn front door.

I stopped when the door screeched open and a woman as wide as the doorjamb peered down at us. Our skin was the same—the color of burnt brownies. Her nose was wide and lay flat on her face. Her lips were turned up in a smile.

"Hello," she said, squeezing me into the tightest bear hug of my life. My nose was squished against her watermelon breasts, she smelled of day-old bread, and I had to flail my arms after a few seconds to let her know I couldn't breathe.

"Sorry," she said, releasing me and cradling my face in her hands. "You all right?"

"Yes," I said, gasping for air. "Just couldn't breathe."

"Chile, I'm sorry. But when Paul called and told me I had another grandbaby, I didn't know what to do! And look at you," she said, squeezing my cheeks. "You are gorgeous!"

"Thank you," I said, pulling my cheeks back and rubbing them.

"Name's Gloria. And yours is Mariah, right?"

"Yes."

"And who's this?"

"This is my sister, Renee."

Renee held out her hand and Gloria slapped it away and engulfed her face in her breasts the same as she did me.

"Chile, we don't believe in handshakes, we hug!" She pulled Renee out of her chest and smiled at her.

"You ain't kidding, you sure enough Beverly's daughter. Spittin' image of her. Well, y'all come in, come in! My show about to start."

We exchanged looks and then went in.

CLOGGED ARTERIES

"Y'all want something to drank?"

"Sure," I said. She gestured for us to sit and we took a seat on a yellow paisley couch. An oscillating fan whirred, stirring the air. The house had a log cabin feel with its fake wood paneling. The royal blue carpet was immaculate, not a spot to be seen. It actually looked new. Who in this day and time picked out royal blue carpet? Glass figurines littered the room, small white children playing, little ones praying, all white. Disturbing.

"I got lemonade. It's Country Time. My favorite. Let me get you girls a glass while you tell me the story."

I watched her walk to the kitchen and was amazed at her size. Her neck was thick as a bull's and she had the shoulders of a quarterback. There was nothing dainty about Gloria. Her feet were covered in yellow athletic socks that sagged around her cankles and her grey hair was curled tightly except for one pink sponge roller in her bangs.

"She's huge," Renee whispered.

"Shush," I said as Gloria came back with two recycled jelly glasses filled with lemonade.

"Thanks," I said, taking a sip. My lips curled at the amount of sugar, and I was sure I was instantly diagnosed with diabetes. Renee shared my expression but managed to put on a smile. "Delicious," she said.

"Can't drink too much of the stuff myself. I'm a diabetical," she said, huffing herself into an oversized chair. "But Paul say it's good. You ever hear of TiVo?"

"Umm, yes . . ."

"They say it tapes shows for you. With a remote. And you can fast forward TV and press pause. On a regular show. Can you imagine? I still have to tape my shows when I want to watch something later. They making VCRs obsolete, like eight-track tapes. But y'all too young to remember that. So, I'm recording my show so you can tell me everything. Go," she said, like I was a race car.

"What show do you watch?" Renee asked.

"*The Rich and the Famous*. You watch it?"

"No . . ."

"You don't know what you're missing! See, today they gonna tell us who killed Rico. See, Rico was a bounty hunter and he fell in love with Jasmine, who was a singer. But Jasmine was married to Shawn, who's a lawyer. But Shawn is a twin, and his brother Chance kidnapped him and took over his life and now Jasmine is pregnant, but she thinks it's Shawn's baby, but it ain't. It's Chance's."

"Interesting story line," Renee said. "Very realistic."

"I know! That's why I like it so much. So, young lady," Gloria said, turning her attention to me. "You're Beverly's daughter? You don't look a thing like her. You look just like your daddy. Now she do," she said, pointing to Renee. "She look just like Beverly."

"I know. We have different fathers."

"Tell me about it. Why did your Mama keep you hidden away?"

"I don't know. Probably the same reason she said that Paul was dead."

"She told you that your daddy was dead?"

I nodded.

"That always was a troubled little girl. When Paul moved away to go to school, I told him, I said, 'Now don't be chasing after no skirts. You keep your mind on those books.' Six months later he telling me he dropping out because he wants to get married. I couldn't believe it. She was the prettiest little thang you ever saw, but I knew right from the start something was wrong with her. She was too attached to Paul, acted like he was her lifejacket or something."

"You didn't like her?"

"I didn't say all that, I just didn't know her. They both came down here to live, and I think that bothered her. She wanted her own place. But what did she expect? Paul ain't have no money. He wasn't even a man yet, he wasn't used to the responsibilities of marriage.

"Her father called her a lot. Too much. Every time she got off the phone with him, she was complaining about something. I think that Daddy of hers was spinning stories, trying to get her to come back home. But she was too in love. Then she got pregnant. I thought that would have made her happy, but she wasn't. Just kept complaining." She shook her head. "I'm sorry, I don't mean to go on like that about your mama."

"No, go ahead. It's nice to hear some of the bad stuff."

She sat quiet for a minute. "I want to show you something." She squeezed herself out of the chair and left the room.

"That woman is huge."

I threw Renee a look.

"Sorry. She seems nice, though. Weird, but nice."

Gloria came rumbling back in the room, her arms full of different colored binders. Photo albums.

"Figured you'd want to see some old pictures of your daddy. I got a bunch of 'em," she said, putting the albums down on the pine coffee table with a loud thwack.

"Start with this one," she said, placing a large, dusty album on my lap. "This is all Paul's baby pictures."

I opened the album, with Renee next to me peering over my shoulder. I added all the necessary oooh's and aaah's—Paul in his crib, Paul at the beach, Paul loses a tooth, Paul gets first haircut—all scribbled in black ink next to each photo. It felt like I was reading the titles to children's books.

"Was Paul your only son?"

"My one and only. Yep, that's my baby."

I closed the album and picked up another one.

"No, save those for later," Gloria said. "I'm getting hungry and was just about to fix myself something for lunch. You girls want to eat?"

"Sure."

We followed her to the kitchen, where we were faced with more fake wood paneling, this time painted a soft yellow. A plastic tablecloth covered the small oak table in the middle of the room, and a large multicolored rooster sat on it. That seemed to be the theme to the room, with a rooster clock on the wall and a large rooster on top of the yellow refrigerator. Roosters everywhere.

"You girls up for a sandwich?"

"A sandwich is fine—I wouldn't want you to go to any trouble."

"No trouble at all." She reached under her cabinet and pulled out a deep cast iron skillet.

"Mariah, go over in the icebox and pick out what meat you want."

I opened the door to the refrigerator and saw salami and bologna. I chose the lesser of two evils and picked the salami.

"Yeah, you a Stevens all right, we love salami sandwiches. Renee, salami all right with you?"

"Actually . . ."

I gave her a warning look.

"Salami's perfect, thank you," she said.

I nodded and handed Gloria the salami. She took it from me and I watched her pour oil into the skillet heating on the stove.

"Won't take me but a minute to fry these up."

"Fry?" Renee and I said in unison.

"Well, how else do y'all eat a salami sandwich? You ain't never had a salami sandwich fried before?"

"No, ma'am."

She shook her head. "Beverly done forgot her roots." She tested the oil to make sure it was hot, and then she dropped several slices of salami into the hot grease. They instantly sizzled and shrunk. She took a slotted spoon and flipped them over while she buttered the bread and added mayo and cheese.

"I thought she wasn't making any trouble," Renee whispered.

"Hush."

"You girls like Oreos?"

"Sure do."

She grabbed a handful of Oreos out of a rooster cookie jar and spread them on the counter as she finished assembling our sandwiches.

"And here we go," she said, sliding the sandwiches in front of us on white paper plates. The grease from the salami had turned the white bread transparent, and yellow cheese oozed out of the sides.

"Looks great," I said.

Renee nodded and I watched in terror as she took a bite. "Delicious," she said as she shuddered.

Gloria looked at me to take my first bite and I did. The heat from the salami had melted the cheese, and all of it stuck on the roof of my mouth like peanut butter. I had to scrape my tongue across it to digest it.

"Yummy." My stomach shook, and I put the sandwich down. "I have a stomach ulcer, so I can't eat all of it, but it sure tastes great."

Gloria dug into her sandwich with the fervor of a homeless person. "When you get diagnosed with that?"

"A little after college."

"Well, you can't eat that. You want a can of soup or something?"

"No, I'm fine. Thanks."

"You got any problems with your stomach?" she asked Renee.

"Actually—"

"She has a cast-iron stomach," I said. "She can eat anything."

We were quiet for a few moments until Gloria asked how Beverly was doing.

"Did she turn out okay?"

"What do you mean?"

"I was always worried about that girl. She had it so hard with her father. Just wanted to know if she's happy."

I looked at Renee to answer. When she didn't, I replied. "She seems okay to me."

"Is William still living?"

"Grandpa? Yes, he's still alive."

"Humph. Well, I guess some dreams don't come true."

I sucked in a breath. "Why would you say something like that?"

"That man was terrible to us. Your mama, too. Did you know he's the reason we never saw you? Paul wrote to your mama for years and heard nothing. Then that William wrote him a letter telling him that he stopped all those letters from ever reaching Beverly."

"Yes, I just learned of that—"

"Downright despicable. Did you know that he tried to pay Paul to annul their marriage? Just came down here and wrote him a check like he could be bought. But I didn't raise no fool. Paul tore that check up right in his face. That didn't stop old William, though. He just kept interfering in their marriage, pointing out all of Paul's flaws to your mother. Nobody's perfect, but if all you see is flaws, then it kills the love. He made having money more important than love." ·

"Beverly never talked of him like that—"

"Since when do you start calling your mother by her given name? What's wrong with you young people today?"

"I don't know . . . I've always called her Beverly."

"I don't know everything that went on with you two, but in this house, you won't disrespect her."

"It's not a sign of disrespect. She actually prefers I call her that."

"Is that so?"

"Yes."

She looked at Renee and she shook her head.

"Renee!"

"Well, what do you want me to do, lie? Mama never liked you calling her Beverly. I told you that."

"I don't believe this," I said under my breath. I didn't drive a thousand miles to be ganged up on. Not again.

I took another bite of my sandwich, gagged, then put it down.

"I'm not trying to get you upset. I'm just trying to catch up. But seems like I'm not the only one who needs catching up."

"What do you mean?"

"Do you even know your mama at all?"

"Of course I do."

"Do you? Does she play the piano for you?"

"Bev . . . I mean, Mama doesn't play the piano."

I looked at Renee.

"Mama plays the piano?"

She nodded her head yes.

"Looks like I'm not the only one who has stuff to learn. Y'all ready for your Oreos?"

"Yes," I said, desperate for something that wasn't slathered in grease.

She walked over to the stove and drained the grease out of the skillet into an old blue coffee can.

"Mariah, could you hand me a stick of butter out of the icebox?"

I got up and handed it to her and watched her heat up the skillet and slowly melt the butter. She then dropped the Oreos in and swirled them around in the butter.

"These will be ready in just a minute."

I sat back down next to Renee.

"I can feel my arteries clogging."

"Oh, shut up."

After I watched Gloria and Renee eat ten pounds of grease, I called Norma.

"So you made it!"

"Yes, we made contact."

"Really? That's great! And on the first day, too."

"Yeah, you wouldn't believe where I am—"

"What is Dynamite!"

"Who's that?"

"My grandmother, Gloria."

"You're in her house? Wow."

"What is Billie Jean Is Not My Lover!"

"What is she doing?"

"Watching *Jeopardy*. She's pretty good, actually."

"Is she nice?"

"Yes. She's tough, but nice. Hey, did you know my mom played the piano?"

"Yes."

"How did you know?"

"What is the theory of relativity! Yes!"

"Renee told me. Why?"

"I didn't know that. Why didn't I know that?"

"Because you never asked?"

"Yeah, but still, I should have known that."

"Mariah, you didn't even want to know what your mother ate for breakfast, let alone what she did as a hobby. You don't like her."

"I know that—"

"What is Some Like It Hot!"

I squeezed the phone closer to my ear. "I know that, but still I should have known more about her. I don't know anything." I sighed. "How's Elizabeth?"

"Good. My nipples look like cow udders, but all in the sake of feeding."

"You're crazy, you know that?"

"So I've been told."

We talked for a few minutes, with me promising to keep her posted through the week, and then I hung up.

I sat back down next to Gloria and finished looking at the albums. The wedding pictures of Beverly and Paul were the ones that garnered the most interest from me. I stared and stared at how happy Beverly looked, and how young she was.

You thought this would last forever. How naïve you were then.

I picked up another album and saw different wedding pictures, to what I assumed was Paul's second wife.

"That's Clarice," she said, pointing to a short woman in the photo. "Paul's second wife. She shorter than sin, but she was nice."

"What happened to her?"

"They divorced. *What is Alaska!*" Gloria shouted to the TV. "Yeah, they only lasted about a year. He got a beautiful girl out of it. Here," she said, turning the page to the picture of a drooling baby in Paul's lap. He was smiling, but his eyes looked tired.

"That's Misty. She about your age. She live close by. She married and got a three-year-old little boy of her own."

"Are they close?" I asked, not seeing many pictures of her in the album.

"Oh, yeah. She over here all the time. I'm sure you'll get to meet her."

"Does she know about me?"

"Yeah, of course she does. I haven't called her yet, I know she gonna want to monopolize all your time. That girl's mouth runs a mile a minute. No, I'll call her tomorrow. But she's gonna be thrilled to meet you. Her boy is something else. Bad as all get out. But I love him."

I looked down at the picture of Paul and Clarice. It looked like they were on some kind of picnic. "Was he happy with her?"

"With who? Clarice? They were okay together, but no, I don't think he was happy with her."

"What about with Bev—I mean, my mama?"

"Oh, yeah. He was happy. But one person being happy in a marriage ain't enough. It takes two. And your mama had high expectations. Too high. He couldn't be what she wanted him to be, so she left. *What is Abraham Lincoln!* Yes! I'm good, ain't I?"

"You are good."

MAN IN THE MIRROR

"So when do you think Paul is coming home?" I asked Gloria, sitting down in a faded blue recliner.

"He'll be walking in that door in just a minute. He always comes home after the six o'clock news. I need to start cooking anyway. You girls staying the night, right?"

"We already have a room in a hotel. We wouldn't want to put you out . . ."

"Girl, it wouldn't be any trouble at all. You don't want to be staying in no hotel—no, ma'am, not the way they clean up. You know one time on *20/20* I saw them inspecting the sheets in this high class hotel with this special light—"

"Ultraviolet," I said.

"Yeah, an ultraviolet light. So, anyway, they check the sheets and see all kinds of bed bugs, and sperm and even doo-doo. Can you believe that? Right there on the sheets. No ma'am, you girls are staying right here. Tomorrow I'm gonna call the rest of my family. I'm fixing a big dinner in a couple of days in honor of you, Mariah."

"Oh, Gloria, you don't have to—"

"I know I don't have to. I want to. Yes, ma'am, it's not every day that a woman finds out she has another grandbaby. This is amazing."

"Amazing," Renee said, smiling.

I hit her thigh.

"You girls ready for dinner?"

"No."

"Yes."

Gloria laughed. "You two do that a lot. Talking at the same time."

I heard the lock in the door turn and in walked Paul. My father. I stood, not sure if I should hug him again or shake his hand . . . How do you act around the father you never had?

He made the decision for both of us by coming toward me and putting me in his arms. He smelled of Old Spice, and I inhaled him like a bag of towels out of the dryer. Which led me to do a long coughing hack like a smoker of fifteen years, with Paul hitting my back and Gloria rushing to the kitchen to retrieve water.

"You all right?" he asked, as I took the glass of water. I took a sip, then nodded.

"I'm fine," I croaked. I cleared my throat, and answered again in my normal voice. "Really, I'm fine. Thanks."

He motioned for us to sit down and I did. Gloria mentioned something about dinner and dragged Renee in to help her. She looked over her shoulder for me to protest, but I just mouthed, 'You'll be okay.'

"So," he said.

"So."

"You're about thirty, right?"

"Almost. Twenty-nine."

"Right, right. Wow."

"Wow."

"So I have another daughter. This is just too—"

"Surreal?"

"I was gonna say strange, but okay. That'll work, too."

Looking at him felt like looking in a mirror. He looked like me. *Someone looked like me.*

"So you know the whole story with me and your mother?"

"Gloria was filling me in on some of the details. How did you two meet?"

"I met your mother at one of my college football games. I played for Texas State. She wasn't even supposed to be there; she told her parents she was at a friend's house studying. There was a big party afterward, and we got introduced and then, well, we fell in love. My mama warned me not to go off to school and fall in love, but I did anyway. Her mother was dead, but her father hated my guts. Beverly was supposed to go to Alvin Ailey, you know, the dance school?"

I nodded.

"But we were so in love, we didn't want to wait. So we got married. Her father had a fit. He was so mad at her. Told her she was throwing her life away, all her dreams. He used to make her feel so guilty—he would tell her how her mother would flip in her grave if she knew about her decision to quit dancing. I didn't want her to quit, either. We called the school and they were willing to hold her slot until the spring semester. We figured that would give us enough time to work and save up money to move. I dropped out of college, temporarily I thought, and we both worked. She was a waitress, and I worked at my uncle's shoe repair.

"Anyway, things didn't go as planned. But that's life for you, huh?" He shook his head. "Nothing went the way we thought it would."

"Gloria told me that my grandfather tried to pay you off?"

"She told you about that? Man, Mama got a big mouth. Yeah, a couple of weeks after we got married, her father came down and said he'd pay me five grand to annul the marriage. I told him no, and he kept raising the price—got all the way to $25,000. But I wouldn't take it. I loved your mother. And no amount of money was gonna buy me off. I thought that would be the end of him, but he was smart, I'll give him that."

He blew out a long breath. "Anyway, the plan was for us to work for a couple of months, and then go to New York. I would go to junior college, and she would go to the Ailey school. But then she got pregnant."

"And she knew she wouldn't be able to dance."

He nodded. "We were careful, you know, but I guess we slipped up . . . Not that we didn't want you, no, we loved you, it's just that—"

"I was an accident." I shrugged. "It's okay, it happens."

He put his hand on my arm. "I'm sorry, baby girl, is this too hard for you?"

I shook my head. "It's okay. I just didn't want to be the reason . . ." I stopped and bit my lip. Mama was a beautiful dancer. Exceptional. And I was the reason she couldn't live her dream.

"Hey, now, we all make choices. She made hers by marrying me."

"Was she happy with you?"

"I think at first she was, but she was scared. It was the first time she was doing something on her own, and without her father's approval. She had a lot of doubt, especially when she got pregnant. I thought her father would stop speaking to her when she told him, but he must have sensed how scared she was. He played on that, kept telling her that she couldn't be a mother, and that we didn't have enough money for a baby. 'Come home and I'll help you. You won't have to work if you just come home.' She started getting resentful. She quit her job, stopped helping out around the house. I should have talked to her, but I was scared, too, I had a lot of responsibilities on my shoulders. We started arguing. A lot. She started blaming me for not being able to dance, and she started . . ."

"Blaming me," I said.

"You have to understand how miserable she was. It didn't mean that she didn't love you. It's just that she never adjusted to this life. It's hard living like this when you've had money all your life. She finally had enough and left. I found out later her father picked her up at the bus station. At first I was angry. Then I thought about how much I loved her and I just couldn't let her go."

"So you went after her."

"Yeah. Found her house, but couldn't get in the gate. I traveled all that way, and couldn't figure out to get past the security at the gate. So I parked outside and waited for her to leave. She had to leave one day, right? I never saw her. So I jumped the gate and scrambled to the front door, but they had some kind of silent alarm or something, because a bunch of police cars showed up, and I got arrested."

"Did she come outside?"

His jaw clenched. "No. I shouted her name as loud as I could, but she never came outside." He looked down and rubbed his hands together. "I sat in jail for a day, and then my mama bailed me out. She wanted me to leave her alone, but I just couldn't. Our baby was about to be born soon, I didn't want to be shut out of that, too."

He sighed. "I started writing letters, begging her to come back. They never got returned so I figured she was reading them. Then I got the divorce papers."

"But you kept writing. Why?"

He shrugged. "I knew Beverly couldn't have been so cold as to not read them. I thought . . . I don't know what I thought. I made a lousy father on paper, so she got full custody and I was granted holidays."

"But I never saw you—"

"I know. I tried those first couple of years, but I could never get in touch with anyone." He shrugged. "I'm sorry, baby girl, but I just got tired of trying." He looked at me, a single tear running down his face. "But I never stopped loving you. I want you to know that."

I put my hand on top of his. "I do."

"Dinner looks great," I said as I looked down at a plate of fried chicken, fried corn on the cob and fried okra.

"I think I'm about to have a heart attack," Renee whispered as we bowed our heads as Paul said the blessing. His prayer was short and eloquent. The food was seasoned well, but left enough grease on my lips to slick down my kinky hair. Renee was right, a few more days of this and we would all be in the hospital. I reminded Gloria of my ulcer and she heated up a can of chicken soup. That and a few saltines was all I ate.

"Ever since the doctor said I was a diabetical, I have to include vegetables in my diet," Gloria said.

"Does it still count as a vegetable if it's battered and fried?" Renee asked.

"Renee . . ." I warned.

"What? I'm just asking . . ."

"Yes, ma'am. Corn is still corn, even if you fry it. You can't change what God made, baby. I don't turn vegetables into anything but what they are, vegetables," she said, tearing into a large chicken leg. "To me the best part of fried chicken is the skin. I always wanted to open up my own restaurant—"

"Mama, don't start with that chicken skins restaurant—"

"Why not? It's a great idea." She looked at us. "What do you think of eating at a chicken skins restaurant?"

We looked at each other. "You mean a restaurant that only sold chicken skins?"

Gloria nodded. "Fried, of course. You could get them by the pound. You know, a pound of fried chicken skins and a side of fries?" She licked her lips. "I can't think of anything better."

"I keep telling you, Mama, that idea won't work. People don't want to eat just fried chicken skins. They want some meat, too. Besides, it's wasteful. What would you do with all the chicken that you didn't use? Throw it out?"

"Absolutely not. We wouldn't just have chicken skins. We would have a variety on our menu. But the focus would be on the skin. Even got the name picked out and everything—*Slide Me Some Skin*. Sounds great, huh?"

"Sounds pornographic," Paul said, taking a bite out of his chicken. We laughed.

"Oh, hush," Gloria said, smiling.

Several times I caught Paul stealing glances at me. After about the fourth time, I asked him if something was wrong.

"I'm sorry, was I staring?"

I nodded.

"It feels weird to sit here and eat with you. My daughter is here." He shook his head. "I knew you would be beautiful, but I didn't think you would be this pretty."

"Thank you."

"How do you like her hair?" Renee asked.

"Renee . . ."

"No, I want to get his opinion. So what do you think?"

"I think it looks nice. It fits your face."

"I love it," Renee said.

"I do, too," I added. "Well, now I do."

"Would you believe that she used to wear a head full of weave?"

Paul laughed and Gloria shook her head.

"Don't go telling Misty. Ever since she started sportin' that natural, she thinks every woman that wears a weave is trying to be white. That's not what you were doing, was it?"

"No, ma'am, I just liked the look." I threw Renee a glance, and she just shrugged.

"You can get away with any hairstyle you want, baby girl."

"Thanks, Paul."

"Why do you keep calling him Paul?" Gloria asked. "He's your daddy. You don't need to be calling him by his first name. Just like you shouldn't be calling your mama by her first name."

"Mama, Mariah can call me whatever she feels comfortable with." He turned and looked at me. "You don't have to call me Daddy. I know all this has to be hard on you."

"No, it's okay. Actually, calling you Daddy sounds good."

He smiled, long and wide.

"You sure you don't mind?"

"Not at all. Daddy."

He smiled again.

"Looking at y'all makes me want to call Maury Povich. He had a show last week talking about finding baby daddies—"

"Mama, we would not fit in on Maury."

"Yeah, now that I think about it, you're right. What about Oprah? Always did want to meet her friend Gayle. It looks like she wears a weave, too, don't it, Mariah?"

"I guess."

"Yep, I think I'm gonna call the Oprah show and tell them I got the perfect show. 'Long-Lost Daughter Comes Home—A Family Reunites.' That's a good idea . . ."

"That is *not* a good idea, and you are not calling them."

Gloria frowned. "Spoil sport." After a few beats she asked, "What about a letter to that magazine of hers?"

"No," we all said in unison. We looked at each other and broke into laughter.

"Yeah, you Paul's daughter, all right. Same attitude." She sighed. "Y'all ready for dessert? I fried up some plantains and Snickers."

"Yum-O," I said.

"Kill me now," Renee whispered.

"Well, who would have thought our day would have ended like this?" Renee asked as she pulled down the comforter on the bed.

After going back to the hotel and getting our things, we were both in Gloria's guest bedroom. The wood paneling was painted dark green and matched the worn carpet. I felt like I was lost in a forest.

"I still feel weird about all this," I said as I changed into my pajamas. I stood in front of a gilded mirror on top of a wooden dresser and smoothed my short hair down and wrapped it with a scarf.

"Your father really has taken a liking to you."

"I know! It's weird how comfortable I feel here."

"This is your family."

I shook my head. "I still can't believe it. And we all look alike. Granted, Gloria's a little—"

"Hippoish?"

"I was going to say statuesque, but still, it feels good to see myself in my family. No offense—"

She flicked her hand. "None taken."

"Did you see how Paul, I mean, my father, kept looking at me? It's like he thinks I'm not real or something."

She shrugged. "I wasn't paying much attention. I sort of blanked out when a pile of grease slid down my throat. I mean seriously, is she going to fry everything?"

I laughed. "Probably. I like her, though. She's so different from Beverly—"

"Mama," Renee corrected.

I rolled my eyes.

"Yeah, well, she's so different from her. She's more real. And she likes me."

"I think she more than likes you, Mariah. She loves you. That reminds me, I need to call Mama so she knows we made it here safely."

"Don't call her."

"Mariah, will you cut it out? I'm not in the mood for your drama. I'm calling her, all right?" She dug in her purse and retrieved her cell phone. I snatched it from her.

"I said no."

"Are you serious? Give me my cell phone back!" I hid it behind my back, and she pushed me on the bed and pried the phone from my fingers.

"You need to grow up, Mariah. I'm tired of you making me feel bad for the relationship that Mama and I have. I'm not going to keep apologizing about it."

I sat up. "This trip is about me! It's not about her."

"It isn't? Mariah, this trip has everything to do with Mama. I saw your face when you were looking through those pictures. You were shocked that Mama was happy. She had a whole other life before you were born. Maybe if you could see her *whole* life, and not just the life that involved you, you would understand her."

"I'm done understanding her. I want to be free from her."

"You'll never be free from her. She's a part of your history. She's a part of you. If you don't get that now, then you'll never get it."

"I get it, all right. I get the fact that no matter what, you want to try to make Beverly a victim in all this. But she's no victim."

"And you are?"

"Yes! My mother, my flesh and blood, denied me love from my father! Do you know he told me that he got arrested because he stood outside her house and screamed for her to take him back? What does that say about her? What kind of coldhearted person does that?"

"You don't have all the answers, Mariah. You're just barely learning the questions. But this victim card you keep throwing around is getting old. Sooner or later you are going to have to take responsibility for your life and stop blaming Mama for everything that went wrong—"

"She is the reason everything went wrong."

"So Mama's the reason that you can't keep a man?"

"In a way, yes."

"And Mama's the reason that you lost your job?"

"No, but . . ."

"And Mama's the reason you're broke?"

"Okay, some of that is my fault—"

"No. No, not some of it. All of it. You can't keep blaming her for everything. She's not perfect by any means, but she's not the devil incarnate, either. You're wasting the purpose of coming here if you're going to keep blaming Mama for your life. How could she be responsible for the mistakes in your life, when you tried so hard to keep her out of it?"

"I don't know. But somehow, she is."

Renee shook her head. "She loves you."

"In my head, I know that. But try telling that to my heart."

HEATHER

The next day I woke up with a crick in my neck and with Renee doubled over in pain as she sat on the toilet.

"What's wrong?" I asked, looking like a stroke victim because I couldn't move my neck as I spoke.

"I have a bad case of the runs. It's all that grease! I don't think I can eat any more of her food."

"Oh, come on, Renee, it's not that bad—"

"Not that bad? My stomach is cramping and I've spent the last three hours on the toilet. If another thing is fried on my plate, I'm leaving. I'm serious."

"What? You can't leave."

"Why not? This trip isn't about me. You don't need me."

"But I do."

I couldn't believe what I just said; I needed my sister. For the first time in a long time, I had come to depend on her. Her opinions, her questions, her reasoning—all of it I needed. But most of all, I needed her by my side in all this. I was tired of doing everything alone.

Renee sat up. "Really?"

"Yes, really. I need you. I can't deal with Gloria by myself. And honestly, I want someone from *my* side of the family with me when I meet Paul's daughter. I can't do that alone. I need you. Please stay."

She groaned. "Of course the one time you need me is when I'm dying from grease overkill."

"Will you stay?"

"Of course I will. How could I not?"

I smiled. "Thanks."

"Now get out so I can wipe my butt in peace."

"No joke, it smells like something died in here."

"Something did."

I left her in the bathroom and walked down the hall to the smell of bacon cooking.

"Good morning."

"Good morning, baby. Come give me some sugar." I walked over and planted a kiss on Gloria's smooth cheek.

"Hungry?" she asked.

"Famished."

"I hope that means hungry, because I fixed you girls a world-class breakfast." I watched in horror as she put several slices of bacon in a vat of grease in a deep fryer.

"You cook your bacon like that?"

"How else you cook bacon? Sit down, it's almost ready." She sniffed the air. "Smells like your sister is out of the bathroom. Let her know it's a can of Lysol under the sink."

I laughed. "I'll let her know." Renee was out of the bathroom when I walked back in, and I held my nose as I grabbed the can of Lysol and sprayed the room. Soon it was baby powder fresh.

"Done," I said, walking back in the kitchen. "Now what?"

"Now you can sit down and let me feed you."

"Good morning," Renee said, smiling weakly.

"Morning," Gloria and I chimed.

"Coffee?" Gloria asked.

"No. I'm not hungry this morning. I think I'll just munch on some saltines—"

"Nonsense! Not after this big breakfast I slaved over."

She filled a plate with fried eggs, bacon, and a bread-like creation with powdered sugar sprinkled over it. She slid the plate to Renee.

"What's this?" she asked.

"A funnel cake. It's like a pancake, only better."

"I think I had this at a carnival once. Isn't it—"

"Deep-fried gold is what it is. Try some," she said, turning her back to fix another plate of food.

"Is she crazy?" Renee whispered.

I just shook my head as I took my plate. "Thanks. It looks delicious."

"It is. Let's dig in, girls."

"Somebody help me."

"What was that?" Gloria asked.

"Oh, I just said I'm going to need help eating all this food."

"Don't worry, whatever you don't eat, I'll finish off. I'll just take me another pill."

"You sure you should do that?" I asked.

"It'll be fine. I can handle it."

I nodded and ate. Surprisingly, the food was good. If you didn't mind your heart skipping a few beats.

"Is Paul, I mean, is my father up yet?"

"Girl, your daddy been up and is already at work."

"Oh."

"Don't worry, you'll have plenty of time to talk to him after work. He really wanted to stay, but he lost some of his workers so he's short-staffed. He would have taken off if he knew you were coming. But don't you worry, because his shop is closed on Sunday, so he'll be here the whole time. Your sister Misty is coming tomorrow."

"Really?"

"Yep. Just got off the phone with her. Charles can't come—that's her husband—but she coming down with her four-year-old son Tyrese. We call him T-bone."

"That's cute."

"Yep, I plan on cooking us a big dinner and I need to go to the store to pick up some things. You girls mind driving me?"

"I'll have to sit that one out," Renee said. "I need some rest. But you two can go. It'll be fun."

"That's what I thought. Well, you take all the rest you need. Me and Mariah will be just fine. Yes, ma'am, we will be just fine."

I smiled and threw a dirty look at Renee.

"Sure, Gloria. We can hang out today."

"You ready?" Gloria called out.

She was standing near the front door in a matching purple track suit and gold glitter tennis shoes. A shiny gold baseball cap was on her head and underneath the hat was that same pink sponge roller in her bangs. I had to work hard not to laugh.

"Yes, I'm ready."

She grabbed her keys and locked the door as I waited for her on the porch, the heat making my tank top stick to my skin. We walked down the concrete steps to the car and got in.

"Fancy car," she said, her hand running over the leather interior. "What did you say you did again?"

"Um . . . I'm currently in between positions."

"You mean you don't have a job?"

"No."

"Then how can you afford this car?"

"I can't. My sister bought me this car."

She whistled. "She sure does love you."

"So where to?" I asked, buckling my seat belt.

"I want to visit my friend first. She's close by."

"That's fine." I started the ignition. "Where does she live?"

"Right there," she said pointing to the yellow house next door.

"She lives next door? Why didn't we just walk over there?"

"I'm not walking in this heat. No, ma'am. Go on, drive over there."

I shook my head and backed out of the driveway. Two seconds later I was unbuckling my seat belt.

"We're here," I chimed, unlocking the door.

"See? That didn't take long."

We climbed out of the car and knocked on the screen door. Feet shuffled and the door opened to a young woman peering down at us.

"Gloria, is that her?"

"Yes, ma'am. My grandbaby raised from the dead. Ain't she pretty?"

"She's gorgeous. Y'all come in, the old man's asleep."

We walked into the home to the scent of antiseptic and BENGAY. A man lay sleeping in an overstuffed arm chair, snoring loudly.

"Come on, let's go sit in the kitchen. I made some iced tea." We walked past the living room and sat down at a chipped-up red vinyl breakfast table.

"This is Mariah, Heather. Heather, Mariah."

We shook hands. Her handshake was firm, her eyes warm.

"Nice to meet you," she said, her blue eyes sparkling. "Gloria was too excited to meet you."

"Wait a minute, so you two are friends?"

Gloria and Heather looked at each other. "Yes. Going on five years. Why?"

"No reason. I just thought that you would have some-body, you know, closer to your age."

They laughed.

"People look at us weird. When I'm wearing my scrubs I think people think I'm her nurse," Heather said. "Gloria's been more a friend to me than anyone I know."

"Age ain't nothing but a number. That's what they say, right? Yes, ma'am, we don't let a silly thing like race or age say we can't be friends. Right, Heather?"

"Right." She opened the refrigerator and pulled out a pitcher of iced tea and poured it into three glasses. I took a sip and crunched on a mouthful of sugar. "Wow, that's sweet."

I watched as Gloria drained her entire glass. "I know. She makes it extra sweet for me."

"You sure you should be drinking this stuff?"

"I know, I know. Paul always telling me to watch what I eat. But this is what I *drink*. So, it don't count." She laughed. "Don't worry. If I start feeling sick I'll just take another pill."

"Gloria, you know the doctor said—"

"I know what the doctor said, Heather. So why keep worrying about everything? It's my life and I'm gonna live it the way I want." She held out her glass for a refill and Heather poured her more iced tea.

"So, isn't she beautiful, Heather? I told you she would be."

"I never denied that she would be beautiful," Heather said, sitting down.

"You guys don't have to do that."

"Do what?"

"Compliment me all the time." I was used to the compliments with my weave, my hair was always beautiful. But now when the compliments were directed toward me, I felt uncomfortable.

"Girl, you better get used to us complimenting you, as pretty as you are. And I don't want to hear you shrug off another compliment. You better take 'em as long as they coming, you hear?"

I nodded.

"Look at her skin, Heather. Her skin is so dark and pretty—"

I laughed.

"What's so funny?"

"Nothing. It's just that . . . never mind."

"What, you can't be cute 'cause you dark?"

"Sure you can, but your life will be harder. Society likes their women light-skinned with long hair."

Heather and Gloria shared a glance and burst out laughing.

"So do you think I have an easier life than you because I'm white?"

"I didn't mean it like that—"

"I think you did. You seem to think that lighter skin and longer hair guarantees a better life. A different life maybe, but not better."

"I hate when people say that. I'm telling you that having darker skin means your life is harder."

"Look at me," Gloria said. "I'm dark as night, and I never once thought that my life would be different if I was a couple of shades lighter. No, ma'am, I would still be me."

"No, you wouldn't. You would be somebody else. Didn't you get made fun of at school?"

"Sure. But everybody does."

"But wouldn't you agree that some people get it harder than others?"

"I guess. But after a while you have to figure out what's true. Am I dark-skinned? Yes. But am I ugly? No. Is my hair nappy? Yes. But is it beautiful? Yes. Your problem is that you take what people say about you and make it true when it's not."

"But I feel like it is the truth."

"Then that's your problem. You need to find your own truth and stop letting people decide what's beautiful for you. We all different. Yes, ma'am, God made all of us different. It makes me mad that you give someone else the power to tell you that you ugly. Girl, you know what people would give to have skin like yours?"

"It's true," Heather said. "You glow."

I touched my cheek. *I did?*

"You see what I'm saying, Heather? This is what I'm talking about. The media got you all twisted up saying thin is in, and fat is out, that being dark is ugly and light is right. It's not healthy. If I had a nickel for every time I thought about something I don't have, then I would go buy Microsoft. You got a lot of things going for you. The sooner you learn that, the better."

"It's hard to see that, the way I grew up. Beverly—"

"Mama," Gloria corrected.

"Beverly was light-skinned with nice hair. So is Renee. I went to an all-white school. Sometimes, when you hear that you're ugly long enough, you start to believe it."

"Girl, you better stop thinking like that. And quick. It don't matter why you feel ugly. It just matter that you feel ugly. And it ain't true."

"When I wore my weave I felt pretty. I felt that people stood at attention when I walked into a room. Don't get me wrong, I'm starting to really like my hair, but it's not the same."

"*You* not the same. Girl, where's your confidence? Nobody looking at you because of your weave. They standing at attention because you command it when you walk in the room. You think you lost that. But I still see it. Don't you, Heather?"

"I do. This is my first time seeing you and I think your hair complements your face well," Heather said.

"You don't count."

"Why not?"

I sighed. "White people are always intrigued by dark skin. They think it's so exotic."

"What's wrong with that?"

"You wouldn't understand."

"She might not," Gloria said, "but I would. You see how you just immediately dismissed what she said? She made a valid point, and she told you the truth. But you trained yourself to listen to the bad, so no good will soak in. That's a shame."

"I don't train myself to listen to the bad. That's not what I'm doing."

"Oh, it isn't?" She took a sip of her iced tea. "Sounds like it to me. Don't it, Heather?"

"Sure do."

"With all due respect, neither of you know me well enough to start judging or giving me unwarranted advice. I know that I have good qualities."

Gloria sat her glass down. "Name 'em."

"Name my qualities?"

"Yes."

"Okay . . ." I thought for a moment and said, "I'm really smart—"

"Nice try. I'm talking about physical qualities."

I sat in silence.

"If you want I'll start," Gloria said.

"Fine."

"I like my big lips. I like that my hair is white as snow. Shows people how smart I am. And dark as I am, I never been afraid of color. That's why my house is green. Yes, ma'am, if God created the color, then I figure it go with everybody."

"I like my hair color," Heather said. "It's natural, by the way, but everybody insists that I color it. And my smile. I have a killer smile," she said, giving me an example.

"Okay. Now it's your turn," Gloria said.

"All right. I like my . . . my eyes?"

"Are you asking me or telling me?"

"I'm telling you. My eyes. I like the shape of them. And I have really thick eyelashes. Never wore fake ones, never had to."

"There you go."

"Heather! LUNCH!" a voice boomed from the living room, making me jump out of my skin.

"Well, the old man's awake." Heather stood and cleared our glasses away. "What time is the dinner party tomorrow?"

"Six. And don't be late this time."

"That was one time. You are never going to let me live that down."

"No, I'm not." They hugged and I felt the weird urge to hug Heather, too. And I did.

"Sorry," I said, backing away from her. "I shouldn't have—"

"Nonsense. I don't get enough hugs in the day. But Gloria was right about you. You are a sight to see."

MRS. MILLIE

"Where to now?" I asked, backing out of the driveway. "Can we stop by my father's job?"

"And do what?"

"I don't know, have lunch?"

"Nah, Paul be too busy to stop for lunch most days. You'll see him this evening. Y'all really have taken a liking to each other. That's real good."

"I expected things to be more awkward, but I feel really comfortable here."

"I'm glad."

I heard my cell phone ringing in my purse and I dug in my bag to get it.

"Hello?"

"I think I just lost my small intestine," Renee said.

"That bad, huh?"

"Yeah. Ask Gloria if she has some Pepto somewhere. I don't want to go digging around in her cabinets."

"Gloria, Renee is still feeling sick. Do you have any Pepto Bismol?"

"Tell her I keep all my medicine in the refrigerator. In the part where you keep the butter."

"Renee?" I said, talking back into the phone.

"Yes?"

"She said it's in the refrigerator. Check the part where you're supposed to keep the butter."

"All right. Where are you guys?"

I looked at the rearview mirror and saw Gloria's lime green house.

"Not that far. We're about to pick up something to eat—"

"Girl, don't even mention food to me."

"You sure you'll be okay by yourself?"

"Trust me, I'm fine."

"Okay, well, we'll be back before dinner. Love you."

"Love you, too. Tell Gloria I said thanks."

"Okay." I hung up and gave Gloria the message.

"Well, one thing you do have is a wonderful sister."

"I know."

"Let's get going. I need to eat something. My sugar's getting low."

"Okay, where to?"

Where to, was a barbeque joint named Miss Millie's. Picnic tables were strewn over a dirt-patched lawn, and you ordered at a trailer, where the legendary seventy-six-year-old Miss Millie took your order.

"You want to eat outside?"

"Got to. Miss Millie don't have any indoor tables."

So she could eat outside, but couldn't walk a few steps to visit her friend? Go figure.

"I'll find a table and you place the order." She grabbed a folded $20 bill from her bra and fit it in my hand. It was wet from sweat. I handed it back to her.

"I got it."

"You sure?"

"I'm positive."

"Well I ain't never been one to turn down a free meal." She slipped the $20 back in her bra. "I want a rib sandwich. And tell her extra bread, last time she forgot. Oh, and two orders of coleslaw. Yes, ma'am, that coleslaw is good. And a Diet Coke. Gotta watch my sugar."

"Okay." I walked over to the trailer and placed her order and added a baked potato for myself.

"That's it?" Miss Millie asked. The few lines that were on her face were around her mouth, which made me think that Miss Millie smiled a lot. She had on a pristine white apron and her gray hair was covered with a black hairnet.

"Yes."

"All right." She handed me a white plastic card with the number sixty-seven on it.

"What do I do with this?"

"You must be new. Stick it on your table and someone will come bring your food."

"All right. Thanks."

"Mm-hmm. Next!" she shouted to the person behind me. I walked back to Gloria with my number in hand.

"What'd you order?"

"Baked potato."

"Loaded?"

"No, just butter."

"I can't eat a potato like that. I need some meat, some sour cream and cheese," she said as she shook out of her purple jacket, revealing a gold tank top.

"I appreciate everything you've done, Gloria. You've made me feel so at home here."

She waved her hand. "This is your home. I hope this won't be your only visit to Memphis. I want you to love it here. Just like I love it."

Our food arrived, and we ate in silence for a few moments.

"Why does my father still live with you?"

Gloria looked up, sauce on her chin.

"You don't pull no punches, do you?"

"I didn't mean to seem rude—"

She shook her head and took a sip of her Diet Coke. "Most people wonder why a fifty-year-old man is staying with me. Paul ain't a loser."

"I didn't mean that."

"But you thought it, right? Don't even try to lie about that one. No, Paul is a good son. He moved in last year when my sugar started to get out of control. I don't drive, so it helps having someone with me."

"That's good."

"Told you I raised a good boy. A good man. Oh, yeah, he take care of his responsibilities. Now you mind if I ask you a few questions, young lady?"

"Go right ahead."

"Why don't you have a job right now? You get fired or something?"

"I was laid off," I said, bristling.

She put her hands up. "I was just asking. Sheesh," she muttered.

I laughed. "I don't know why I'm so sensitive. I've always worked. This is the first time in my life that I haven't. It takes a little getting used to."

"Well, your sister is taking good care of you. Yes, ma'am, for her to buy a brand new BMW. I take it Beverly still got a load of money?"

"Beverly still has money, but my sister has her own money."

"How did she get all that money?"

"She married well."

"Humph. That seems to run in y'all's family. Wanna get rich? Marry a rich man." She laughed. "What did you do before? At work?"

"I was the book review editor for *Spirit Magazine*. Have you ever read it?"

"Naw, it was too uppity for me. Don't like to read nothing that I need a dictionary with. But I'm sure it was a nice job."

"It was."

"Why'd you get fired?"

"Technically I didn't. The magazine folded."

"Folded?"

"Closed. No more *Spirit Magazine*."

"Oh. Well, I wouldn't take that too personal. It's not like you weren't doing a good job."

I nodded.

"So what are you going to do now?"

"I don't know. I really liked writing reviews and reading. My two loves."

"Not everyone is fortunate to do what they love to do. With that rich sister of yours, you can take your time and find out what you really want to do."

"You sound just like her. I have to admit it is nice to take my time and figure things out."

"My thoughts exactly." She belched. "I need another Diet Coke." She lifted her Styrofoam cup. "Yoo-hoo? A little more soda, please?"

After a two-hour stint at the grocery store, I was finally pulling up in Gloria's driveway.

"You go on inside, I'll bring the groceries in."

"You sure?" Gloria asked.

"Positive," I said, as I popped the trunk.

"Well, if you think you can handle it, that's fine by me. Yes, ma'am, I've never been one to turn down some help."

I got out of the car and grabbed as many plastic bags as I could handle and walked to the front door. Gloria was standing there, blocking my entrance.

"Gloria, do you mind? These bags are heavy."

She moved, and then I understood why she stood like a statue.

Beverly was sitting on Gloria's couch.

The hair is real—it's the head that's fake.
—Steve Allen

IT WAS AN ACCIDENT

I dropped the groceries.

Fortunately, most of what I was carrying was canned goods and paper products, so no harm was done to the food. But a lot of harm needed to be to done to the woman who held my gaze. For the first time in—well, *ever*—she had no makeup on. Her bouncy hair was slicked back in a bun and revealed the prominent dark circles under her eyes. She was dressed simply in a long, blue sundress. She rose and picked up all the bent-up cans around me as I stood silently, mouth agape.

"What are you doing here?" I asked after several seconds. I searched the room and saw Renee standing in the corner. "What is she doing here, Renee?"

"She called me—"

"Why is she here, Renee?"

"I knew you would be upset, but she asked me if we made it Memphis and I told her that we were here."

"She had no idea I was coming," Beverly said, her hands full of cans. She walked them to the kitchen, comfortable in the surroundings of Gloria's home.

"You brought her here," I said to Renee. "I can't believe you."

"Mariah—"

I walked outside to get the rest of the groceries. Beverly came up behind me and reached in to grab a bag just as I slammed the trunk closed.

"OWWWW!" she screamed, her eyes smarting with tears.

I dropped the bags, this time breaking eggs and other perishable items.

"Oh, Mama, I'm sorry!"

Tears were running down her face, and she held her hand out. Her knuckles were bloody, and before my eyes her fingers began to swell.

"I think it's broken," she said.

"What happened?" Renee said, running outside. "Who's screaming?"

"I closed the trunk on Mama's hand—"

"Oh, my goodness! Mama, let me see!"

Beverly showed Renee her swollen, bloody hand. Renee looked at me.

"It was an accident."

"Sure it was."

"Do you think I would do something like this on purpose?"

Renee just stared at me.

"It was an accident!"

Gloria came outside.

"What's all the hooping and hollering about?"

Beverly outstretched her hand.

"Ooo, that looks bad. What happened?"

"Mariah slammed the trunk on my hand—"

"A total accident, by the way—"

"Mm-hmm. Yep, you got banged up. Some of your fingers look broken. Mariah, drive her to the hospital."

"I think Renee should—"

"What did I say? You did the damage, so you help fix it. Drive your mama to the hospital."

I hesitated.

"Now, Mariah," Gloria said. "Renee, help me pick up the rest of these groceries before they get run over."

Renee picked up the spilled groceries while Gloria opened the door for Beverly and helped her in the passenger seat. After buckling her seat belt, I saw her whisper something in Beverly's ear, which only made her cry harder.

"Okay, the closest hospital is a couple of miles away." I listened as Gloria rattled off directions and we were on our way.

Beverly was still sniffling and crying, a few moans escaping her lips.

"I'm really sorry."

"I know."

"It really was an accident."

"Okay."

"You believe me, don't you?"

She sighed. "After everything I've done to you, I wouldn't be surprised that this wasn't done on purpose. But don't worry, I know this was an accident."

"It was."

"Okay."

"Why did you come?"

She sucked in a breath. "I didn't want you facing Paul alone."

"I'm not alone. Just be honest, you just didn't want me hearing the truth about you and my father."

"I came to right some wrongs. I figured you should hear the truth from *both* of us. Not just him. You should hear my side of the story, too."

"Why? So I could feel sorry for you? So we can be all lovey-dovey, mother and daughter? I used to want that, too, but it's not going to happen. You've done too much."

Tears fell from her chin. "I know. But a girl can try, can't she?"

"We're on our way back. Four of her fingers are broken, and her hand was fractured. We need to fill a prescription and then we'll be there."

I was cradling the phone under my chin as I helped Beverly back into the car.

"Her hand is in a cast?" Renee asked.

"Pretty much. She's fine, though. In a little bit of pain, but otherwise okay."

"Well, I'm glad. Your dad's here. And your sister Misty," she whispered.

"Okay. What does she look like?" I asked, buckling Beverly into the car.

"Like a bigger version of you."

I shut her car door, and leaned against it. "You should have called me—"

"Look, I had no idea she was coming. She surprised me, too."

"Give me a break, Renee. You knew—"

"I told you I didn't."

"You want to wrap this up in some neat little package. *Stevens Family Reunion.* Stop playing peacemaker!"

"I wasn't. You've some nerve telling me off. The way you broke Mama's hand like some kind of Mafia goon."

"That was an accident!"

"Sure it was."

She clicked off before I could yell at her more. I walked over to the driver's side and yanked the car door open.

"You're still angry?" Beverly asked quietly.

"No," I said, my hands clenching the steering wheel.

She sighed. "I didn't mean to upset you. I really came to help—"

"Do you have any idea what you've done by coming here? This trip was about me, about me finding the truth about my father. Now you've turned this whole thing into something about you. I'm sick of you, can't you tell? All my life I've been trying to get your approval, and now I don't care what you think of me. I just want to be as far away from you as possible. But no, you had to ruin that, too."

"I'm sorry. I thought if I explained my side, you would understand." She looked out the window. "I can see it's too late for that now."

"You bet it is," I said, keeping my attention on the road. For the first time in years I didn't care if she listened to me or heard me. I just wanted her away from me.

⌒

After picking up her prescription we were finally back at Gloria's house. We came into the living room and Paul jumped up at the sight of Beverly and her cast.

"Beverly," he breathed. He straightened. "You all right?"

"It's good to see you, Paul," she said, stiffly. He paused for a minute and gave her a side hug, something more appropriate for an ex-wife.

"Mariah, this is your sister, Misty."

Renee wasn't kidding when she said she looked like me. Her dark skin glowed and her kinky hair was twisted up in an elegant updo. She hugged me almost as hard as Gloria.

"I can't believe I have a sister. This is amazing." She pulled away and examined me, head to toe. When she reached my hair, she stopped. "You wear a relaxer?"

My hand flew to my hair. "Yes . . . Why?"

"I can't believe you put that stuff in your hair. Why would you ruin what God created? He meant for us to be nappy—"

"Misty, save your natural hair speeches for later. Your sister just got into the door, and I don't think she feels like being preached at."

"Grandma, I was just letting her know how damaging relaxers are." She shook her head. "Well, at least you don't have a head full of weave."

Renee laughed.

"Mama, I need to take a dump."

I looked down and saw a small boy tugging on Misty's pant leg. I knelt down. "And you must be Tyrese." I held out my hand. "I'm Mariah."

He looked up at his mother.

"Go on," Misty said. "It's okay."

He placed his little hand in mine.

"Nice to meet you, Tyrese."

"T-Bone."

"Sorry, T-Bone."

He looked up at Misty again. "Mama, I need to boo-boo."

She shrugged. "That's kids for you." She reached out and hugged me again. "I'm so glad you're here."

"I'm glad, too."

Misty left the room and Beverly coughed.

"I need to rest," she said, turning to Gloria. "Could you—"

"Yes, you can sleep in the girls' room. I have a pull-out bed. Paul, go set it up. Dinner's ready if everybody's hungry. Come on, Mariah, help me dip up the plates."

I watched as Paul led Beverly to our room. I followed Gloria to the kitchen, Renee on my heels.

"I'm still mad at you," I said.

"Good," Renee said, "cause I'm still mad at you."

"You girls just hush. Neither one of you is mad. It was an accident. On both parts." She pulled down dishes from the cabinet. "Now if you two don't mind, fix the plates while I go wash my hands."

"You okay?" I asked. She was sweating profusely, and her hands were shaking.

"Just fine. The events of the day just got me a little riled up. You girls fix the plates and start eating. I'll be back in a minute." She kissed my cheek, then walked to the back of the house toward her bedroom.

Paul came back in the kitchen.

"How's she doing?" Renee asked.

"She was falling asleep when I left."

"You think I should—"

He shook his head. "She'll be fine. The best thing to do is let her sleep." He walked over to me and hugged me. "Mama told me what happened, you okay?"

"It was an accident!"

He backed up. "Okay, just calm down. Who said you would do anything like that on purpose?"

I looked at Renee, and his eyes followed my gaze.

"You think your sister did it on purpose?"

Renee crossed her arms over her chest.

"You don't know her like I do."

"Girls, that's enough," Gloria said, coming back from her bedroom. Her dark skin had taken a grayish tone and she was still sweating. "I think we've all had enough drama for today."

"Mama, you okay?" Paul asked, walking over to Gloria. She waved him off. "Boy, I'm fine. Just a little winded."

She looked around the kitchen. "You girls get those plates down. I don't want to have to tell y'all again."

We both got plates and glasses from her upper cabinet near the stove, rolling our eyes at each other. Misty came back from the bathroom with T-Bone. After setting him up in a booster seat at the kitchen table, she fell right into step with us, and we made an assembly line of dishing out the food.

We sat down to eat, and Paul said another short eloquent prayer. Misty kept up the conversation, asking me questions every few minutes.

"So you don't have any kids?" Misty asked.

"No."

"And you're not married?"

"No."

"And you don't have a boyfriend, either?"

I sighed. "No."

"Man, I was hoping you at least had a kid or something. T-bone wants a little playmate, don't ya, T-Bone?"

"Mm-hmm," he said, chewing on an ear of corn.

"Stop pestering her with questions, Misty. This isn't a job interview," Paul said.

"Daddy, I'm just trying to get to know my older sister. So what do you do for a living?"

I sighed again. This was going to be a long night.

WHAT I'M GOOD AT

After dinner, everyone piled up to watch a few family movies, *to catch me up to speed*, Misty said.

"I'm going to check on Mama first," Renee said.

"Good idea. Why don't you both go check on her?" Gloria said.

I opened my mouth in protest, then quickly closed it when I caught Gloria's look. I followed Renee into the guest bedroom where Beverly was propped up with pillows, her hand laying on another bunch of pillows.

"How you doing, Mama?" Renee asked, sitting down on the bed next to Beverly.

"Better," she said, looking down at her hand.

"Does it still hurt?"

She nodded. "A little bit."

I stood like a statue, refusing to look at them.

"Renee, will you do me a favor and look in my bag on the floor? I have something I need to give to Mariah."

"If you think that you can win me over with gifts, think again," I said.

Out of the corner of my eye, I saw Renee hand Beverly what looked like a present.

"Will you give us some privacy?"

"Sure," Renee said, placing a kiss on Beverly's cheek. "I'll come check on you later."

"Thanks."

Renee walked past me, but not without rolling her eyes first. I crossed my arms over my chest.

"Come here," Beverly said, patting a spot next to her on the bed with her good hand.

I sighed heavily to let her know I was irritated and sat on the bed, still refusing to look at her.

"I know you still don't want to talk to me. But I need you to look at me."

I turned to face her.

"I made a really bad mistake. Horrible. Unforgivable." A tear slid down her face and she wiped it away. "There's nothing I can do to take it back, nothing I can do to change what I did. But I was hoping . . ." She shook her head and pointed to what looked like a shoe box. "Open it."

"I can't believe you thought you could just buy me off. You can't undo what you did."

She closed her eyes and lay back on the pillows. "Just open it, Mariah."

I picked up the box and opened the lid.

"Oh," I said, picking up a pink, leather journal. "This is my journal from junior high." I ruffled through the box. "These are *all* my old journals. I thought I lost them . . ."

"Remember how you used to write all the time? Stories, essays, anything that tickled your fancy?"

I nodded, memories flooding back. "I remember."

"And you were good, too. Better than good. I loved your stories."

I flipped through the pages and saw my prim cursive writing, trying to make every letter perfect.

"I was thinking, with all this time off and everything, that's what you should do."

"Do what? Write? For a living?" I shook my head.

"Yes."

"That's ridiculous. I'm not a writer."

"Says who? You've been writing for years, you just didn't know it yet. That's why you surrounded yourself with books, worked at a magazine reviewing books. It's what you do. It's what you're good at. Pick up the last one, the book at the bottom."

I reached in and pulled out a small blue photo album.

"That one's mine."

I opened it and saw all my old articles from college, my first book review from *Spirit Magazine*—all my writing achievements in one little book.

"You kept these?" I whispered.

"Of course I kept them. Even when you went off to school and didn't write or call enough, I found out what you were doing and would get the school to mail me a copy of whatever it was. I've read just about everything you've written."

"I didn't know . . ."

"I know I treated you girls different. But I'd like to think I brought out the best in both of you. I love you, Mariah. I do."

I nodded. "Thank you for this. It means a lot."

She smiled.

"I was hoping it would."

SUNDAY ROLLERS

I left Beverly only to bump into Renee in the hallway.

"What are you doing out here?"

"Nothing," she said, walking away.

"You are such a bad liar. You were listening, weren't you?"

She crossed her arms over her chest. "Yes. But I didn't get to hear the end part. What did she give you?"

I showed her the box. "It's a bunch of my old journals. She kept them."

"That was nice."

"She thinks I should start writing."

"You're always writing—"

"Professionally. She thinks I should write a book."

"And be like a real writer? Like for a living?"

I nodded.

"Are you going to do it?"

"I don't know . . ." But the more I thought about it, the more my hands itched to try. "I might."

"You can stay with us. Until you finish your book."

"Thanks. It wouldn't be forever or anything—"

"I know. But if you want to take this on you're going to need some support. At least financially. Writers don't make a lot of money."

"Thanks. I think," I said, trying to figure out if she was helping me or trying to diss me. "And for the record, I didn't hurt on her purpose. It was an accident."

She smiled. "I know."

⌇

"Everything all right?" Paul asked when we entered the living room.

"Just fine." I sat next to him on the couch. "Thanks for letting Beverly stay here."

His jaw tightened. "It's no problem. Misty, go ahead and play the movie."

"I wanna watch *Spongebob*," Tyrese whined, thumb in mouth.

"Later," Misty said as she pushed play on the remote. She pulled him on her lap and after a few minutes he was asleep.

I sat back and watched the images come on the screen, a montage of photos set to song.

"When did you guys do this?" I asked.

"Couple of years back," Misty said. "I thought I was going to be a wedding videographer."

"Was that before or after the idea to be a florist?"

"I think it was after she wanted to be a designer. Too much *Project Runway*, in my book," Gloria added.

"Forget y'all. Don't listen to them, Mariah. A person has a right to change their mind if they want to."

"We don't mind you changing your mind, just stick with something, for goodness sake."

"Whatever." She kissed Tyrese on the cheek and announced that she was putting him to bed.

"I'll do it," Paul said, kneeling down to pick him up. "My little man is all tired out." He placed him over his shoulder and walked out of the room.

Misty tapped my arm. "Anyway, now I'm a hairstylist. I would offer to do your hair, but these hands," she said, holding her hands up, "only touch natural hair."

"You should have seen me a couple of months ago," I said. "I wore a head full of weave."

Misty shrieked in horror.

"Here we go," Gloria said.

"Do you know where all that hair comes from?"

"No, but I'm sure you're going to enlighten me."

"Dead people," Misty whispered.

"Misty, stop lying," Gloria said.

"I'm not lying. It's true. They shave the hair off dead people and then sell it to hair dealers. It's true!" she added, when she caught a bunch of shocked stares.

"Technically, hair is dead as soon as it grows from the hair follicle. So cutting it off a dead person or someone who's living is the same. If you're dead or alive, the hair is already dead."

"But, still, wearing *dead* people's hair is gross. How could you do that?"

I shrugged. "Easy. Went to the salon and paid for it."

Gloria laughed, and then stopped when she saw Misty's face. "Really, Misty, you need to take a chill pill. Ain't nothing wrong with wearing weave." She patted the pink sponge roller in her head. "Been thinking of getting some myself."

"You better not, your hair is fine." She turned to look at me. "What is it with black women and weaves? It's such an obvious form of self-hatred."

"How?"

"Putting all that fake hair in, tossing it around like you're some kind of white girl. It means you're not comfortable in your skin."

"I never looked at it like that. It was just an accessory, like a pair of earrings." *A pair of earrings I couldn't live without* . . .

"Why don't you wear it now?"

I smoothed my hair at my nape. "I like my hair short. But who knows? I might get it again, to change things up. But I don't *need* to wear it." I shrugged. "It's just hair."

"Yes, ma'am, that's what I say—it's just hair. People talk about hair like they talking about world peace or something. Especially black folk. If you get a relaxer you hate yourself, and if you go natural you some kind of hippie freak. It's a bunch of nonsense. People ought to wear their hair how they want."

"Speaking of hair, why do you wear that roller all the time?" I asked.

"What, this?" she asked, pointing to the pink-sponged atrocity sitting on her head. "This here is my Sunday roller."

"Your Sunday roller?"

"I only take it out on Sundays."

"Why?"

"Sabbath, girl. God said to rest, and that includes your hair."

"Oh, my goodness," Misty said, holding her face in her hands.

Renee and I laughed.

SMELLS LIKE HOME

"Gloria, what can I do to help?" I asked, coming into the kitchen.

After a night of watching old home videos, I woke up to the smell of Gloria cooking. Thankfully, it wasn't breakfast, so Renee and I fixed a bowl of cereal. Paul had cut the grass this morning, getting the yard and house ready for the party, and after smelling the good smells coming from the kitchen, I wanted to help.

"How good are you with a knife?"

"Average, I guess."

"Well, it will have to do. Here," she said, handing me an onion. "Start chopping. Cutting board is behind the toaster."

I grabbed the knife and onion, and reached behind the white toaster to get the wood chopping board. After a few rough starts I finally got the hang of it. "What are you making?"

"Gumbo."

"Smells delicious."

"Just wait until you taste it. Here," she said, handing me a spoon full of broth. I swallowed, then coughed.

"You all right?" she said, patting my back.

I nodded. She stopped patting.

"Spicy," I said, my voice strangled.

"Oh, yeah, I should have warned you. We like our food spicy. Since you're a Stevens, you should be able to handle it, but I don't think Beverly cooked spicy food for y'all, did she?"

I shook my head.

"Figures."

"Who's all coming?"

"Not that many people. Let's see, Heather, my two brothers, Chauncey and David, and their wives and children, and a few friends. Of course Misty—this time she bringing her husband."

"Oh."

"Now, don't be nervous. I called them and told them all about you. They can't wait to meet you."

"What did they think about my story?"

"They were shocked, of course. But most were just glad that things had worked out and that you're here. They're thrilled to meet you at last."

"What do you think about my story?"

She sighed. "You mean what Beverly did?"

"Yes."

"I think she was wrong, no doubt about it. But she was young, confused, scared. And her father didn't help."

"It feels so strange to hear you say that about him. He's always been so loving to me. It was Bev—I mean, Mama, that was cold. To hear that he was mean," I shook my head. "I don't get it."

"Not everything looks the way it seems. It never is." She paused. "Have you ever talked to your mama?"

"Recently? We talked a little last night."

"And?"

"She thinks I should be a writer."

"What do you think?"

"I think she's right."

"Hard to imagine your mama being right about something, huh?"

I nodded.

She blew out a long breath. "It's hard to be a mother. It's the hardest job ever. And you don't know if you've screwed up 'til it's almost over. Your mama messed up, yes. But how long should she have to pay for it?"

"I don't know."

"I think twenty-nine years is long enough, don't you?"

"I guess."

"You don't guess, you know. It's time to let it go."

I wiped a tear from my eye on my sleeve. "The onion . . ."

"Oh, baby . . ." She scooped me in her arms, and I cried in her chest, feeling her warmth. She smelled like home.

I stopped when I heard raised voices coming from the bedroom.

"Did you hear that?" I asked.

"Yeah. Go check what's going on. I'll finish up here."

I hugged her again and left. I went down the hall and started to knock on the door when I heard my name.

"Mariah is fine. Yes, I made a mistake, but I'm trying to make it right," Beverly said.

"I'm not talking about Mariah, I'm talking about ME," Paul yelled. "How could you just up and leave like that? What happened to '*til death do us part*'? What happened to that?"

"I was scared. I didn't know how to be a wife to you, let alone a mother to her. How could I stay here? How could I raise our daughter like this?"

"You could try! I drove to your house to see you, screaming your name in the street like some kind of fool, and you never came out. You never said one word to me. I didn't care if you screamed or yelled at me or anything. I just wanted you to talk to me."

"I didn't know! My father never told me that. I would never have let you suffer like that if I'd known. Imagine how hurt I felt when you weren't there to hold Mariah for the first time. I thought you never loved me, but . . ."

"I did love you. I never stopped loving you."

I pressed my ear onto the door. I couldn't hear anything. I turned the knob and entered the room, and caught them.

They broke free from each other's arms as soon as I entered, but any dummy could see that they had been kissing.

"I, um, I was just—"

A loud crash came from the kitchen that interrupted anything else I could say. Paul rushed past me and we followed him. A small scream escaped my lips as I saw Gloria sprawled on the floor, covered in cut-up onion.

"Call 911," Paul yelled as he knelt by her and turned her over. He listened for a pulse and started CPR.

"Mama, don't you do this, you hear me? Don't you die on me."

For three days after death
hair and fingernails continue to grow,
but phone calls taper off.
—Johnny Carson

MOUNTAIN OF MACHINES

Why are hospitals so cold? It's freezing in here. I haven't been in to see Gloria yet. The doctors are saying she had a stroke. Paul is in there right now, Misty, too. They're only letting two people in at a time. They had to wear face masks, something about germs. I was in too much shock to pay much attention.

But I did see Paul holding Mama's hand in the waiting room. I'm sure this is what every child hopes for, that their parents will get back together. But I never knew I even had that chance, what with my mother being a liar and all.

Please, God, don't let Gloria die. I just met her; it seems so unfair that she die without me really knowing her. I'm tired of not knowing people, especially my family. I'm tired of secrets. I'm tired of hating my mother. I'm just plain old tired.

I stopped writing when I saw Paul and Misty come back in the waiting room. I didn't have time to grab my journal, so I wrote on a scrap of paper Renee found in her purse.

We all stood.

"How is she?" Beverly asked, going up to Paul and grabbing his hand. There it was again. I threw a look at Renee. Her eyebrow was quirked up, but she said nothing. *So I wasn't the only one who knew . . .*

"She's still unconscious—"

"It's bad," Misty said, looking down. "The doctors say that her brain lost a lot of oxygen—"

"Will she be okay?" I asked.

Paul looked at me. "We don't know, baby girl. We hope so."

Beverly kept rubbing his hand.

"I know this is a sad moment and everything, but Mama, what's going on?" Renee asked.

As if finally realizing she was holding Paul's hand, she dropped it. "What do you mean?"

"You know what she means," I said.

"Did I miss something here?" Misty said. "I mean, besides the fact that Grandma had a stroke?"

No one spoke.

"Daddy? What's going on?"

Paul looked at her. "Nothing, baby. Weren't you supposed to call your husband?"

Misty looked at her watch. "Oh, yeah, I forgot. He needs to pick up T-Bone—" She walked away, punching numbers into her cell phone.

"Look, baby girl," Paul said, facing me. "Your mother and I need to do some talking."

"I saw you two. Looked like you weren't doing much talking."

"What were they doing?" Renee asked.

"Kissing. Like a couple of teenagers."

"Mama?"

Beverly's cheeks flushed. "I'm sorry. I know my behavior was inappropriate." She looked at Paul. "But Paul and I have a lot of sorting out to do—"

"Do you know how hard this stuff is to hear, Mama? All this time I thought you were in love with my father—"

"I did love Anthony. Don't do that, Renee."

"Do what? I called you down here to support Mariah, but you're down here making everything worse. You're complicating things—"

"Thing have *been* complicated, Renee." She shook her head. "But you're right. I shouldn't have come." She started to walk off, but Paul caught her hand.

"Stop running away. I need you here, especially now. Stay." He held her gaze for the longest time, and I saw something in Mama's eyes shift. She nodded.

"Can I go see Gloria now?" I asked.

Paul nodded.

I looked at Renee. "Will you come with me?"

"Of course."

We followed the directions the nurse gave us and entered the room where Gloria lay unconscious. She was surrounded by a mountain of machines, and her dark skin was ashy and grey.

"Oh, Gloria," I said, covering my mouth with my hand. The only comfort I had in looking at her was seeing that pink sponge roller still in her hair.

"Renee . . ."

"I know," she said, standing next to me.

Our hands found each other and she squeezed my hand just as tight as I squeezed hers.

SUNNY SKIES

Paul and Mama sat with Gloria during her final hours. She died Sunday morning. Paul asked if I wanted to go in and say my goodbyes, but I couldn't do it. Gloria was gone and I couldn't go in and say goodbye to her cold body.

Cold. That was the last word that I would use to describe Gloria. She was so warm and funny. I can't believe it's been a week already. The house is quiet; even with all the people mulling around, it's quiet in here.

I keep looking at the stove, waiting to see if Gloria will come out her bedroom and start frying something. It seems I'm not the only one who thinks about her cooking, Paul instructed that no one touch her stove. Like she would ever know if someone touched anything.

Seems unfair how sunny the sky was today when Gloria went into the ground. Where was the rain, the clouds, the thunderstorms and lightning? Who got buried with the sun shining as bright as it did today? But then again, besides Renee's husband, how many funerals had I gone to?

How do you end up loving somebody so much that you just met? My heart ached for her, and I know she had more wisdom to share with me. But now? No more. I had so much to learn and now she was gone.

And now I have to deal with my parents. (I can't believe I'm writing that, it still feels too surreal to write. Parents?

Wow.) They can't keep their hands off each other, always reaching out for each other like no one notices. I notice. It bothered Renee, I could tell, yet she kept her mouth shut. Me? Not so much.

What would Gloria say about it? She didn't like Mama, yet she still made her feel welcome. Would she have hated the two of them back together?

I heard footsteps approach and I closed my journal.

I knew it was her before I even turned to look at her.

"Want some company?"

I shrugged.

She sat down next to me on the porch steps. She fingered the cast on her arm.

"I can't believe she's gone," Beverly said.

"I know."

"She was such a big part of Paul's life. He's devastated."

"He'll be okay, won't he?"

Beverly nodded. "He's strong. He'll survive."

"What about you?"

"I'll be fine."

"No, I mean—" I blew out a breath. "I mean what about you . . . and my father. What's going on with you two?"

"I know it bothers you—"

"Bothers isn't quite the right word."

"I know you don't like it. But we want to try again. Give it a real go this time. We never gave ourselves a real chance before."

I nodded. "I'm happy for you."

"You are? You seemed upset all week—"

I held my hand up. "I know. But really, I'm glad. Everyone around me has grown up, making real adult decisions. Life's too short to be upset with you. Gloria would want me to be happy for you, too, and move on."

She smiled. "I think she would have been happy for us. I'm glad you are too. I've made a real mess of things. I look at my life and I have so many regrets, too many. I can't take back what I did to you. You reminded me of everything I lost, and I guess I blamed you for it. I didn't want to take responsibility for the fact that I was to blame for losing the one man I've ever loved. I didn't mean to make you feel so bad about yourself . . ."

She started crying and I resisted the urge to reach out and touch her. She wiped her eyes and continued, "Thanks for being the bigger woman. You turned out so much better than me—"

"I'm not better than you."

She shook her head. "You are. You came down here with so much courage and, and—"

"Hope," I said. "I never imagined that my father would be so loving. But he is. I can see why you loved him." I sighed. "Love him, I mean."

"Thank you for forgiving me." She held up her hand. "I think I've truly paid for my mistakes in blood."

"It was an accident!"

She hugged me. "I know, baby, I know."

"Well, that's it. You girls are all packed up."

"Thanks," I said.

"Who's driving?" Paul asked.

"I'm driving the first leg," Renee said.

"Come here, baby girl." Paul gave me a tight hug and a kiss on the cheek. "Call me as soon as you get back?"

"I promise."

"And I'm coming to see you in a couple of weeks, okay? Just need to get some stuff settled first."

I saw Beverly come out of the house and stand next to Paul. I stepped from him.

"Where are your bags?" I asked.

She looked at Paul and reached for his hand. "I'm staying." Paul looked down at her with so much love, I had to look away.

"Mama, are you serious?" Renee asked.

Beverly nodded.

Renee walked over and hugged Beverly. She said something in Beverly's ear and then walked back to the car.

I walked to Beverly and hugged her. When the urge to cry came, I let it come and didn't fight it. All my fighting was over.

"Be happy," I whispered into her hair.

"I plan to."

"Goodbye. *Mama*."

BIOGRAPHY

Katrina Spencer is the author of *Six O'clock* and lives in Texas with her husband and daughter. She readily admits that if she were trapped on a desert island, the three things she couldn't live without are her family, her Bible, and her hair weave. Learn more about her at katrinaspencer.com and stop by her blog, Curl Up and Write, where she dishes about writing, hair and more.

2010 Mass Market Titles

January

Show Me The Sun
Miriam Shumba
ISBN: 978-158571-405-6
$6.99

Promises of Forever
Celya Bowers
ISBN: 978-1-58571-380-6
$6.99

February

Love Out Of Order
Nicole Green
ISBN: 978-1-58571-381-3
$6.99

Unclear and Present Danger
Michele Cameron
ISBN: 978-158571-408-7
$6.99

March

Stolen Jewels
Michele Sudler
ISBN: 978-158571-409-4
$6.99

Not Quite Right
Tammy Williams
ISBN: 978-158571-410-0
$6.99

April

Oak Bluffs
Joan Early
ISBN: 978-1-58571-379-0
$6.99

Crossing The Line
Bernice Layton
ISBN: 978-158571-412-4
$6.99

How To Kill Your Husband
Keith Walker
ISBN: 978-158571-421-6
$6.99

May

The Business of Love
Cheris F. Hodges
ISBN: 978-158571-373-8
$6.99

Wayward Dreams
Gail McFarland
ISBN: 978-158571-422-3
$6.99

June

The Doctor's Wife
Mildred Riley
ISBN: 978-158571-424-7
$6.99

Mixed Reality
Chamein Canton
ISBN: 978-158571-423-0
$6.99

2010 Mass Market Titles (continued)
July

Blue Interlude
Keisha Mennefee
ISBN: 978-158571-378-3
$6.99

Always You
Crystal Hubbard
ISBN: 978-158571-371-4
$6.99

Unbeweavable
Katrina Spencer
ISBN: 978-158571-426-1
$6.99

August

Small Sensations
Crystal V. Rhodes
ISBN: 978-158571-376-9
$6.99

Let's Get It On
Dyanne Davis
ISBN: 978-158571-416-2
$6.99

September

Unconditional
A.C. Arthur
ISBN: 978-158571-413-1
$6.99

Swan
Africa Fine
ISBN: 978-158571-377-6
$6.99$6.99

October

Friends in Need
Joan Early
ISBN:978-1-58571-428-5
$6.99

Against the Wind
Gwynne Forster
ISBN:978-158571-429-2
$6.99

That Which Has Horns
Miriam Shumba
ISBN:978-1-58571-430-8
$6.99

November

A Good Dude
Keith Walker
ISBN:978-1-58571-431-5
$6.99

Reye's Gold
Ruthie Robinson
ISBN:978-1-58571-432-2
$6.99

December

Still Waters...
Crystal V. Rhodes
ISBN:978-1-58571-433-9
$6.99

Burn
Crystal Hubbard
ISBN: 978-1-58571-406-3
$6.99

Other Genesis Press, Inc. Titles

Other Genesis Press, Inc. Titles (continued)

Other Genesis Press, Inc. Titles (continued)

Eve's Prescription	Edwina Martin Arnold	$8.95
Everlastin' Love	Gay G. Gunn	$8.95
Everlasting Moments	Dorothy Elizabeth Love	$8.95
Everything and More	Sinclair Lebeau	$8.95
Everything But Love	Natalie Dunbar	$8.95
Falling	Natalie Dunbar	$9.95
Fate	Pamela Leigh Starr	$8.95
Finding Isabella	A.J. Garrotto	$8.95
Fireflies	Joan Early	$6.99
Fixin' Tyrone	Keith Walker	$6.99
Forbidden Quest	Dar Tomlinson	$10.95
Forever Love	Wanda Y. Thomas	$8.95
From the Ashes	Kathleen Suzanne	$8.95
	Jeanne Sumerix	
Frost On My Window	Angela Weaver	$6.99
Gentle Yearning	Rochelle Alers	$10.95
Glory of Love	Sinclair LeBeau	$10.95
Go Gentle Into That Good Night	Malcom Boyd	$12.95
Goldengroove	Mary Beth Craft	$16.95
Groove, Bang, and Jive	Steve Cannon	$8.99
Hand in Glove	Andrea Jackson	$9.95
Hard to Love	Kimberley White	$9.95
Hart & Soul	Angie Daniels	$8.95
Heart of the Phoenix	A.C. Arthur	$9.95
Heartbeat	Stephanie Bedwell-Grime	$8.95
Hearts Remember	M. Loui Quezada	$8.95
Hidden Memories	Robin Allen	$10.95
Higher Ground	Leah Latimer	$19.95
Hitler, the War, and the Pope	Ronald Rychiak	$26.95
How to Write a Romance	Kathryn Falk	$18.95
I Married a Reclining Chair	Lisa M. Fuhs	$8.95
I'll Be Your Shelter	Giselle Carmichael	$8.95
I'll Paint a Sun	A.J. Garrotto	$9.95
Icie	Pamela Leigh Starr	$8.95
If I Were Your Woman	LaConnie Taylor-Jones	$6.99
Illusions	Pamela Leigh Starr	$8.95
Indigo After Dark Vol. I	Nia Dixon/Angelique	$10.95
Indigo After Dark Vol. II	Dolores Bundy/	$10.95
	Cole Riley	
Indigo After Dark Vol. III	Montana Blue/	$10.95
	Coco Morena	

Other Genesis Press, Inc. Titles (continued)

Indigo After Dark Vol. IV	Cassandra Colt/	$14.95
Indigo After Dark Vol. V	Delilah Dawson	$14.95
Indiscretions	Donna Hill	$8.95
Intentional Mistakes	Michele Sudler	$9.95
Interlude	Donna Hill	$8.95
Intimate Intentions	Angie Daniels	$8.95
It's in the Rhythm	Sammie Ward	$6.99
It's Not Over Yet	J.J. Michael	$9.95
Jolie's Surrender	Edwina Martin-Arnold	$8.95
Kiss or Keep	Debra Phillips	$8.95
Lace	Giselle Carmichael	$9.95
Lady Preacher	K.T. Richey	$6.99
Last Train to Memphis	Elsa Cook	$12.95
Lasting Valor	Ken Olsen	$24.95
Let Us Prey	Hunter Lundy	$25.95
Lies Too Long	Pamela Ridley	$13.95
Life Is Never As It Seems	J.J. Michael	$12.95
Lighter Shade of Brown	Vicki Andrews	$8.95
Look Both Ways	Joan Early	$6.99
Looking for Lily	Africa Fine	$6.99
Love Always	Mildred E. Riley	$10.95
Love Doesn't Come Easy	Charlyne Dickerson	$8.95
Love Unveiled	Gloria Greene	$10.95
Love's Deception	Charlene Berry	$10.95
Love's Destiny	M. Loui Quezada	$8.95
Love's Secrets	Yolanda McVey	$6.99
Mae's Promise	Melody Walcott	$8.95
Magnolia Sunset	Giselle Carmichael	$8.95
Many Shades of Gray	Dyanne Davis	$6.99
Matters of Life and Death	Lesego Malepe, Ph.D.	$15.95
Meant to Be	Jeanne Sumerix	$8.95
Midnight Clear	Leslie Esdaile	$10.95
(Anthology)	Gwynne Forster	
	Carmen Green	
	Monica Jackson	
Midnight Magic	Gwynne Forster	$8.95
Midnight Peril	Vicki Andrews	$10.95
Misconceptions	Pamela Leigh Starr	$9.95
Moments of Clarity	Michele Cameron	$6.99
Montgomery's Children	Richard Perry	$14.95
Mr. Fix-It	Crystal Hubbard	$6.99
My Buffalo Soldier	Barbara B.K. Reeves	$8.95

Other Genesis Press, Inc. Titles (continued)

Other Genesis Press, Inc. Titles (continued)

Secret Library Vol. 1	Nina Sheridan	$18.95
Secret Library Vol. 2	Cassandra Colt	$8.95
Secret Thunder	Annetta P. Lee	$9.95
Shades of Brown	Denise Becker	$8.95
Shades of Desire	Monica White	$8.95
Shadows in the Moonlight	Jeanne Sumerix	$8.95
Sin	Crystal Rhodes	$8.95
Singing A Song…	Crystal Rhodes	$6.99
Six O'Clock	Katrina Spencer	$6.99
Small Whispers	Annetta P. Lee	$6.99
So Amazing	Sinclair LeBeau	$8.95
Somebody's Someone	Sinclair LeBeau	$8.95
Someone to Love	Alicia Wiggins	$8.95
Song in the Park	Martin Brant	$15.95
Soul Eyes	Wayne L. Wilson	$12.95
Soul to Soul	Donna Hill	$8.95
Southern Comfort	J.M. Jeffries	$8.95
Southern Fried Standards	S.R. Maddox	$6.99
Still the Storm	Sharon Robinson	$8.95
Still Waters Run Deep	Leslie Esdaile	$8.95
Stolen Memories	Michele Sudler	$6.99
Stories to Excite You	Anna Forrest/Divine	$14.95
Storm	Pamela Leigh Starr	$6.99
Subtle Secrets	Wanda Y. Thomas	$8.95
Suddenly You	Crystal Hubbard	$9.95
Sweet Repercussions	Kimberley White	$9.95
Sweet Sensations	Gwyneth Bolton	$9.95
Sweet Tomorrows	Kimberly White	$8.95
Taken by You	Dorothy Elizabeth Love	$9.95
Tattooed Tears	T. T. Henderson	$8.95
Tempting Faith	Crystal Hubbard	$6.99
The Color Line	Lizzette Grayson Carter	$9.95
The Color of Trouble	Dyanne Davis	$8.95
The Disappearance of Allison Jones	Kayla Perrin	$5.95
The Fires Within	Beverly Clark	$9.95
The Foursome	Celya Bowers	$6.99
The Honey Dipper's Legacy	Myra Pannell-Allen	$14.95
The Joker's Love Tune	Sidney Rickman	$15.95
The Little Pretender	Barbara Cartland	$10.95
The Love We Had	Natalie Dunbar	$8.95
The Man Who Could Fly	Bob & Milana Beamon	$18.95

Other Genesis Press, Inc. Titles (continued)

Order Form

Mail to: Genesis Press, Inc.
P.O. Box 101
Columbus, MS 39703

Name _____
Address _____
City/State _____ Zip _____
Telephone _____

Ship to (if different from above)
Name _____
Address _____
City/State _____ Zip _____
Telephone _____

Credit Card Information
Credit Card # _____ ☐ Visa ☐ Mastercard
Expiration Date (mm/yy) _____ ☐ AmEx ☐ Discover

Qty.	Author	Title	Price	Total

Use this order form, or call **1-888-INDIGO-1**	Total for books _____
	Shipping and handling:
	  $5 first two books,
	  $1 each additional book _____
	Total S & H _____
	Total amount enclosed _____
	Mississippi residents add 7% sales tax